I0652688

www.wispvine.com

978-1-939997-89-0

1st Edition

BOOKS BY OLIVIA ASH

**Dragon Dojo Brotherhood**

Reign of Dragons

Fate of Dragons

Blood of Dragons

Age of Dragons

Fall of Dragons

Death of Dragons

War of Dragons

**Blackbriar Academy**

The Trials of Blackbriar Academy

The Shadows of Blackbriar Academy

**The Nighthelm Guardian Series**

City of the Sleeping Gods

City of Fractured Souls

City of the Enchanted Queen

**Demon Queen Saga**

Princes of the Underworld

Wars of the Underworld

**Sentinel Saga**

*By Dahlia Leigh and Olivia Ash*

The Shadow Shifter

Join the exclusive group where all the cool kids hang out… Olivia's secret club for cool ladies! Consider this your formal invitation to a world of hot guys, fun people, and your fellow book lovers. Olivia hangs out in this group all the time. She made the group specifically for readers like you to come together and share their lives and interests, especially regarding the hot guys from her novels.

Check it out! Everyone in there is amazing, and you'll fit right in.

*https://www.facebook.com/groups/LilaJeanO-liviaAsh/*

Sign up for email alerts of new releases AND an exclusive bonus novella from the Nighthelm Guardian series, *City of the Rebel Runes*, the prequel to *City of Sleeping Gods* only available to subscribers.

*https://wispvine.com/newsletter/olivia-ash-email-signup/*

Enjoying the series? Awesome! Help others discover Blackbriar Academy by leaving a review at Amazon.

# THE TRIALS OF
# BLACKBRIAR ACADEMY

BOOK ONE OF THE BLACKBRIAR ACADEMY SERIES

OLIVIA ASH

**I shouldn't be here, and everyone knows it.**

Blackbriar Academy is an enchanted school on a magical island, and *everyone* wants in. It's a home away from home for the most advanced mages in the world—and only the best of the *best* are given an invitation.

By some freak accident, I managed to get one.

If I pass the trials, I get to stay. It's my one shot at having a meaningful life, and I won't let *anyone* take this from me.

But there's a catch.

**It turns out the people on this island are trained to hunt the darkness—basically, they're being trained to hunt *me*.**

I'm being watched.

To survive, I have to hide what I am. I'm half-human and half-mage, but my magic is mind-blowing—and incredibly *illegal*. It puts even the most skilled mages to shame.

**As the trials get harder, it's clear I'm being hunted. If I'm caught... I die.**

Magic like mine? Over history, it has corrupted the souls of those who were born with it. They've all gone dark—razing towns and murdering hundreds of thousands throughout history.

All but me.

**At Blackbriar Academy, nothing is ever as it seems. I want in, and absolutely *no one* will stand in my way.**

The Trials of Blackbriar Academy is a full-length novel with an alternative relationship dynamic that supports our badass heroine's right to choose more than one man. Get ready for a breathtaking story, soulmate romance, lip-biting love scenes, mind-blowing magic, one kickass heroine, four gorgeous men, lots of toned muscles, fights to the death, and edge-of-your-seat action.

*Warning: The Blackbriar Academy Series is an academy fantasy reverse harem series with explicit scenes and is meant for adult readers who enjoy steamy scenes and lip-biting action.*

**The Trials of Blackbriar Academy is a full-length novel with a badass heroine, a riveting storyline, and an alternative relationship dynamic. Get ready for a heart-pounding story filled with an academy fantasy romance unlike anything you've read before.**

Buckle in for heart-pounding action, breathtaking magic, deadly assassins, four drop-dead gorgeous leading men, lots of toned muscles, **and most importantly—a young woman's journey of justice, self-discovery, and freedom.**

# CONTENTS

I'm alone... sort of.

Hiding within a dense crop of trees, deep in the enchanted forest I've been trapped in for six years, I know I'm close.

So very, very close.

After three years of trying to beat those jackass forest trolls at their own game, I will finally win. I'm faster, stronger, and no amount of cheating is going to stop me.

I will be *free*. I can finally live on my own terms, for the first time in six years.

I weave my way through the trees and edge toward a long-dead oak so I can duck out of sight. A bead of sweat drips into my eyes, and I use the back of my dirt-covered hand to wipe it away. With a quick check around me, finding only the silent woods, not so much as a branch or a leaf moves with the gentle breeze blowing around me.

I'm in the clear.

The sacred horn is close. I can practically *feel* it —and it's not far off from where I stand.

It will be mine.

If I get the horn, that means I'm free. By earning my freedom, they won't keep dragging me back once I leave.

Because that's the deal they made me.

It's the same as every year. They think I won't be able to do it. That I'm too weak. Too human. They want to give me false hope, but this year is different.

This year, the horn is as good as *mine*.

The snap of a twig behind me draws my attention and I narrow my eyes in the direction the sound came from. That's the difference between me and the trolls. I know how to sidestep a twig on the ground and avoid giving away my position.

I hasten my steps as I draw nearer to the horn.

The sacred horn is legendary among this village of trolls. It's a thing of myth. Of ancient lore. It's been around for eons—longer than this forest, probably. Whoever gets the horn is granted honor and brings prosperity to their family for the coming months' harvests.

Most importantly, to them, it brings respect.

But I don't want their respect. I want freedom. And for a human living among trolls, that's something I've never had. I'm always treated like a monster.

A slave.

Soon, I can go home to my aunt. Get answers. Find out who killed my family.

Hell, I could go anywhere I damn well please.

I shuffle my feet to the right, around a large oak, before jumping down a short slope toward a river rushing through the forest below me. Landing on my feet, I grip a narrow aspen for support and rake my gaze around my surroundings.

No shadows move.

And no shadows means no trolls.

Moving on. I can almost taste the mouthpiece on my lips as I press it to my mouth and prepare to give it a blow. But that's moving ahead of myself. Too soon to get my hopes up just yet. Too soon to celebrate.

Six years ago, when I was only fourteen years old, the trolls kidnapped me. Now, I'm twenty and used to fending for myself, surviving on scraps and exploring the woods when I'm not being harassed by my captors.

They probably didn't know it, but they gave me everything I needed to survive without them. Without anyone. I once made it three entire days on my own before they finally caught up to me.

Because they always do. Every time I try to escape, they find me. It's only a matter of time.

Not anymore.

I'm done with them all.

But first, I need that horn.

I hop into the riverbed and look toward the east. The horn is within my sight now, sitting at the base of an ancient tree near the basin, north of the troll village. I'm so close to the damn thing.

The sweet bliss of freedom is about to finally be mine.

To be perfectly honest, I don't know what is so important about a relic such as that horn. None of the trolls ever told me. And though the deal is to give me freedom if I get the horn first, they all treated my participation as a joke.

*Silly, puny human.*

*You're our slave. You belong to us.*

*You will never win.*

And I don't.

Because Gnars does.

He always wins.

He cheats, but he wins.

I'm done with losing to a cheater like him. It's not fair, and I'm finally just *done*. I'm going to ensure things change for me from here on out. I refuse to spend another year as a slave, as an escapee, recaptured and forced to do their dirty work for them while they feast on legs of elk, drink their spirits, and praise themselves for the lords of the world they think they are.

I glance behind me once more and slowly inch my way to the ancient tree, trying not to slosh my boots in the water. The heavy thud of footsteps pounds against the ground behind me, thick and clunky as the troll sprints toward the finish line.

Out of time, I push myself forward and storm through the water.

Something hits my back, and a weight knocks me off balance. I land in the riverbed, holding my breath to keep my lungs from being filled with cold water, as drowning is a very unpleasant experience. The weight leaves me, and I roll onto my back and stare at Gnars' wart-covered face.

"Stupid human." His moss-green skin wrinkling as he sneers down at me. "I followed you. I do every year. Always. You make it so damn easy for me to win."

I narrow my eyes at him, wishing I could just shoot him with my magic—but the last time I used my powers on one of them, they broke my conduit and beat me for days. Magic is powerful, but trolls have thick skin and are quick to overwhelm their prey. Back then, I was only fifteen, and I didn't stand a chance against dozens of full-grown trolls. It was brutal. I suffered a broken arm, broken ribs, and a punctured lung, and they forbade me from ever getting another conduit.

They thought they could break me by taking away the one thing that allows me to use my magic. Without a conduit, I would be nothing but a frail human, easy for them to bruise and break.

But I made another one.

I reach for the homemade conduit tucked in my pocket and feel that it remains in one piece. My fingers slide along all the grooves of the small branch of birchwood with pretty, clear crystals I found during one of my adventures in the woods, wrapped with straw and mud. I've memorized every bump and groove over the years, and it's perfect.

My little secret, safe and sound.

Good.

I tune him out as he continues to berate me for being an irritating human and recites the various punishments he will force me to endure for the coming year. He laughs, but he won't be for much longer.

This year, the damn horn is mine—no matter the cost.

It's just me and him. There's no one to outnumber me this time, and Gnars is truly on his own.

I pull out my conduit and aim it at his big, stupid face.

He stops talking, voice caught in his large throat which leaves his mouth hanging open like a dumb animal. He stares at my short wand in a blend of disgust and disbelief. "You *dare*—"

"That's right asshole," I growl. "Back up."

He edges closer to the horn. His fingers flinch as they get ever so close to touching it.

I sigh and roll my eyes. "The other direction, Gnars."

He growls and does as he is told.

Keeping an eye on him, my conduit pointed dangerously at his chest, I climb to my feet. Cold water sloshes between my toes and I try to ignore the chill overcoming my body as the cool breeze blows like ice through my clothes.

"Farther," I say, voice deadpan and leaving no room for argument.

"I won," Gnars growls.

"Not yet you haven't."

He doesn't win until he blows the horn, and I'll be damned if he gets to it first.

"You're making everything worse for yourself, human," he says with disgust, like I'm nothing more than an ant beneath his boot.

"My name is *Wren*," I snap. "And I won't let you cheat your way to winning this year, Gnars."

His eyes dart toward the horn and he goes to grab it. Furious, unwilling to let him win yet again, I shoot a blast of my magic at his chest. It hits his arm instead, blowing a hole in his sleeve. He yells in pain, the cry echoing through the forest as he's blown backward.

As smoke spirals from his arm, he scrambles toward the horn. If he blows it, he can get help— and I won't let that happen.

I jump into a dead run, cutting him off before he can get a hand on the trophy of this hunt. He manages to get on his feet as I near, but I'm faster.

Wrapping an arm around his waist, I throw all my weight into him.

Lucky for me, trolls are top-heavy.

We fall together to the forest floor. Furious, practically seething at my audacity, he pounds his hands into my back, and I bite against the pain as my magic fills me. It burns and swirls within my body, boiling my blood with all the rage and fire of battle.

Time to end this.

I aim my conduit at his shoulder and blast him with a shock of electric light.

He cries out and releases me.

This is my chance.

I bolt to my feet, my eyes on the horn.

It's *so* close.

Gnars grabs my ankle and tugs hard. I fall, and my chin hits a rock embedded in the leaves beneath us. My world spins, and I can't stop myself from teetering as I try to regain my balance. "Enough," Gnars says, his voice dripping with hatred. "You will pay for daring to touch me, you disgusting human."

Murmurs echo from around me, banging around in my aching skull as I try to clear my head. My vision slowly clears, and to my horror, Gnars and I are no longer alone. The thirteen other trolls that were participating in the hunt slowly emerge from the shadows, one by one, cutting off every possible exit.

They surround me, sneering. Some lift their clubs, ready to bash my head in if I so much as dare to move. They cluster around me, ignoring the horn despite the fact that it's barely five feet away from my outstretched palm.

They... they were all in on it.

I can't help but gape in dismay as I figure it out. They're not going for the horn because they don't *want* it. Whatever deal Gnars made with them, they refuse to let anyone else win.

I knew he was a cheating bastard, but this is an entirely new low. Even for *him*.

There's only *one* rule of the hunt. Every troll for himself.

They were willing to work together if it means I fail. If it means they get to keep their puny little human slave for another year.

"You're never going to let me go," I say quietly, finally understanding. "All this—even if I got the horn, you wouldn't honor your promise."

Gnars chuckles darkly, brushing off his still-sizzling shirt as he stands. "You finally understand how the game works." He looks me over briefly. "You're just a toy we play with, but it's fun to watch you fail."

My hope shatters.

I can't possibly take them all on at once. It'll mean another six months of healing, of shattered bones, of trudging their laundry to the river even as I gasp to breathe.

But I don't care.

I won't give up that easy.

Gnars has seen the conduit, which means they're going to beat me regardless of what I do. I only used it because I thought I would escape this place, but now I realize that's never going to happen.

If I want out, I have to fight my way free.

The other trolls inch toward me as Gnars calmly walks toward the horn, rubbing salt in the wound as he casually goes to claim what's mine.

Briefly, I debate blowing the stupid thing to smithereens, but that would only fuel their hatred. They would kick me harder for destroying their ancient relic. No, as much as I want to destroy everything around me, I rein in my anger.

Mostly.

The nearest troll—Fek, the dumbass that he is— smirks, gently slapping his club against the palm of his hand as he scans my body for where he wants to hit me first. Three more flank him, each sizing me up, each ready to hurt the weak little human in their midst.

But none of them seem to notice the conduit in my hands. Trolls are evil, but at least most of them are fairly stupid.

I should have known better. I should have known they would never honor their promise. I should have known they would keep me here, forever, doing whatever it took to keep their frail little human slave.

Lesson learned.

The betrayal still stings. I can barely breathe. My magic bites at me from within, desperate to break free, eager to destroy something.

Fek swings his club at my head, and I duck. Lost in my rage, I fire at his chest. It hits him hard, knocking him into the trolls standing behind him. Sizzling blasts of my magic dart in every direction as I fire randomly, knowing I'll hit something because I'm entirely surrounded.

I mostly hit trees, but I manage to take down three of the trolls. They fall, groaning in pain as the others swarm me. Something hits me hard in the small of my back, and I fall to my knees in agony. I grimace, trying to bite back my scream of pain. Someone else grabs my hand, twisting it violently until the conduit falls to the ground.

But I'm not done.

I'm not going down without a fight.

I reach for the knife in my boot, the dull one they gave me to gut fish and tie off rope. My fingers brush the hilt as another troll knees me in the face, knocking me to the ground.

They pile on top of me as I struggle beneath them, trying to reach my conduit, trying desperately to wrestle my way out of their grip and blast them all to dust.

But I can't.

Trolls don't have magic, but they do have incredible strength—and I have six of them either grabbing my limbs or lying on my back.

I'm pinned.

*Damn it.*

"Grab it, Gnars!" Fek shouts as he slowly sits up, one hand on his chest as he nurses the smoking wound I gave him.

"Get it!" another troll chimes in.

Their voices clamor together as they rub my defeat in my face, forcing me to watch as Gnars puffs out his chest with pride. He smirks, arrogant and full of himself, like I didn't just damn near own his ass only moments ago. He steps casually to the tree, reaches for the horn, wraps the item in his chubby, dingy hands, and brings the mouthpiece to his sorry excuse for lips.

Sucking in a deep breath, he blows. And the last of my strength leaves me.

The sound shudders the trees. More hoots and hollers come from the trolls around me. They chant in Gnars's honor. Then they turn their unwavering attention to me.

Here it comes…

"You will never win, slave," one says, and I absolutely don't give a damn who it is. I don't care anymore.

They laugh as they sling blends of insults at me from left and right. I tune it out. I've heard them all before, and none of it matters now.

They want to see me cry. They want to feel stronger than and superior to me. They need to prove to themselves—and to me, in some twisted way—that they are stronger than me. I'm beneath them. My place is to do their bidding and kiss their mud-covered feet. All because they say so.

But they're wrong, and I don't cry. I never cry. Not in front of them, and never in private.

Tears are weakness. One I can't afford.

"You're just inferior, human girl. Always have been, and always will be." Gnars hooks the horn to his belt and gives it a proud little pat, like he's daring me to do something about it. Say something about it. But I don't.

He gives a nod, and his cronies slowly stand. They lift me to my feet, only to toss me to the ground. I land hard, but I don't stay down long. I quickly jump to my feet and eye my conduit.

I need to grab it. To be done with this place and these trolls. My magic pools beneath my skin, and I let it gather so that I can take them all out once I reach my conduit.

Because I'm done with being pushed around.

Gnars nods to the conduit, barely four feet away. "Take that stick and break it. She can never have something like that again."

My eyes widen. Now or never, then.

I dive for it, but Fek is closer. As my fingers brush along the crystals, he grabs it and elbows me hard in the face. I fall, my world spinning as the trolls pile on me again. They grab my arms, pinning me down. I growl, cuss, and buck against them. It's mine. They can't have it.

My magic churns within me, and even from this

distance, the wand starts to glow with my power.

My heart flutters with hope.

Seemingly oblivious, Gnars grabs the conduit out of Fek's hands and looks it over. "Ugly little thing. Just like you."

He squeezes my wand in his hands, breaking it, reducing the crystals to glittering dust and the wood to little more than kindling. He tosses the remnants to the ground in front of my face, and the trolls pinning me down finally let go.

I sit up and look at the rubble in front of me as Gnars steps toward me. I don't look at him. I won't give him the satisfaction of seeing the pain in my eyes, because what he did broke me.

No mage can perform magic without a conduit.

I'm so, *so* screwed.

Gnars kneels until his putrid face is level with mine. "You need to accept this, girl. You will never be one of us, and you will never have freedom. I'll rule this place someday, and when I do, you will finally experience *true* hell."

He laughs, and the rest join in as they leave, celebrating Gnars's victory again.

Fucking cheater.

As they retreat into the trees, leaving me broken and battered on the dead leaves of the forest floor, I stare at the shattered remnants of my beautiful conduit. My last shred of hope. Tenderly, I scoop the fractured remains of the wand into my palms, my throat tightening in dread and horror as I stare into the lifeless crystals.

It'll take *years* to make another one. To find the ingredients. To find a moment alone to perform the ritual. To create a bond strong and beautiful enough to cast my magic once again.

I'm… I'm screwed.

Looking at what is left of the conduit I made, I can practically feel my heart shredding to pieces. I can practically feel myself break.

Still, I don't allow a tear to fall.

Building the conduit was the hardest thing I've ever done in my life. My father showed me how, when I was little, and it took ages to remember all the steps. In a way, it was the last thing I had to remember him by, and Gnars…

He will pay for this one way or another.

As if in response to my rising anger, my magic swirls within me, pooling in my hands, trying to come out, but it doesn't. Because, it can't.

All magic has to have a conduit.

All I can do is sit there and stare at the ground, the dust, the splinters of wood, and wait for my magic to calm. After a while, I collect the pieces and shards that I could salvage of the conduit and tuck them inside my pockets.

Standing, I dust myself off and look back in the direction of the troll village.

I don't want to go back. I can't. The moment I do, my punishment will begin. I attacked them, and I broke the first rule of my imprisonment—I'm forbidden to have a conduit.

They're distracted now with the feast and celebration of Gnars' victory, and that buys me some time.

I'm leaving. Maybe I can just take a nice long walk and never return. There has to be a limit to how far even the trolls will go before giving up on me. They despise humanity, live in secrecy, and won't risk exposure of their existence for me. Especially with as often as they remind me that I'm nothing to them but a slave.

It's a long shot. But I can at least attempt freedom. If not for just a little while.

Regardless of how I spin the possibilities or how little I matter to them, I have to face the facts. I'm still their property, and they will always find me.

Next time they find me, however, I'm determined to make them regret trying to bring me back.

## CHAPTER TWO

I belong somewhere.

I know it. Deep down.

Though it may not be with the trolls, there is some place for me. A place to belong.

The town nearby is full of humans. Ones who smile and say hello. Ones that don't look down on me for being one of them. For being human. I look like them. Not like a troll. I'm the furthest thing from a troll as I could possibly get.

Strangely, I don't think that my position among the trolls would be any different even if I did look like them. However you skin it, I'm still an outsider.

I make my way toward the sleepy town of Lakeview, Idaho, weaving my way through the trees on the downward sloping mountainside as the sun rises high overhead, inching its way toward the other side of the world. This town has become a welcome escape for me. I visit as often as I can.

And after today, I may never see it again.

Though the trolls usually keep me busy with burying their shit within the trees, discarding of rotting remains from animals they don't finish eating, washing their rags called clothing, or serving as a form of entertainment, I still find time to make it here. It has been a while since I've been able to come. I usually have to sneak off to get time away. Much like this visit.

The trolls won't look for me until tomorrow morning at the earliest. They'll be too preoccupied with their celebration of Gnars's victory to worry about me. Hell, maybe I'll get lucky and they'll give up on finding me ever again.

Wishful thinking, but still.

I leave the shelter of the trees and make my way across the highway where the town sits nestled against a large, blue lake that mirrors the sky. The sun reflects off the water like a beacon, and at night, that's my favorite. The moon and stars are painted along the clear waters as if a whole world rests within the water.

Absolutely beautiful.

Sometimes I would sneak off during the night just for that view alone. Hope and the knowledge that a better life is out there for me somewhere would brew in me. I would become resolved, encouraged in my faith there was something more in the world for me than living beneath the feet of the trolls.

I step off the road and into the trees bordering the streets of Lakeview. I find the walking path that leads into town and take my time, watching as the leaves in the canopy above me dance in the sunlight and the breeze gently blows around me. Warmth and the smell of earth surround me.

The soft twinkling of laughter echoes toward me. I smile and follow the sound. In my life of constant misery, to hear genuine, happy laughs is quite something to experience. I want to know more, and the sweet music leads me toward a pair of children playing in their yard set back from the main road.

The kids are playing tag while their mother sleeps on the porch of their small cabin-like home. It's a peacefulness that I'm rarely graced with seeing. The girl can't be more than six, and the boy no more than eight years old as they chase each other in circles a short distance from their front door.

The sight makes me nostalgic about my own childhood. I miss the time when I played in my yard, chasing fireflies while my dad held open a mason jar.

But that was another time altogether.

Now was the time that even small, quaint towns like this have nightmares.

The last time I was here, I saw notices from small towns surrounding the area reporting abductions of small children. There's something in these woods—something that takes kids.

Nervously, I glance again at their mother. Her weary expression makes me wonder when she last slept, and her eyes keep fluttering open even as she drifts to sleep.

My magic courses through me, pulsating with warning. It detected something I missed.

There's danger in these shadows.

A pinch forms in my forehead as I process the sudden change in the tension in the air. With their mom sleeping in the chair, I don't think there would be enough time to keep them safe if something were to happen.

Strange. Nothing seems off.

A nagging sensation to leave burns through me. I need to get out of here, to put as much distance between me and the trolls as possible. It's my only hope of escaping them once and for all.

But my conscience won't let me. If there really is danger here, I can't let these kids be hurt.

I scan the shadows of the woods surrounding the home and nothing moves. Maybe it's just me, but just to be safe, I remain in the shadows and watch the kids a little longer.

The mother stirs, and I think she's about to wake. I take that as a sign and proceed on my way toward the main road.

I was probably worried about nothing.

As I leave, I cast one last wary look over my shoulders—only to catch a pair of glowing red eyes hovering in the shadows of the woods opposite where I was standing before. They're so close to the ground, so dim that I couldn't see them before, but at this angle I can't miss them. They hover low to the ground, almost completely blending in with the colorful leaves collected on the ground at the base of the trees.

I'm on high alert and don't know what I can do. I don't have my conduit, so I can't perform magic. But I can't leave these kids to a fate I don't care to imagine, because the creature in the woods stalking them would certainly lead the poor things to a grisly, nightmarish end.

I can't let that happen.

With the life Gnars has laid out for me, I'm as good as dead. Even if I escape now, he'll hunt me for the rest of my life. Without a conduit, I don't stand much of a chance, so whatever happens to me is fine. But these kids have a long life ahead of them, and I'll be damned if the light in their eyes is snuffed out before their time.

Taking a deep breath, I run my hands down the length of my sides and straighten my shoulders, preparing myself for what has to be done.

I casually step into the yard and calmly walk toward the playing children. The boy sees me first and stops laughing as he faces me, and his expression is a mix of questioning and curiosity. The girl follows suit, turning to face me as well, probably wondering why brother stopped playing.

I stop a few feet in front of them.

"Who are you?" the boy asks.

I smile at them, trying to make myself seem as friendly, warm, and casual as possible. "I was chasing a rabid dog," I lie, winging it, "and with the playful sounds you two were making, I'm worried he's headed this way."

Their eyes widen as their mouths form wide "O" shapes.

"What should we do?" the girl asks.

"As calm and as quickly as you can, go inside, and please take your mom with you. Can you both be brave and do that, please?"

They nod, and the brother takes his sister's hand as they walk toward the house and up the steps, and I make my way toward the creature that watches the kids walk away.

In my pockets, my palms are slick with sweat. The red eyes in the darkness shift toward me and narrow.

I rack my brain for a plan. I still have the dagger in my boot, thankfully, but that's not going to be much good if this is a magical being.

"You cost me a meal, wench," the creature hisses. Its chilling voice sends a shiver up my spine, and it sounds like I imagine Death itself would sound if it came for me.

"Sorry," I say with a shrug even as my heart thuds painfully in my chest.

The eyes slowly raise through the growing darkness as the creature lifts its head, growing staggeringly taller with every passing second. "Never fret, child. I shall eat you instead."

Oh, joy. I'm a meal now.

I take a deep, calming breath as my magic pulses through me in warning. It wants me to run, but going into the field would mean those kids might see what was stalking them.

A sight like that, and so young—it would shatter them.

Careful to keep my distance, I step into the woods so that no one can see me take on this creature I'm not even sure I will be able to kill.

My dagger is crude at best, but it will have to work. I hope it will be enough.

As my eyes quickly adjust to the darkness in the forest, a beam of sunlight cutting through the canopy glints off silver scales a short distance away. The scales move through the shadows, slithering through the darkness as the coiled body of a massive snake comes into view.

A woman's face appears between two branches, her red eyes narrowed on me as she hovers impossibly high in the air. As she nears, I wonder what I'm up against—a rogue mage, maybe, with a snake for a pet.

But, as she steps into the light, I realize the

smooth skin on her naked torso slowly fades into the silver scales.

She *is* the snake.

This is a lamia.

*Shit.*

My father told me stories of the lamias when I was a little girl, and none of them end happily. These beasts eat children that stray too far from their parents.

Now, I'm about to become her dinner.

I should feel dread. Maybe even fear. But as I stare into the cruel monster's glowing eyes, all I can feel is numbness.

If she wants to eat me, she's going to have to *work* for it.

"You don't really want to eat me, do you?" I grin, gesturing to my body. "I'm probably all tough and chewy."

The creature stretches high above me as she unhinges her mouth. It almost seems to grow in size to accommodate my body, but I refuse to stand here and let this horrifying creature eat me.

I'm thankful the children are safe and sound inside their home. If they saw this thing, their fragile minds would be forever shattered.

I pull on the dagger, forcing back the shudder

that threatens to rush through me at the unhinged jaw on this woman's face. My hand grips the handle tightly as the blade points toward the lamia.

She chuckles, her words garbled thanks to her stretched jaw. "That won't do you any good against me, human."

"Maybe." I shrug. "Maybe not. I guess we'll see."

I charge the snake-like creature. As the wind blows my hair from my face, making my sight clear, I aim the blade for the scaled belly button on the body of the lamia. It lands true. The lamia lets out an ear-splitting scream, but I don't let go.

She claws my arm, leaving four deep gashes. A stinging pain burns through my shoulder. I bite my lip and jump back, rolling to my feet before she could land another blow like that. The blade of my dagger is coated in slimy, green ichor and I do my best to wipe it on my pants.

The lamia is quick. Almost quicker than me as she slithers toward me and slashes again. I dodge in time to barely avoid another slash of her sharp claws. My magic grows stronger within me and I bite my lip against it, wishing I had a conduit right about now. This fight would be over already if I could just use the power within me.

I lunge and sink my blade into her side. She

growls and claws at me as I wrench the blade in a long slash. She flings me from her, and I land hard against the trunk of a tree and topple to the ground. My dagger is gone. I must have lost my grip on it when I hit the tree, and I have no idea where it is. Rolling to my back, I face the creature as she coils for her attack.

She launches.

I flip myself over and quickly duck behind the tree.

There are two choices, here—try desperately to find a dull knife somewhere in the dark, or run.

She crashes into the trunk and splinters of bark shatter from the impact.

Looks like I'm running.

I run deeper into the woods. This fight was too close to the cabin and too close to the village. I can't let the lamia be seen. It would cause chaos and fear, and these people are too kind to live with such nightmares.

The lamia follows me, growling and screaming and repeatedly demanding that I stop dragging this out any longer than necessary.

"You're only making your death sweeter for me and more painful for you," she hauntingly calls after me.

Not if I can help it.

"Gotta make you work for your dinner. Can't eat for free," I shout over my shoulder.

That pisses her off more.

Her claws swipe at my legs, and she knocks me clear off my feet. I fall on my back, rolling, and scramble backward as she slowly coils to spring.

We should be far enough from civilization, hoping and praying to whoever is out there listening there aren't more of her kind hanging around, waiting for dinner to come home. I doubt it, because lamias aren't exactly common in these parts, but if anyone had asked me if I expected to run into one of these creatures on my trip to the human town, I would've laughed at them.

The lamia is seething now, breathing exaggerated and with each exhale she sprays saliva, poison, or both from her scaly lips.

"Enough of this nonsense!" A string of saliva oozes from her lips. "It's time to die."

I jump to my feet and beckon her closer with my hands. "You first."

She launches and I dodge the blow. I notice a stick with a semi-pointed end laying off to the side, so I grab it. It won't do much damage, but dammit, it will keep her teeth busy instead of embedded in my flesh.

She slaps my side with her tail, and I fly through the air and hit a tree. This hit takes a lot out of me. My head spins and my vision blurs. I won't be able to take many more hits like that before I'm as good as dinner.

My magic begs to be freed as she wraps her tail around the bottom half of my legs and holds me upside down in the air. But I can't let it free. I have no conduit.

I'm caught between a rock and hard place. Her mouth opens wide and I see into the cavernous hole that I'm about to be taken into.

As my magic boils with fury and rage, I hold my hands up to brace for her impact.

A torrent of purplish pink light shoots from my hands in a strong burst that obliterates the creature. Her tail releases me, and I fall as I shut my eyes against the painful burst of light. I hit the ground hard, groaning in agony as pain splinters down my back. The brunt force seems to shut off the blast of light from my palms, and for a moment, the world is staggeringly silent.

Once my magic ebbs, I blink away the dots of light amidst the ashes that fill the space surrounding me. Soot wafts on a gentle breeze, coating the grass with gray powder.

The lamia is gone.

I… I destroyed it.

With my bare hands.

I want to feel victory. To feel joy. To feel *something.*

But mostly, I'm still just numb.

My eyes drift toward the shadows of the woods as the lamia's ashes float weightlessly toward the ground.

Oh shit.

I just performed magic. *Without* a conduit.

This is bad.

Really, really bad.

Ever since I was a little girl, my father was my greatest teacher. He taught me the laws of magic. Number one being, all magic must be used with a conduit. But I was such a challenging, inquisitive child. I never took what I was told at face value. I always wanted to know more, try things out for myself to see if the rules could be bent or broken.

So, when the topic arose, I faced my father and asked, "What would happen if I did use magic without a conduit?"

He became serious as his brown eyes met my

own. He lowered himself to my height and gripped my shoulders. I thought maybe I had made him mad, that he was going to shake me, but his firm grip never wavered as he said, "Only those who are dark and have dark intentions will be able to break the laws and perform magic under such circumstances. Anyone who uses magic without a conduit is *always* dark. Even if they were born with good hearts, the power corrupts them. It's inevitable."

As silence weighs on the trees and the final remnants of what I had done collects on the ground around me, I know what this means. My breaths quicken as my thoughts begin to race.

Oh. My. God.

I'm dark?

It has to mean I'm dark.

But I don't *feel* dark.

I want to figure this out. Come up with any other options or possibilities that would explain my magic away. To make it mean I'm not going dark. But the shouts of men reach me, and I have to get out of here quick. I can't be caught.

Climbing to my feet, I glance one final time at the collection of ashes scattered among leaves, dirt, and twigs. I turn away, running for freedom.

There has to be an explanation for me doing

magic beyond me being dark that would somehow make what I had just done okay. And I have to figure that out soon.

Because, as Dad had emphatically told me, there was no coming back from going dark.

## CHAPTER THREE

I know in my heart that I should move faster, to put as much distance between me and the trolls as possible, but the weight of what I did to the lamia is almost too much to handle.

The moon is already high in the night sky, shining beams of silvery light through the treetops, lighting my way as I slowly make my way to a new life.

I ran in a wide circle from the lamia's remains, in case the humans had dogs with them. When I came across a spring, I cleaned out my wound and covered it with some moss and mud. My head and body both ache, screaming with some of the harder hitting movements like landing after a jump or climbing over boulders, but all in all I know my injuries could have been much, much worse.

"I need a break," I mumble to myself, rubbing my stinging eyes.

Taking a seat on the ground at the base of a tree, I watch the moon as it struggles to push its light through the canopy of the trees above me, filtering the thick shadows with silver light alive with mystical nightlife that remains secret and safe from most of humanity.

Faeries step between trees a short distance from me. They have seen me before, but they are still wary of me. I'm half-mage, sure, but I'm still half-human, and faeries are distrusting of humans thanks to their penchant to destroy things they don't understand. I know there's more to that, but that's the best answer I know. So, that's what I stick with.

Fireflies, or sprites, dance in and out of the shadows, weaving through the bushes and trees. I wish I hadn't caught them when I was a little girl. They are so tiny, harmless, and had I known they die in captivity, I would never have done it. But that was a lesson I learned the hard way, and I always leave them bits and pieces of my few, small meals as a means of making amends for my childhood mistakes.

A branch snaps from my right and my head snaps in that direction. I narrow my eyes as I see a glimpse of something I had yet to see but had read stories of.

A stag with soft, glowing white antlers steps into view and turns his head toward me, his eyes meet mine and I can tell he's trying to decide if I mean danger. The edges of his body shimmer like fog, iridescent and indistinct.

I lower my head in a small bow to show my respect and to signal that I'm not going to bring him harm.

He watches me for a moment longer before he continues on his way, peaceful and quiet.

I smile, despite myself. The legend surrounding the stags are as long as I'm tall and range widely from granting wishes to being just a symbol of good luck. I don't know which is correct, and honestly, I don't want to find out. He's a life. An innocent creature that just wants to live without disruption of greedy hands. Who am I to stand in his way?

Small yellow lights fill the hollow of a tree not far off to my left. Gnomes. They are small delights but vicious when backed into a corner. Rabbits hop across my path, one stopping to sniff the air around me before hopping off.

This is the reminder that I needed. Life can be beautiful. Seeing these creatures gives me belief that things can be better than what they are now. I just need to get there first.

But I can't sit here forever.

I watch for just a little while longer before forcing myself up to my feet and dusting off the back of my pants with my hands. Time to go. Whether I like it or not.

Before long, I get the creeping sensation of someone following me. Though as I look around, I can't see anything out of the ordinary. Or anyone for that matter. But as I continue on, that feeling only continues to grow. And as I reach a small dirt path that cuts through the forest, I spot someone sitting on a toppled down tree not far off from me. No more than fifty feet or so ahead of me.

I pause briefly to weigh my options.

One: I can continue on and see who this person is. I know he's not a troll. He's too small.

Two: I can walk back the other direction, circle around, and hope that I throw this person off my trail, if they are waiting for me.

Three... I really don't have a three. Those are

pretty much the possibilities that I have to work with, as going in the opposite direction is just wasting precious time.

The person turns their attention toward me, and I blow a raspberry and cross my arms over my chest in defeat. Well, crap. Now I *have* to go with option number one. I start moving toward him.

The figure stands and says, "Wren Blackwood?"

I stop mid-step and hold my breath. This person definitely was looking for me. "Who are you, and how do you know my name?"

He slowly makes his way toward me and says, "My name is Deacon Lawrence. I'm a professor of alchemy at Blackbriar Academy. As to how I know your name? Magic, of course."

"Blackbriar Academy?" I gape, breathless. I go still, simply watching the man who *lives* at the most historic academy for magic in the world. Mages would kill just to visit, much less attend.

When I was little, I dreamed about going. But now, I dream about vengeance. About finding the people who killed my family. Nowadays, I dream about freedom.

I take a steadying breath, trying to clear my head and focus. He glossed over how he found me, and I suspect he figured he could drop the academy's name and make my knees go weak.

I'm not that easy to win over.

This guy is gonna have to do a lot better with his answers if I'm going to believe him.

"Explain how you found me, then." I stand taller to look more imposing than I probably am. It's a trick I learned from the trolls, but hey, it works.

Deacon approaches me. "I have a machine that allows me to track specific magic throughout the world. You recently performed magic, yes?"

I hesitate, but nod.

He stands less than two feet in front of me now and I can see that he is tall, with short, grey hair. His stature suggests that he's accustomed to his position with his long brown coat and business slacks. A scarf drapes over his shoulders. He smiles, as if he notices me sizing him up.

"That's how I found you," he admits. "I tracked the signature to the area where the magic was performed and traces of it led me to this place," he gestures around him. "It took a little while to figure out which direction you'd take, but I'm fairly good at ironing out little details like that." He winks proudly.

"But why?" I ask.

He nods, his smile fading, and that strikes me as odd for some reason. "Each year, I'm given one invitation to the school's trials for admittance to the academy. I give mine to those whom I believe show promise in their magical abilities." He takes a step closer, watching me with an intense gaze. "I find talented mages, Wren, and I make them truly *great.*"

He reaches into the inside pocket of his coat and pulls out a black envelope and holds it out to me.

Rustling sounds surround us, and if Deacon hears it, he doesn't let on. But I notice it as loud as ever, and the hairs on my arms stand on end.

"She's not going anywhere. She belongs to us," the troll chief says.

Shit.

The trolls are here.

I turn to face them, brimming with the rage I've tried so hard to swallow over the years. "But *why*? You hate me. You only want to keep me to empty bed pans and be a punching bag when nothing goes your way. I'm your scapegoat. Anything wrong gets blamed on me. Just for *existing* and annoying you with my mere presence. Let me simply leave!"

"You will not go," the chief says. "You will be put in chains if you push further. You think we hate you now? You have not seen anything yet. As I see it, we have been more than lenient with you."

The trolls step out of the shadows. We are surrounded. Damn near the whole village is here. They must have had something special planned for me upon my return, and they were *pissed* when I didn't show. Chains were likely just the beginning of that little treat.

How sweet.

"You," Gnars says, voice a low growl, and points to the professor. "You will die for trespassing on troll land."

"What?" I ask. "You have got to be joking."

"Humans can't know of us," the chief says. "All humans die. Can't let him rattle off about us and our location."

"He's a mage," I snap. "If you think—"

"Shut up," Gnars interrupts.

I bristle, my hatred simmering beneath my skin. "No."

Gnars tilts his head, clearly astonished. "What did you—"

"Never again," I say with a grimace. "I'm not your toy anymore."

I killed a lamia with my bare hands. Dark or not, I don't have to put up with them anymore. I don't entirely know how I used my magic without a conduit, sure, but if I did it once, I can do it again. This man's life isn't going to be taken because of me, and I'm *never* going back to the trolls.

I turn toward the professor. "The academy is a lot of things to a lot of people," I admit. "But I want the truth. Is where you want me to go better than this place?"

All I need is a promise of things being a fraction better, and that would work for me. If only to get away from the trolls. Once I'm free, I'll press for more information. And if I don't like what I hear, I'll go off on my own.

Simple as that.

Deacon Lawrence smiles, but it doesn't quite reach his eyes. "Undoubtedly," he says.

I know he isn't telling me everything. To be the best, you have to make sacrifices, and I suspect Blackbriar Academy is so much more than people think.

But it's good enough for now. I won't find out what it is if we don't get away from here, so I nod. For the time being, that answer will suffice.

"Wren," Professor Lawrence says sternly. "Do you accept?"

Do I accept his invitation to Blackbriar Academy?

To the trials he has told me nothing about?

"If it means I get the hell out of here," I say with a nod to the trolls around me. "Then hell yes."

"Very well," he says calmly, withdrawing his conduit from his pocket as he turns his attention to the chief. "Sir, I'm afraid Miss Blackwood is under my protection, now. If you attempt to take her, you will answer to me."

Despite the fact that I don't totally trust this man, I smile. It's nice to not be totally alone.

As the trolls lift their clubs, ready to swarm us, I square my shoulders. This man is my ticket to a better life, and I won't use magic without a conduit unless I absolutely have to.

I don't want him to know what I can do. Dad never told me what happens to the mages who go dark, but I can guess.

I ball my hands into fists, ready to do what it takes to finally win my freedom. And, for the second time in one day, I will literally fight for my life.

## CHAPTER FOUR

My first mark is the chief, and I punch him square in the face. Years of getting my knuckles broken as they beat me to a pulp gave me a wicked right jab, and he goes down like a pile of bricks.

Of course, I just signed my own death warrant by attacking the chief of the troll village, but I will not go down easy.

The trolls charge.

Trolls are mean, nasty creatures and will sink to any low if it means they win. No one knows this better than I do. To win this fight, both Deacon and I will have to be smart about each move we make and try to outwit them as much as possible.

It dawns on me to let the professor know this. "They cheat!"

"Thanks for the warning," he shouts as he twists around and blasts the trolls running up behind him with a blast of light that looks a lot like bolts of lightning but bluer. A loud boom resonates through the forest as it connects with the trolls. He doesn't stop, instead moving on to the next troll.

Meanwhile, I dodge the club aimed for my head as a fist connects with my gut.

"Hold still so I can hit you," Fek says.

"Don't count on it," I retort as I slide to the ground and slam my foot into the troll's kneecap. He groans in pain as another troll comes to take Fek's place.

I dodge and weave between them, knowing my erratic movements are going to do nothing but piss them off more. And that's exactly what I want. A pissed-off troll makes mistakes.

As I duck blow after blow, a delightful little tremor shoots through me. My magic burns and boils in my blood, and I'm surprised to find that I actually enjoy this.

The fight.

In fact, the rush of slurs and growls the trolls keep throwing at me is hard not to laugh at.

The chief charges into the fray, his furious glare trained on me. When he finally goes to land a blow to my face, I duck, and he hits the troll that was sneaking up on me. He slams his club into the other's head, and I chuckle.

This is kind of *fun*.

A red blast of heat rushes behind me and I turn to find another troll ignite in flames. I face Deacon, and he nods, lips in a grim line. I nod and return to the fight as a female charges me with a makeshift knife made of sharpened stone. Her eyes are full of rage and fury. "No one hits the chief!"

"Well, I just did. Now what?"

I fall to my butt and roll, kicking up my feet in the air. As she goes to land on me, I plant my feet in her stomach and use her momentum to roll back, sending her into a tumble on the ground, and I follow through, landing on my feet.

All around us is chaos. Magic flares and burning flesh and wood, mixed with screams, growls, and the electric snaps of the professor's magic. My own magic pulsates and rushes through me, but I can't use my magic. Not in front of Deacon. It's too dangerous. At least until I know about how I was able to perform magic without a conduit.

That will have to remain my secret.

For now.

Even if Deacon Lawrence conveniently showed up at the right time, there is still something about him I'm not quite sure about. There is more he needs to tell me before I will trust him completely. Even though he is able to hold his own in a fight, I will never get the answers I need if the trolls somehow outwit this man and kill him.

And with each troll downed, two more seem to come.

That confirms it. The whole village came looking for me. I can't help but wonder what sort of unpleasant things they had planned for me for losing the hunt again as I continue to stay out of reach of the trolls. If Deacon hadn't shown up, I probably would have been put in those chains like the chief threatened.

A force hits me hard in the back and I fall to my hands and knees. Sharp stabbing pain shoots up my arms and legs as bits of rock and bark embed into my skin. I don't let that distract me for long. Looking over my shoulder, Gnars is about to kick me in my stomach. I quickly roll out of the way, and his foot slides out from underneath him. He seems to hover in the air for a moment as the realization dawns on him that he's about to land on his back.

And he does. With a loud thud.

"Serves you right, cheater," I say.

He groans and slowly climbs to his feet. When he faces me, he says, "You will pay for that."

"I'm afraid I'm not in charge of gravity, so that one's on you."

I dodge the fist aimed for my gut by twisting out of the way and ramming my elbow into the back of his ribs. He gasps and tries to recover as one of his buddies runs up with a club, ready to swing at my head.

Without hesitation, I chamber my left leg in front of me and as soon as he is close enough, I kick with all the force I have in me. He's knocked back, taking down two others with him.

My magic pulsates stronger, and I bite my lip against it. I cannot lose control over the power within me. Not this close. I could kill Deacon—or, worse, he could discover my darkness.

I'm kicking ass, sure. But I would totally own this fight with my magic.

I try to shove that thought and my magic down as Gnars finally recovers. I face him, eye to eye.

"What will it be, Gnars?" I ask. "Fight and lose more of your people, or end this and let us go?"

"You belong to us." He huffs. "You will never go

anywhere else. When we're back, I'll chop off your legs so you can never run away again."

I square my shoulders and lift my head higher. "You'll have to catch me first."

"Cowards run," he says.

I narrow my eyes. "I never said I was going to run."

Without missing a beat, I land a roundhouse to his side, a punch to his gut, and an upper cut to his face. I finish this beauty of a move by front kicking the shit out of his sternum. Gnars quickly recovers, much to my chagrin, and lands a solid blow to my face and another to my gut.

I stumble backward, knowing the last time I got myself into a situation where it looked like I was nearing the end of the line, my magic took control and released a torrent of destruction, vaporizing my foe into nothing but ash.

But I would rather do that than lose.

I would rather lose control and expose everything than go back to the trolls.

My hands start to glow as I regain my balance and form fists. I keep an eye on Deacon, who has a nice collection of trolls scattered around him, all of the trolls either unconscious or dead. I can't be sure.

My attention switches to Gnars as he is popping his knuckles.

"Time to learn your place once and for all. He cocks his arm to land a devastating blow.

I swallow hard and charge him, slamming into his torso, sending him backward. He lands hard on the ground as his head cracks against the earth in a sickening thud that will likely haunt my dreams for many years to come. His arms go limp and I stand. As I stare at him, I think of all the times he had cheated his way to the horn during the hunts, the many days of endless torment, and the hurtful words and horrifying promises of torture he would always give.

No more.

The chief climbs to his feet and shouts, "Enough!"

The fighting stops as all eyes look toward him, even mine and Deacon's.

"Enough loss has been had tonight. We will let you leave. But on one condition," the chief says.

Deacon looks to me before turning his attention back to the chief. "What is the condition?"

The chief lifts his head. "You are hereby banished. Should you or any of your people ever return, you will incite a war."

"I can't imagine she'll want to come back," Deacon says. "It's a deal."

"Good." The chief turns and gestures to his people who gather their dead and wounded and carry them back to the village.

And I'm staring, holding my breath, unable to fully process that I had just been given my freedom. It's too much. I suck in a breath and watch as the trolls leave me behind. My gaze shifts to Deacon and I'm caught off guard. He seems irritated.

"What?" I ask.

"Why didn't you use magic?" he asks.

"No conduit. They shattered mine earlier," I say. It's not the truth, but it's not a lie either. To prove it, I reach into my pocket and pull out the remains of the conduit to show him and prove myself to him.

He nods. "We'll have to get you another one then."

At first, I don't know what to say. I just stand there.

"Why live with the trolls?" he asked and makes a disgusted expression.

Trust me buddy, it wasn't a choice. "I was kidnapped from my bed when I was fourteen. That was shortly after I went to live with my Aunt Patricia."

"Where are your parents?" he asked as he starts dusting himself off and readjusting his clothes.

I shrug and wrap my arms around myself. "My parents were..." A knot forms in my throat, and I look quickly away to hide the flicker of pain I'm sure is crossing my face. I clear my throat, eager to get this over with. "My parents were killed, okay? My aunt took me in."

"Your Aunt is Patricia Blackwood?"

I hesitate, but eventually nod.

"I know of her." A quick smile breaks his stoic mask as he looks me over. "Wren, she has been looking for you. She'll be thrilled to know you're okay. I'll send word once we arrive." He turns to walk into the woods.

"Not so fast, Mr. Lawrence," I say, still standing in my spot, not moving an inch.

He stops and twists to face me. "It's *Professor* Lawrence, if you don't mind."

"I never said I would go with you. First I want some questions answered." I stand straighter to drive my point home.

He laughs under his breath and gestures for me to continue. "Ask away."

"Tell me more about Blackbriar." I start with the

most basic information first. "Everything. The truth."

"Blackbriar is a school for mages," he says, crossing his arms. "Only the best of the best go there, and admission is by invitation only. Students who receive an invitation are expected to go through trials, or tests, to determine if they are a good fit for the school. We train students in magic, to be powerful, influential, and renowned. It's the Ivy League for mages who go on to live full, enriched lives and are often the wealthiest most powerful of all mages.

"The school is exquisite, tropical, and magical. Full of wonderous, fantastic opportunities that only our students have a chance to participate in. You'll be in the top class of mages, a vied-for position, I assure you. You will never want for anything while there. Maybe even make lifelong friends and live a fulfilling life that you may not get if you don't choose to accept the invitation."

He snaps his fingers. "That reminds me." He pulls the invitation out of his coat again and holds it out to me.

I walk up to him and take it. The paper shimmers with a purplish-blue aura. I slide my finger under the seal and pull out the thick cardstock that reads:

*Wren Blackwood,*

*You are hereby cordially invited to participate in the initiate trials at Blackbriar Academy.*

As I stare at the paper. "What's the catch?"

"There is a catch to everything, Wren, but you're not obliged to stay. Come to the Academy, see for yourself, and then make a decision. What say you?"

I think about it for a moment, but I don't want to take too long. I'm sure there was more he wasn't saying, but honestly, what did I have going for me that was a better option? The academy sounds beautiful and could be worth going to. It could be life changing for me, and more importantly than that, I could learn more about my magic.

"I'll do it." My words echo around me slightly.

He smiles. "Excellent. Let's get going. We're running late as it is."

"Late?" I ask, confused. "For what?"

Professor Lawrence doesn't answer. Instead, he leads me through the woods to a small shimmering tube of light glowing from the ground into the air about six feet or so. He pauses outside of it and faces me again. "This is your last chance to refuse the invitation. Are you absolutely sure you want to go through with this?"

"I'm sure."

"Very well," he says and nods. "That there is my only invitation. Don't let me down."

Great. No pressure.

He holds his hand out toward what I assume is some magical portal, ushering me ahead of him. I take a deep breath and then step into it.

Into my new life.

Into my second chance.

And I absolutely will *not* fail.

## CHAPTER FIVE

The feeling within the portal is one that reminds me of being inside an elevator as it slows from its ascent and descends quickly to catch the destination floor. That sensation that makes me feel like my stomach is in my chest. The one that fades just as quickly as it starts, and I find myself surrounded by chilling, salt-filled air, near the ocean, at some port harbor.

A few street lights line the wooden walkway with sheds spaced out every ten feet or so. Only one boat is sitting in the dock, and it looks like we're the only ones here. Well, me, Deacon Lawrence, and this old man who is carrying on a rather heated sounding debate with himself. His long grey hair has seen better days as it sticks up in every direction.

Deacon's hand rests on the small of my back, and I look to him as he nods in the direction of the man.

Oh. Oh, no.

We're not seriously walking toward the crazy guy, are we?

As we move, the answer becomes blatantly clear. We are definitely heading toward the crazy old man, and he doesn't seem to stop arguing with himself as we arrive.

"Your invitation, Wren?" Deacon says.

I look at the piece of paper and then to the professor as he nods toward the old man. Assuming I understand what all these gestures mean, I hold out the invite to him.

At last, the old man stops his ramblings and grabs the invitation. He takes a moment to read it through his spectacle dangling over his rather tattered, old-fashioned, tunic style shirt and vest, hums to himself, and then looks between me and Deacon. "Well, what are you waiting for? All aboard."

The old man steps onto the boat, and it's the first time I had a good look at the vessel. I had been so pre-occupied with the old man's appearance and show, I never thought to pay attention to the thing he stood in front of. I question the sea worthiness, but I also don't know enough about sailing to know for sure. But I have to trust that Deacon wouldn't go through the effort of seeking me out and fighting off a village of trolls just to have me get on a rickety boat that will sink five minutes after departure.

Carefully, I test the surface before putting my full weight on the boat as I step a foot over the edge and climb aboard. I stop once I'm fully on and look back, noticing that he didn't get on.

"You're not coming?"

He grins slightly. "I'll meet you at the academy."

"Whoa, I'm going on this boat with him," I point to the crazy old man, "by myself?"

"Yes," he says simply.

"Why?" I cross my arms in front of me.

"This initial trip is required to get to the island for the first time, because of the wards placed around the castle. No other way will let you through. I'll meet you there." He waves his hands over the ground in front of him and a portal appears.

"See you soon." He nods curtly before stepping through and disappearing through the portal.

I sigh and take my seat on one of the built-in benches that line the back and sides of the boat. The old man mutters something about death and the boat's engine roars to life. The vessel propels forward, and I'm forced to catch myself to keep from falling out of my seat.

In mere moments, I settle in for the ride and get caught off guard by how clear and unobstructed the sky above me is. I thought the image in the lake was beautiful, but this… this is even better than I could ever imagine.

Ribbons of purple that fade into pink weave through the sky and wave up and down in the sky. I know this is the aurora borealis, but I have never seen it in such beauty and vivid color like this. The stars fill nearly every inch of sky above me, and the Milky Way glows against the backdrop of the midnight blue sky. I suck in a breath and the awe that enters my voice as I whisper, "Wow," lets me know that I had made a good decision.

I shift and something jumps out of water, diving back in before I can catch it. My attention is now claimed by the shadows in the water. I marvel at the strange creatures, unsure of what they are. But my moment of awe is cut short by the boat's sudden jump in speed. I'm forced to clutch the railing on the boat for fear of being tossed off.

The crazy old man laughs as he keeps looking over his shoulder at me. I question his ability to drive and keep his eyes on what is going on in front of him. Hell, I worry I may just wash ashore some remote island worse for the wear.

Ahead of us, a swirling cloud rises over the water and grows. It barrels toward us and surrounds us in mist. My skin feels like the water collecting on my cheeks will freeze as sharp prickling sensations fill them. Just as I think nothing else could possibly happen, sharp rocks jutting out of the water come awfully close to the boat. I suck in my breath, hoping and praying that this boat isn't a fraction of an inch off course for fear of crashing into one of those rocks and being chewed up into humanburger.

There's a sharp turn to the left only to quickly veer to the right and I'm starting to believe this is all some kind of cosmic joke. Come to this academy and die on the way there.

Physical forms aren't allowed. Sorry. Fine print is a bitch.

The boat straightens and slows, and I watch the dense fog surrounding us dissipate like it was never there in the first place. As though it was a fragment of my imagination. Once the boat docks, I jump off and nearly fall to my knees to kiss the ground for being back under my feet, right where it belongs.

I take in a deep breath and inhale the air, and it smells… different, sweeter, fuller. Like it has a life of its own, and it surrounds me in welcome.

"Wait until you see the mermaids!" the crazy old man says and rattles off riddles that don't make any sense. I pay little attention to the words and more to the way he laughs at me when I look at him like he's lost his mind completely. He leads me to a set of wooden stairs that climb the side of the mountainous island. As I take the steps, I can't help but let my eyes wander over the woods and the twinkling lights in colors of green, blue, purple, pink, and yellow. I wonder if they are sprites, but I can't be sure unless I get closer. I have never seen sprites with so many colors.

Gnomes climb a smaller set of stairs to the right of where I am, and every so often, there's little tunnels they walk in and out of as they carry things I can't make out along with tiny lanterns. My eyes rove over the woods that seem to breathe and move and to shadows that blend in and stand out all at the same time.

And with that comes the idea that I'm already more at home here than I was anywhere else in the world. It's like I belong here, and I can feel my magic churn with excitement at just being here.

But I don't allow myself to get too carried away. I have to pass the trials first.

The top of the stairs come into view with the top tiers of what I assume is the academy's towers. The light burning within the windows seem so warm and draw me closer, inviting me in. I don't know what to expect, but I'm far better off now than I was with the trolls.

I arrive at the gate at the top of the stairs. Deacon is waiting for me on the other side, and my gaze quickly moves from him to the massive castle behind him. I'm once again struck with awe as the numerous towers seem to stretch into the sky as if they are all racing to touch the stars. Some windows show a scene glowing with yellow light behind the images, and I catch myself staring and trying to make out the shapes. In front of me is a large walk path lined with groomed bushes in the shape of a strange bird, dog, dragon, and some weird octopus.

The door to the castle stands open and I'm caught by the ivory backdrop with burgundy trimmings.

"Enjoy your trip?" Deacon asks, and my attention is pulled toward him.

"Not exactly the term I would use," I say and step through the gate.

He chuckles. "It's different for sure. That will be all, Captain."

The man salutes Deacon and heads back down the stairs. I shake my head as he starts arguing with himself again.

"What do you think of the academy so far?" Deacon asks.

I stare around me—it's so much to take in. There's so much detail, awe, and the magic within me pulls me closer to the door. "It's a beautiful place."

"I knew that you would like it. Wait until you get inside."

I follow him through the door, and I'm impressed at the two massive staircases that curve along either wall toward the door, ending at the opening of a hall on both sides. In the center stands a large fountain with a stone tree rising high into the air. Behind that is a tapestry, embroidered in burgundy and gold, with the shape of a woman with antlers on her head. She's holding her hands up high, reaching toward a giant golden orb above her head.

I glance down each hall. The one to my right cuts off short, but judging by the size of the castle from the outside, it's just a turn. There's so much more to the hall in that direction, I can feel it. The left is lined with windows and statues between those. Paintings of various scenes and people line the wall opposite of the windows. Doors interrupt the wall every so often, and the hall cuts off toward the back of the castle as well.

"This place is massive," I say, unable to hide the amazement in my voice.

Deacon chuckles. "Follow me," he moves toward the stairs to the right and I take them behind him, absorbing everything I possibly can.

Once we reach the top, we turn left and follow the hall that turns left again.

After a series of left and right turns, and a slight sense of this place being a maze that I may get lost in for the first few months that I'm here, we arrive at a door. Deacon gestures toward it and tells me this is my room.

I open the door, eager to see what's inside and stop short at a guy who has his bare back facing me. He turns, showing impressive pecs and abs, and I force back the rush of heat filling my cheeks. Smiling, he says, "Well, I wasn't expecting guests, but what the heck, come in and make yourself at home."

I look at the professor. His face is a mix of expressions. From being less than impressed to completely outraged. "This here is Jesse Taylor. He's your roommate."

"My what?" I ask. My magic rushes through my body, refreshing and cool. I wonder what the hell is going on. My magic didn't react to Deacon. It did pull me toward the castle, so maybe it's just a nice side-effect? All of this is something I will have to figure out later.

"Your roomie! Aren't you a lucky girl," Jesse says and I swear I hear Deacon growl.

"It's only temporary. For the time of the trials at most. And Taylor, you'll do well to remember this and keep your hands to yourself. Lest you want to throw away your chance at acceptance with the academy." He points a finger at the guy, and I sort of wonder if my "roomie" comes with a certain reputation.

"Relax, Professor. I can look but I can't touch… yet." He winks at me and I shake my head to keep myself from blushing again. First time was a mistake.

"I won't be doing any touching," I say. Besides, nearly everyone hates me, and I don't expect it to be different with him. Though he is freaking hot, charming, and has a nice smile, it's probably all a ruse.

"Challenge accepted," Jesse says.

I roll my eyes as the professor changes the topic. "You are one of three girls who've accepted an invitation. Unfortunately, we only have five rooms available for initiates. If he becomes a problem, come to me and I will appeal a sixth room from the headmaster."

I nod. "Thank you. But I can take care of myself. Just don't blame me for any damage done."

"Ouch. I love girls that pack a lot of spice." Jesse smiles and pulls on a shirt. "I'll cover the temptation, to put the professor's mind at ease."

I shake my head.

"Everything will be explained at breakfast tomorrow morning. Seven sharp. You should get to sleep soon so that you are rested. You've had one hell of a day."

"You can say that again," I say.

"Goodnight," he says and leaves the room, closing the door behind him.

My magic rushes through me still, and I try to

ignore that and Jesse as I move to the closet and find it stocked with clothing far more expensive than I could ever afford. They must be gifts from the school, which include several sets of school uniforms. I softly touch the fabrics. The nicest thing I had was a shirt I had outgrown long ago. It was the last thing my mother had given me.

"So, here for the trials?" Jesse asks.

I look at him from over my shoulder. He's lying on his back with his hands tucked behind his head and his legs crossed at his ankles. He's all relaxed and sexy and… I push that thought to the side. I'm here to learn what I can about magic, not get caught up with sexy guys.

"Looks like it," I say, setting my gaze to a set of drawers in the middle of my closet. I pull the top drawer open to reveal comfortable, soft pajamas and pull out a matching t-shirt and pants.

"Well, I'm glad to share a room with you. It will be fun to see what trouble we can get into while we're here."

"I'm not getting into any trouble, least of all with you." I continue to feel my magic rush through me, and I don't want to say anything about it just yet. I need to see if it continues to happen. I face Jesse, and there is something sharp and intelligent about his eyes that has my intuitions flaring.

There is definitely more to him than meets the eye. That may be a good thing. Maybe not. I'll have to see.

"You gotta name?" Jesse asks and I realize I didn't tell him that.

"Wren Blackwood."

He jumps up from the mattress and does an extravagant, over-dramatic bow. "Pleasure to meet you, Wren. Pretty name for a pretty girl."

I lift an eyebrow. "Cool it, Romeo."

"Just when I'm getting started? Come on now, I have much more up my sleeve."

"I'm sure you do, but as Professor Lawrence said, we have an early morning and—"

"Eh," he waves me away, "live a little. What's wrong with getting to know who you're sleeping with."

"I'm not sleeping with you. I just happen to be sleeping in the same room. That's it." I pick up my clothes and make my way to the bathroom, hoping he gets the hint. But as soon as I change and leave the bathroom, he's there, expectantly.

"What?" I ask.

"I'm glad you asked, Wren." He holds up his hand

and counts off his fingers. "Yes, I'm an initiate. I come from a very rich family. I'm bunking with a crazy hot woman, and I'm a Capricorn. What about you?"

I shake my head, and though I try not to, I laugh.

"I lost my parents when I was fourteen and was kidnapped from my aunt's house by a village of trolls, where I lived until a few hours ago. That pretty much sums me up. Goodnight, Jesse."

His face turns into an expression of shock, but his eyes look like they are trying to piece together a puzzle missing too many pieces.

"Trolls don't exist, Wren. I'm hurt you would tell me that." He places a hand over his chest.

"Well, they do, and they're assholes, so… if you have an issue with my story, I'm sure Professor Lawrence will vouch. He helped me fight them to get my freedom."

"Really?" He says, and it's all serious. I don't think he's accustomed to that.

"Goodnight, Jesse." I crawl into bed and turn off my bedside lamp. The mattress is so soft, it's like lying on a cloud. The day's aches seem to fade away, and I'm pulled into sleep almost instantly.

## CHAPTER SIX

S even in the morning came quick.

Too quick.

After pulling myself from bed, showering for the first time in years after bathing in rivers and lakes, I dress in the school uniform, which is a long sleeve, black button up with a golden B embroidered on the upper left part of my chest, just above my breast, and a black straight skirt that reaches my knees with burgundy tights and black shoes. Jesse and I walk to breakfast together. His uniform is similar except that he has a more preppy look with his black pants and a polo shirt with the same emblem and a burgundy tie.

Once we finish eating, all ten of us initiates are gathered together and given a tour of the castle.

What I saw last night was just a fraction of the sheer size of the castle. The thing is *massive*. It's like an entire town of its own. Four wings for the four houses, and the center of the castle is filled with classrooms, the kitchen, cafeteria, and arena (like a gym from a regular school, but this room changes its interior according to the desired purpose). Eventually, we end at a massive garden full of beautiful budding bushes in all colors imaginable lined with marble benches and square stones.

In the center of this garden is a life-sized statue of a woman dressed like a Greek goddess with a crown of antlers on her head.

"This, initiates, is Lady Alene," the tour guide says. He's got a soldier-esque feel to him, but with a kind voice and eyes that are bluer than anything I've ever seen before. He's gorgeous. My magic doesn't react to him though. I tested it by getting closer to him. Nothing. Jesse is the only one, it seems. I'm curious about that, though. But one thing I wonder is if it's somehow a requirement to be gorgeous to attend here.

He continues, "She is our Patron Mage. Everyone, say hello."

A cacophony of hellos ripple through the small crowd.

The statue moves—I jump, eyes wide and mouth hanging open.

"Hello, initiates," Lady Alene says, her voice soft as a whisper but powerful and enchanting. "I'm pleased to meet our next group of hopefuls for this wonderful school."

I must be the only one new to this concept as no one else seems impressed by this statue coming to life. Honestly, I can't pull my eyes away. It's hard to follow the conversation because I'm so floored by the sight in front of me.

Oh, I'm going to *love* it here.

The tour guide says, "It's said that Lady Alene's soul actually resides in the statue, but she isn't telling, are you Lady?"

"Some mysteries are fun to keep to myself," she says.

I giggle. Not only does the statue come to life, but she has a sense of humor.

"Initiates," the guide says, "I'll leave you in our Lady's capable hands." He bows to the lady, who in turn lowers her head in such a regal way that I'm mesmerized.

She turns her attention to us and says, "Gather around initiates, get comfortable, there is much to discuss."

I sit on a bench next to Jesse who tries to put his arm around me. I narrow my eyes at him and shake my head.

He smiles and shrugs like it's no big deal.

Though I'm grinning, I roll my eyes and return my attention to Lady Alene as she smiles at each of us. My magic rushes through me, cool and refreshing again. It's puzzling, but I can't focus on that right now. My attention is once again caught by the speaking statue.

"Your trials will begin soon. But before they do, I'm going to give you a history of the trials and let you know what to expect. I'm sure you all will have questions, but please refrain from asking them until the end of my story."

She takes a moment to look at each of us and, once satisfied, she waves her arms in an arc. White light surrounds her and encompasses the whole garden. It's like being shrouded by clouds. Before long, images start to play out before my eyes, and I'm lost in what I see.

Men and women are performing magic, battling strange and terrifying creatures I can't understand or recognize as the images shift and move too quickly for me to process every detail. There's a blend of darkness and light, and I can almost feel each blast of magic that the mages perform.

"Long ago…" the lady's voice echoes, surrounding me in a live-action story, narrating the images before me. "Our predecessors were required to go through a single trial that was both dangerous and rewarding…"

An image of a mage stands before me, shrouded by a hood as a sword of fire arcs toward him. He ducks in the nick of time, but the hood catches fire. He manages to douse the flames but not before enduring burns on his forehead.

"These trials were reserved for those who wanted to become masters of their craft, to be one of the very few who would carry the label Master Mage. Many died…"

The images shift to scenes of mages who lay lifeless on the ground, succumbing to their multiple injuries, or falling to their deaths into a pit of endless darkness.

Chills erupt over my arms and I can't help but wonder just what the trials here are going to hold for us. Are they just as dangerous? How many students have died taking these trials just to be admitted into this academy?

"But those who survived became masters…"

Pictures of men and women standing tall and proud, smiling, powerful, flash before my eyes. The images slowly fade, as does the white light that surrounds the garden. As the garden comes back into focus, Lady Alene looks to each student and says, "The trials of old are the basis of the trials that each of you will face. Because Blackbriar is the best academy for mages thus far, these trials were developed to challenge each initiate with four basic principles—knowledge, physical strength, mental endurance, and skill."

Lady Alene steps forward, turning to face each student as she speaks. "The trials you will face are based off those you just witnessed. You must pass each trial in order to be accepted into the academy. If you fail even one, you will not be accepted into Blackbriar."

Jesse whistles and shakes his head. "Man, that's a tall order. Get into school or die trying. Talk about fine print."

I elbow him and glare at him as I press my finger to my lips.

He holds up his hands as if to ward off an attack and smiles. "Got it, boss." He presses his fingers to his lips and makes the motion of locking them shut and throwing away the key.

"These trials were developed in such a way that only the best and most promising student mages are allowed to study here, as it takes a great deal of devotion, study, and commitment to become a leading mage in your community."

I'm still waiting for the catch. Surely, the powers that be wouldn't let a school kill their potential students. That's a bit excessive. I catch glimpses of the other students who have turned pale and look seconds from vomiting up breakfast. I shake my head. There's a catch, I know it, but dying isn't it.

I hope.

"Though I cannot say specifically what your trials will be like," Lady Alene continues, "as they are slightly unique to each initiate, I strongly urge you to take them seriously. These trials are, and will be, the foundation to your learning here at Blackbriar."

This is it. We're getting close to the catch.

"Any questions so far?"

I raise my hand.

Lady Alene smiles and nods at me.

"What's the catch? Not death, right?" I ask.

She laughs under her breath. "Of course not. Students who don't pass the trials are not allowed to attend Blackbriar. However, it's a little deeper than just denied admittance. We take pride in the secrecy of our school. Though mages around the world know we exist, only those who graduate from here can know of the lessons, activities, and preparations that are specific to this school and *only* this school. As such, each initiate who doesn't pass every trial will have their memories of this place erased and will be removed from the grounds."

That is not okay with me. I don't want anyone messing with my mind. Ever.

She settles her gaze on each of us once more as she says, "This is the condition that each of you must accept in order to participate in the trials." She holds up a finger. "This brings me to the rules. No initiate is allowed to discuss the trials, as they are different for each student, and must be presented without knowing what to expect. Any initiate caught discussing the trials—believe me when I say there are ears everywhere—your admittance to the academy will be revoked."

Wow. These people like their rules. But I can't really blame them for that. Not really. Just as the trolls relied on the protection of secrecy for their community, so must the academy. The rules are in place for the safety of the island and everyone who stays here. It feels like a very special thing to be invited to the school. I, for one, have no intentions of leaving. Or risking my place here, for that matter.

"Each initiate must formally announce to me they are willing participants in the trials. Once you formally accept the invitation, you will be marked with a special symbol unique to each initiate, which will be placed on the inside of your wrist. Refusal of acceptance is your decision, but you will be faced with having this placed erased from your memories and you will be removed from the island."

I look around at the other nine initiates invited to take the trials and not a single one is batting their eyes at the possibility of their minds being messed with. Either they are that confident they will pass, or they accept the consequences of failing.

I, for one, don't intend to fail or have my mind messed with, thank you very much. Though there are some down sides to the trials, it seems the benefits far outweigh the risks of failing. But I won't fail. Failing is not an option.

"Take time, deliberate on your options. This isn't a decision to be made lightly. Once you have announced your decision, there is no turning back. As soon as you are ready, come to me."

She reclaims her original position in the center of the garden.

I sit back and wait, not wanting to be the first person up there. Jesse jumps up and winks at me from over his shoulder as he approaches the statue first. Lady Alene turns to him, smiles, nods, and takes his hand into hers. With her other hand, she covers his wrist, and a bright white flash forms under her hand. Just as quick as it flares up, it fades and is over.

Jesse turns to face me winks, and hops off to do what I assume is flirting with the ladies of the academy.

As he walks off, my magic settles.

Four more people have approached Lady Alene and received a mark. Time for me to go.

I stand and approach the amazing figure in front of me. She turns her gaze to me and smiles in greeting. It's a soft smile, a kind one.

"Miss Blackwood, it's an honor for you to grace our school. I trust you have made your decision?" she asks.

"Something tells me you already know what my decision is," I say, and that doesn't seem to bother me. There is something about the spirit of the school that calls to me and makes me feel like I can trust her. She's safe, and that gives me hope.

"Indeed, but it must be official," she states

matter-of-factly. "Do you accept the invitation to the trials?"

"I do, Lady Alene," I respond, and this strange excitement burns through me and makes me giddy inside. I want to giggle and run and dance like I used to when I was a little girl.

I give the lady my hand, and she does the same thing I have observed her doing for the last five initiates. The light is cold, but warm at the same time, and strange tingling ripples through my wrist and into my arm and hand. It's not unpleasant, but tickles. And just like with those before me, the flash is over as quick as it starts. I hold my wrist up and a faint, glittering outline of a shape, slightly lighter than the rest of my skin, takes up the inside of my wrist.

Three sets of circular-swirling lines that meet in the middle at a single point. If I were to trace the outer perimeter of the swirls, they would be perfectly enclosed within a triangle.

"A triskele?"

The lady nods. "You have some time before lunch to enjoy. Go have fun. Good luck, Wren. I look forward to our talks."

I smile. "Thank you. And me too."

## CHAPTER SEVEN

This place is *enchanting*.

I walk through the grounds, mingling in the sunlight, absorbing the warmth and enjoying the butterflies, gnomes working in the gardens, and the way the trees seem to breathe.

This place is so magical, I love it. Nothing will stop me from passing the trials. I will do anything not to be sent away from here. Whatever it takes, I won't leave this place.

I find a bench close to the ocean, although I can't see it beyond the small wall that seals off this court-yard I'm in. I can hear the waves crashing against the shoreline. The birds sing a melody that is inviting and peaceful and pulls me into a serene mindset from the tree that shades the bench I sit on.

Walkways surround and circle around me, wrapping around buildings, huts, and gazebos. The gardens and trees seem to be in constant bloom.

As soon as I give into this peaceful moment, crunching of grass and dirt pulls my attention to a guy stepping out of a shadowy pathway nearby. I set my eyes on him and he is beyond hot. He's tall, and by the look of his bulging muscles against his polo shirt, he clearly loves to work out. He sets his gaze on me and I can't tell if it's the sun that shines in his eyes or if it's me, but he seems to glower. Beyond that, his mouth has that kissable attraction to it, and I force myself to look away from them before I do something embarrassing like lick my lips.

He starts to walk off and I close my eyes, listening to the sound of the waves mix with the song of the birds.

But the rhythmic sound of boots thumping against the sidewalk that encircles me interrupts the wonderful music.

I open my eyes to find the guy sort of pacing around me, his eyes focused on me.

What the actual…

My magic erupts in heat. Like a ball of flame burning inside me. It's a pleasant warmth though, and as it moves through me, I'm embarrassed to find myself a little aroused. I try to ignore that feeling, but it's almost like this guy is causing this. I open my mouth to ask what the hell he is doing, but he beats me to the point.

"You're new here?" he asks.

I gawk for a moment, thinking that has to be obvious, but if not, I guess I can spell it out for this guy. "Yes. I'm an initiate."

"Name?" he made it sound more like a demand and I bite my tongue on the remark that wants to escape my mouth.

Instead, I say, "Wren Blackwood. You?"

He nods and continues to slowly march around me. "Where are you from?"

"You wouldn't believe me if I told you," I say, and it's true. Jesse didn't believe me when I told him, and I realize it's because the existence of trolls is something of a secret in the world. A sort of Big Foot legend.

"Why here?" he asks.

This guy is nosey. Not pushy, but nosey.

"Because I was invited. And it's a far cry better from where I was before, so why not?"

"But you don't want to tell me where you are from?" he asks.

"I'm not so sure why that matters. I'm here to

participate in the trials as an initiate. What does it matter to you?"

"Do you come from a magic family?" he asks.

At first, I want to demand he answer my questions first, but I really dislike the idea of getting into a heated argument and ruin what is left of the mood I was just in. Besides, he strikes me as someone militant and used to being in charge and having his orders followed. If I cross him, it could spell disaster for me, and I need to avoid that. Especially since I want to stay here for as long as I possibly can. He strikes me as someone that doesn't get crossed without repercussions, and I don't need him throwing me off my trials to keep me from being here.

"Sort of. My father is Michael Blackwood."

He stops in front of me and his glower softens slightly, but his eyes take in everything. They are a beautiful, unique shade of amber, and I'll be damned if they don't make me feel like he can see into my very soul.

But more frighteningly of all... they almost seem like they already know my dark little secret.

"You're half-human?" he asks. It comes off as though he doesn't believe it himself. And I can't help but wonder if I just told him too much.

"Who are you, and why is what I am matter to you?" I ask.

"Name is Soren McCallister, First Lieutenant of Blackbriar Academy Special Forces. I'm here to keep the school safe. My instincts are never wrong, and right now they tell me that you're hiding something. Something you don't want anyone to know." He points at me. "Mark my words, Wren Blackwood, I will find out what that is. It's only a matter of time."

I cross my arms over my chest and arch an eyebrow. "So, you're a glorified hall monitor. Good luck with your mission. If you don't mind, I was enjoying my peace and quiet until your little inquisition came along, I'd appreciate it if you'd go about your merry little way and leave me alone."

His mouth slightly hangs open in shock, but he quickly recovers and returns to his stern face. Yep, definitely a guy used to giving orders and not accustomed to someone like me. He steps closer, and that sets my magic even more on fire. Blissful, sweet burning… go away.

Up until now, I thought my magic only responded to Jesse, but it seems like Soren is one of the lucky ones too.

Yay me.

"How good are you at keeping secrets?" His voice is dark, seductive, and does nothing for the pressure that is pooling between my legs. I want to grab him and kiss him, but that's absurd. Clearly, my magic and body are confused.

Don't get me wrong, this guy is totally fuckable.

But he's an asshole.

"You may be Lawrence's pet project, but you will not get special treatment from me. You are expected to uphold all the rules and laws of the academy. Fail to do so, and you'll find how little of an issue it is for me to administer the proper punishments." He looks me up and down. If I didn't know any better, I'd swear he was checking me out. He turns away and starts to walk off.

I stand, ready to just go to my room and keep my head low to keep from bumping into him again. "Thanks for the warning, jerk."

He spins around to face me with a glare that is meant to make me cower. But what he doesn't know is compared to the trolls, this is nothing. I stand there staring at him, unwavering, not willing to back down. After all, I've done nothing to this guy, and he's delivering ultimatums like I'm a branded criminal.

Screw him.

He doesn't scare me. Nor does his threats. Small potatoes.

"I'll be keeping an eye on you."

"Looking forward to it." My voice is flat, deadpan.

We glare at each other. Each of us probably waiting for the other to back down first. I don't. I won't. Finally, with a growl, he storms off. My eyes drift to the nice ass he has.

Such a waste.

And that, ladies and gents, is a beautiful start here in this new life of mine.

My magic cools as I wait until Soren is out of sight before turning to go in the opposite direction. A girl, about my height, with dark brown hair and purple streaks walks up to me with a smile as bright as the sun. My magic doesn't react to her, and I'm unsure of what the deal is. Clearly, it doesn't react to everyone. I definitely need to find out more about these little reactions.

"What's that guy's problem? You have history together or something?" she asks.

"Oh, him?" I point behind me. "That's just my amazing charm working its magic."

"So, no history?" she asks with her eyebrows raised above her silvery eyes that hold their own purple hue. There's something about this girl that makes me want to talk with her. She's just so happy. It's contagious.

I chuckle. "Nope. None whatsoever."

"Ah, too bad. Maybe there can be history, huh?" She bobs her eyebrows.

I don't know who this girl is, but she makes it easy to laugh.

She holds out her hand and says, "I'm Savannah Fey. I saw you in the garden earlier. We're fellow initiates."

I take her hand and say, "Wren Blackwood."

"I know," she says with a casual bounce of a shoulder.

"Y-you do?" I ask, surprised that anyone knows my name here besides the obvious ones who should.

She winks as she says, "It's a gift. So, that guy, I hear he's totally a hard ass. I don't know what you did, but a friendly bit of advice, try not to stay on his bad side. He's the youngest member of the Academy Special Forces, which means, he could probably kill with a look."

My eyebrows knit together as I cock my head to the side and say, "Thanks for the warning."

She grabs my hand and pulls me back to the bench. "So, are you ready for the trials to start?"

I shrug. "I don't know. I guess so."

"Well, I heard that there is a secret fifth trial that only certain students go through. It's the hardest trial. Puts the fourth one to shame. Do you think we'll have to do that?"

"I hope not. Sounds like a horrible thing to be selected for if it's that hard. Especially after what we saw earlier." It's just so damn easy to talk to her. I sort of don't mind that at all.

"Right?" She smiles and it reaches her eyes, making them shine brighter. Not like Deacon's.

She slides her arm into the crook of mine and it's like we've been best friends forever. But I don't know if I should get attached to anyone. Everyone I care about has a bad habit of leaving me in one way or another, and until we pass the trials, I feel like it would be best to keep her at arm's length.

But damn it all if there isn't something purely magnetic about her. Maybe that's one of her gifts.

After we share a few laughs and exchange a little more small talk, I wonder if there wouldn't be any harm in having someone to talk to after all.

## CHAPTER EIGHT

I could have spent the whole afternoon talking with Savannah. And I nearly did. After eating lunch together, we went our separate ways. Now, I'm in the academy's library, and it's huge. There are endless rows of bookshelves taller than any house I've ever seen, and all of them are stocked full of books. It will probably take a lifetime to read all the books that are housed here.

One look at the massive room, and I know this place will be a sanctuary. But first, I have to get through the trials. Still, this is definitely finding itself at the top of my list of favorite places.

The sweet smell of leather, paper, and ink is a scent all of its own and lures me deeper into the room. Before long, I'm in full-on research mode, practically dying to learn all I can about using magic without a conduit.

To be honest, I have no idea where to start. I begin with the histories of some of the more notable mages in history, focusing on some epic battles they've had with shadow mages. One particular account I find interesting is Isaac Blackwood. I pause to wonder if he's a distant relative. He saved a small human town against a shadow mage that had called on several lamias to destroy the town's children. I shudder, remembering my recent encounter with the lamia right before meeting Professor Lawrence.

The book's historical account dutifully describes how Isaac defeated the lamias and the shadow mage, but it seems to skip over the spells used by the shadow mage or the manner in which he had used magic without a conduit. Not very helpful for me. I then backtrack to try and see if there are any accounts of good mages who may have used magic without conduits, but again, I find no record.

Is using magic without a conduit evidence of darkness, or is it all in the person's heart and intentions? I'm certain I'm neither the first nor the last person with magical abilities who has encountered something like this, so there *has* to be a historical account or story about this. But the books so far would lead me to believe that all those who use magic without a conduit are dark—but I can't accept that I'm dark, that's not who I am.

I keep searching, thumbing through crisp pages. No hints of someone going dark much less using magic without a conduit. I figure I'll have to refine my search, but for the first go, I consider this an okay result. At least I know where to look next time.

Three hours into it, and nothing to show beyond basic information is getting frustrating. I'm no closer to an answer than I was when I started. But at least I can check these books off my list. There are undoubtably hundreds more here that I could use to find answers. I just have to find them.

At least, that is my hope.

When I first came into the library, I scanned the shelves for certain categories of books before settling on the ones I picked from. But there is a room that was locked up with a barred door. There are hundreds more books in that room, but I have no way to get into it. I wonder who I have to talk to gain access?

"Well, hello new girl," a guy says.

I jump a little and look toward a guy wearing the

academy's uniform, leaning against a bookshelf near the table I'm sitting at. He's cute, in a basic way, with the way his dirty blond hair is disheveled on the top of his head in a sort of purposeful way, and his ice-blue eyes settle on me. But my magic is calm. Not that I'm sure what I would do if it had reacted toward him. There is something about this guy that sets my intuitions on high alert. So, honestly, I'm relieved.

A little.

Jesse and Soren must be special. I just don't know how. That's something I will have to look into further later. For now, figuring out my magic is my number one priority.

"Um… hi," I say and turn my attention back to the book that lays open in front of me.

"Enjoying your research?" he asks as he steps closer, drawing my attention toward him once more. He fingers a title I had cast aside a few hours ago.

"I guess you could say that," I say as he takes a seat across from me. Never mind there are ten other tables in the library—at least—and I clearly had *my* area claimed with books and my notes. But he doesn't let that stop him. He simply pushes the pile of books in front of him to the side and props his elbows on the table.

"I was using those," I say, gesturing to the books he just casually discarded to the side. I wasn't done with them, and I expect him to put them back in the exact order I had them laid out in.

"Allow me to introduce myself…" He holds out his hand. "Anderson Stone, second year student."

I stare at his hand and then lift my gaze to his. "I'm Wren. And I'm busy. If you don't mind, I would really like to get back to my research."

He moves his hand back, but he doesn't seem bothered that I snubbed him. Instead he asks, "Are you liking the school so far?"

I shrug, returning my attention to the opened book in front of me. "What's not to like?"

"I like that response. In fact, I think I like you. Wanna get some coffee? Maybe get to know each other better?"

I raise my eyes to him. "I don't like coffee. And I'm not looking for a relationship right now."

That's a lie. I don't really know if I like coffee or not. I've never had it.

But I don't want him knowing anything about me. Something about him is off and I don't like it. I don't like him. He just has this something about him that makes me want to get as far away from him as possible. Not that I'm going to move. I was here first. So there.

I continue my research, a few moments pass before he starts to hum, flipping through one of the books.

"Are you always this annoying or am I just special?"

"Oh, you're special. But I'm guessing you have no idea why, and that makes this even more exciting for me."

"Lucky me."

His eyes turn cold, in the same way the trolls would look at me before raising their hands to slam me to the ground. A sense of dread comes over me. He's dangerous, and my intuition is telling me to get the hell away from him. He says, "Indeed. Even Professor Lawrence lucked out giving you his one precious invitation."

I settle my gaze on him, forcing myself to be as calm as possible. Though it's difficult, my voice manages to come out even. "I don't know what you are dancing around with all this, but I'm busy and really would like to continue my research. Please, be quiet or leave."

He doesn't seem to get the hint I want to be

alone, and I truly dislike being overly direct. But it's like this guy is either getting a kick out of making me uncomfortable or he is just that dense. Direct is apparently the only thing that's going to work.

"Why history of mages? What are you looking for?" he smiles from over the book in front of him.

So much for being direct.

"Personal reasons." I hope he doesn't continue pushing. I don't want to be unpleasant and have another enemy. But if push comes to shove, I have no problems with handling this in a less than lady-like manner.

"Rather ambitious of you, don't you think?" The way he spoke makes me narrow my eyes on him. He sits in front of me, unfazed by anything I have thrown at him to show him I'm not interested.

Yet, he persists.

I groan and roll my eyes. My last nerve is being worked on, and the sense of dread is doing nothing good for my research. This guy doesn't seem to take no for an answer and apparently is after specific information and won't leave me alone until he gets it.

"How so?" I ask, hoping if I entertain a few more of his questions, I can tell him to leave me alone and he will.

Probably.

"Well, you could fail a trial, and that would force you to leave. You'll forget all the wonderful information you are learning here."

"Your point?" I ask, a little harsher this time.

He shrugs, unfazed. "Seems pointless."

I get the feeling there is a threat hidden somewhere in his words and I'm not positive I'm okay with that settling there between us. The dread that something is wrong here quickly grows more intense and makes my stomach twist.

"And I suppose you just want a date for the sake of putting another notch in your belt? Or do you keep your collection on a bed post? Journal perhaps? I'm not interested." I say.

"My, my, does the kitten have some claws wanting to come out? Calm down, precious. I only want to help." He chuckles and it makes me feel like this is all just a game to him.

I try not to bite his head off for referring to me as a cat, but I let that go. The knots in my stomach have won. I have to leave, and that means my research is over for the day. But maybe I can ask him about that room. I won't know if he's telling me the truth with his answer, but I could always ask someone else later.

"That locked room back there, what is it?" I ask.

Anderson sits back in his seat and grins at me. "Wanting to do a little B&E?"

"No. Of course not. I'm trying to find information on something and I'm having trouble with the books here."

"Yes, I see the research. Interesting, indeed. Sorry. That room is off-limits to initiates."

I nod. Sadly, I believe him. We're only allowed access to certain parts of the castle until we pass the trials. And even if we don't, our memories are erased. But I still don't want to risk my place here by breaking the rules, and I certainly don't want to encourage this guy any more than I have.

Finally, I stand and gather my things. "I have a headache. I need to go lie down. Excuse me."

He stands and joins my side. "I'll escort you."

"No," I say too quickly and too sharply. He raises an eyebrow and I clear my throat and say, "I'm fine on my own. Thanks anyway."

He grabs my hand and brings it to his lips. The feel of his skin is like holding a snake. Cold and clammy. A strange vibration enters my skin as his lips touch the top of my hand. I feel drained, light-headed, and nauseated.

Whatever he's doing. I don't like it.

And though it lasts only a split second, it feels like longer.

I snap my hand away and walk off before he can do anything else to me. But I can't shake the feeling coursing through me. As I gain a little distance from him, I speak over my shoulder. "It was nice to meet you."

Not.

Really, I was just trying to be nice.

"You too." His words echo behind me, almost sounding ethereal, and a cold chill creeps up my spine, but I force myself not to shiver. I don't want him getting the impression he affects me. He does, and it's a negative effect, but I would prefer to avoid all future encounters with him entirely.

He spells trouble for me. With a capital "T". And I don't need any more trouble than what I'm currently dealing with. Especially his brand of trouble.

Not now.

Not ever.

I need to figure out what he did to me before he has a chance to do that again.

As I move through the halls, I check every so often to make sure he isn't following me. So far, so good. But I'm not in the clear yet.

Once I make it to my door, I check one last time to make sure he didn't follow me. The halls are clear. And I sigh in relief against the door before turning and stepping into the room with a polite wish that it's empty.

It is.

Thank the gods or whoever is listening.

No offense to Jesse, but I just don't know if I have the patience to deal with his antics on top of what I had just gone through. I feel like a piece of my soul was sucked away. I need to refresh myself with a hot shower. I lock the handle and find a change of clothes.

I desperately need to scrub his lips from my hand, and the effects of that—whatever it was— sensation off me. Dinner will be soon, and I could use the time to figure out more about this Anderson Stone if I can find Savannah. She's a wealth of information and gossip. I only hope she knows something.

CHAPTER NINE

I have to say, the more time that passes since that little interaction with Anderson, the better I feel. A hot shower was also just the right thing to jump start that feeling.

Jesse didn't even mind that I had locked the door. I could tell he wanted to know more about what happened, but I told him I wasn't in a sharing mood. Instead, he walked with me, silently for once, to the arena for the dinner celebration in honor of all the new initiates. The second he was near, my magic rushed through me, cooling me, creating comfort. As strange as it may seem, I'm glad my magic reacts to Jesse.

As I stand in line, waiting for the rest of the students to be seated, someone taps on my shoulder. I turn to find Savannah's smiling face. She says, "Surprise!" and gives me a hug.

This girl is too much happy in such a tiny package. But she is just that good. And just like before, her happiness is contagious. I feel the last of the dwindling effects from Anderson fade away, and the only thing I'm left with is the unfortunate memory of that event.

"We are sitting together," she says.

"Of course we are," I add, and it's so easy to be at ease around her.

Just as I go to introduce Jesse to Savannah, we are allowed into the arena.

Had I not been here before, to see that it looks like a plain, large room, I would think this is the normal set up.

Balls of burning light float within glass orbs, hanging from the ceiling that seems to go on forever, ending in darkness. Small shelves line the walls in a never-ending ring, every so often a gnome would pop out of a dark hole and rush to another, carrying only god knows what. They are such tiny creatures, and I hope that I can get to know more about them once I finish the trials and become a full-fledged student here. Tiny lanterns light up along the wall and I'm caught in awe. This place is so magical. So wonderous. I'm loving it.

"Whoa," I whisper.

Savannah leans in and whispers as we move. "See those tapestries?"

I nod.

"Each of the four symbols is a mascot for the house that sits before them." She points to each and says, "House of Phoenix, House of Drakon, House of Kraken, and House of Winterwolf."

"You sure are full of information." I'm amazed she learned all of that so quickly.

She smiles. "Well, I love to gossip. Just sharing the juicy bits with you."

"Thanks." I chuckle as we are led to our seats, which is a table along the opposite wall of where the houses sit. It spans the length of the houses and holds all the professors and the headmaster. I only recognize one, though—Deacon Lawrence who nods as I pass him.

I nod back and take my seat as soon as I get to it. Jesse takes the seat to my left while Savannah takes the one to my right. And I'm glad to be surrounded by people who seem to enjoy my company.

I'm sitting in front of the House of Kraken's

tapestry and its students, and I notice in the center, it looks like an ocean that is moving. Tentacles poke out of the surface and I gasp. I look to the house of Winterwolf, it's a scene of a cliff overlooking a forest at night. A bright moon shines through and a wolf as white as snow and as massive as a house takes a stand on the cliff and silently howls into the night.

Anxious, I look to the Drakon's house image. I lean a little closer to Jesse to get a better view, but he chuckles and wraps an arm around my shoulders. "I knew you would come around eventually."

I narrow my eyes on him. "Really?" My voice comes out flat.

He winks. "All in due time, love. All in due time."

I shake my head. "You're ridiculous."

"Yeah, but I'm adorable too." He smiles all charming and devilish.

Instead of falling into the enchantment he very easily casts upon me, I sit up and remove his arm from my shoulders, pretending to be unaffected by him. "You're cute, but you're not that cute."

"We'll see." He settles into his seat, folding his fingers behind his head just as at ease as ever.

I shake my head and breathe through the coursing coolness of my magic flowing through me. My eyes take in the sheer number of students and it's like a sea of faces all studying us like meat in a meat market. Their gazes show they are curious to see which of us will make it through the trials to become one of them. As I meet more than a few of their glances, I square my shoulders and let out a breath of air from my pursed lips and find a spot for my gaze to fixate on. I decide to watch the Kraken's image, swirling in its magical waters. This way, I won't be too distracted by the eyes that seem to all look at me.

Because I'm not used to the attention. Not this kind anyway. After all, I was an outcast.

"Oh, there's Mr. Hottie McMoody," Savannah says and points out Soren under the House of Phoenix tapestry.

Yup. There he is. All six foot whatever of brooding anger all directed at little ol' me.

Super fabulous.

It seems he is definitely doing what he promised by keeping an eye on me. He didn't use those words exactly, but that's most definitely his intention.

Savannah says, "I asked around about him for you." She winks. "This is what I found out... He's the headmaster's best friend."

"Oh good, the headmaster's best friend hates me. That makes this start even more fabulous."

"His loss if he hates you," Jesse says. "Personally, I think there is a whole lot to love about you."

I shake my head. "Of course, you do, Jesse."

Savannah pokes me in the side. "Well, he's single too."

"Trust me, that is the least of my worries," I say.

Jesse sits forward and says, "You could do better." He winks when I look at him.

I sigh. And dammit, I also smile. "That's not why she was getting information for me."

"Oh?" He smiles and sits a little straighter. "Do tell me more..." His hand grazes mine and it's a pleasant buzz of cool energy that rushes through me.

I gently slide my hand away and say, "It's nothing. Really."

"Word is," Savannah continues, "He's from the McCallister family. Which means he was bred for the military life. He's deadly, kills without mercy."

Suddenly that threat from before resonates within me with just a little bit more dread. *You'll find how little of an issue it is for me to administer the proper punishments.*

Sheesh. After getting into that back-and-forth argument with him, he doesn't just hate me. He despises me.

"That also means he's an elite, set up to be one of the top soldiers of all time," Savannah's voice pulls me back from my thoughts. "General, in fact."

I feel the same icky feel from earlier and catch the gaze of Anderson. "Oh great. Of course, *he's* here."

"Who?" Savannah and Jesse say at the same time.

"Anderson Stone." My voice is flat, cold, deadpan. I can't stand him, but he can't seem to get enough of me as he waves at me like we are best friends.

Ugh. Not.

He winks.

I almost gag. Almost.

I point him out. "Under the Winterwolf tapestry. Dirty blond, smiling like a dork, waving like I'm going to respond."

When he doesn't stop waving at me like a fool, I half-ass wave and roll my eyes. He finally stops and I'm suddenly not okay with sitting up here.

"I really need to find out what his power is. Do you know anything about him?" I ask and look to Savannah.

Jesse leans in closer, bobs his eyebrows. I shove him back and laugh.

Speaking of dorks. But this one I actually like.

Savannah looks in the direction of Anderson and turns her gaze back to me. She smiles wide, "Well, aren't you filling your days with sexy hunks. You sure can pick 'em too. How many men do you need? Two? Three?" Her smile widens even more as she adds, "More?"

I don't know how to answer that. Trolls don't believe in one partner. It's whoever is more promising to give them a son on a year-to-year basis. I never had a boyfriend before. Far as I know, my mom and dad were devoted entirely to each other. I never thought about it before.

Relationships are weird.

That's not to say that I wouldn't be open to having a relationship with someone or a few someones.

I say, "Trust me, he is not even a blip on my radar as far as hot guys go."

"Good. I would hate to show him up and demonstrate what a real man looks like," Jesse interjects.

Savannah and I look at him and just... laugh. He comes up with some of the weirdest things to say.

"Look, he saw me researching something in the library earlier, and when I got up to leave, he kissed my hand, and it felt like my soul was being sucked from me."

"Oh," Savannah says. "Bummer."

Jesse's hand clenches and his eyes narrow in Anderson's direction, and I feel like I suddenly need to diffuse the situation before it gets out of hand.

"Down, killer," I say.

Jesse sets his dagger-filled stare on me, and he says, "That is a zacar."

"A what?" I ask.

"An energy vampire," Savannah says. Her violet eyes soften and fill with worry. "He stole some of your energy from you. The fact that he did that is very much not okay. He broke about six school rules, if I counted correctly, and that's not even the worst of it."

The words resonate within me and everything makes so much more sense. I wasn't willing to give him what he wanted, and so he took it. Thought he'd be slick about it. Well, not anymore, buddy. I don't want to look at Anderson. Don't want to give him the satisfaction of seeing me squirm under his gaze. Nope.

That settles it. I refuse to be alone with him ever again. Much less allow him to touch me. I'm not a foodbank, and I'm certainly not here for his feeding pleasure.

Moreover, something needs to be done. But what?

"Are you okay?" Savannah asks. Her eyebrows are knitted together, and I force my thoughts aside to reassure her that I am.

"Yes. Now. But he can't be allowed to do that again," I say.

Jesse chimes in, "I'll kick his ass." He thinks about his words for a moment then adds, "Well, at the very least kick him where it counts."

"I'll help," Savannah says.

It dawns on me that I've never introduced them, but they are already willing to take up arms for me. "Thanks guys, that means a lot, but I can handle it. By the way," I gesture between them as I say, "Savannah, Jesse. Jesse, Savannah."

"Charmed," Jesse says, holding out his hand.

Savannah giggles, takes his hand, and says, "Likewise."

"We need to figure out a way he can't feed off initiates like that," I say. "It's wrong."

"I've always wondered what healthy competition would look like," Jesse says, sounding like he's back to himself with his carefree attitude, but there is a serious look in his eyes, and I have a feeling he's formulating a plan. One that could get him hurt if he's not careful. I wonder if he's had his own personal run-in with them before. From the moment he uttered "zacar" his body language shifted.

"Don't worry, I would choose you over him any day," I say and pat him on the shoulder.

He smiles at me. And it's a charming bright smile that I can't help but return.

"You need to let Professor Lawrence know," Savannah says. "I highly doubt he would look kindly on your little run-in."

I open my mouth to answer, but a bell rings through the room.

Everyone quiets and turns their attention to a sexy, dark blond-haired man dressed in a burgundy button up stretched over his muscular arms and torso, black pants and tie. His expression is hard, serious. But by god if that doesn't make him even more lip biting hot, I don't know what does. I have to know who he is.

He glances my way, and my heart skips a beat.

Whoever this man is, he has my full attention now.

## CHAPTER TEN

G ideon Storm.

The young-looking and handsome as hell headmaster, has me on the edge of my seat. My mind goes to places one shouldn't go when surrounded by people. I think of the number of ways I could get him alone, and I think the thing that turns me on the most is he's completely untouchable.

Regular schools frown upon student-teacher relationships. This one has yet to give me a different impression.

As the temperature seems to rise around me, I wiggle a little in my seat and fan myself with the fabric napkin sitting next to my plate.

Savannah looks down at my napkin, meets my gaze, and she smiles knowingly too.

I can't deny it. I'm hot for headmaster.

But that's not going to keep me from *trying*.

The places my mind goes shocks even me. I had no idea I was capable of such thoughts, but I imagine that his strong capable hands could put me in positions I've never even heard of. Send me to new heights that...

I shake my head and fan myself more.

Glancing at Jesse, who has a knowing little smirk on his face, I sit back in my chair and cross my arms over my chest.

Gideon's eyes glance toward me as he's talking to the whole room about traditions–that I'm too distracted to listen to—almost as if he knows. A small smirk pulls at the corner of his mouth and I force myself to look away as my cheeks burn with fire. Even my cooling magic, the effect from Jesse, rushing through my body is doing little to quench the disastrous heat.

He moves closer, stopping at the first initiate and introduces him. The guy stands up and shakes his hand, waves to the students, and then takes his seat.

This process repeats until he gets to Jesse, and

my magic flares again. This time I feel strength and renewed energy. My magic feels recharged, and I wonder what the *hell* is going on with me.

He stands next to me, touches the back of my shoulder, and says, "Wren Blackwood."

I stand on wobbly legs as he introduces me. All eyes in the room drift to me, and the attention makes me slightly uncomfortable. I just pray my legs don't give out on me. But I know they won't because they feel rooted, but I *am* weak in the knees.

His eyes meet mine and I'm caught in a sea of blue-green. He shakes my hand, smiles, and I... I can't breathe. The touch of his hand is rough from years of whatever it is that he does, and warm. And the feel of his skin on just my hand sends my mind crashing through other scenarios of us. Naked. Grinding against each other.

He pulls his hand away, and I snap back to the room, taking my seat as I learn to breathe again.

As Gideon Storm stands next to Savannah, his hand slides across the top of my back and stays there as he speaks. And I'm flushed with heat and sexual desires. I'm wrought with a mix of wanting him to remove his hand and me taking him right here and now.

This man knows *exactly* what he is doing to me, and he's enjoying it.

The sexy bastard.

Too soon, before I could make up my own damn mind, his hand is gone, and he's off to the last few initiates left to be introduced.

Good. Freaking. *God.*

My eyes switch to Soren. I practically screwed his best friend in my thoughts, and he stares at me with what I can only assume is malice. I glance to Anderson, and he's all grins and with adoration filling his eyes.

Or... is that hunger?

"Nice ass," Jesse says in a whisper. His hot breath not helping my raging hormones. I close my eyes and try not to groan. Of course, I have to contend with Jesse.

These men are going to kill me.

Gideon returns to his seat and I feel my magic slowly return to the level I need it to be for a clear mind. And thankfully, it happens. Mostly. I still feel some of the effects that blend deliciously with Jesse's effects, and I'm loving it.

Three men make my magic react in different ways.

Lord help me if there are any more.

Ice water appears at the table and I take a nice, long pull of the cooling liquid before clearing my throat and refocusing on what's being said.

"Now that the introductions are out of the way," Gideon says, voice dark, even, and *sexy*. "Let's lay down the rules for initiates to abide by as guests of Blackbriar Academy."

Oh good. These are probably important to listen to.

"During the time of the trials," Gideon says, "all students and initiates are to be in their rooms by eleven. That is when curfew begins. Lights out at eleven-thirty. Rise and shine at six AM. Initiates must spend their days with their mentor to better prepare for the trials. When not with a mentor, we ask that you remain in your room or in the main common areas. Nowhere else."

"Lame," Jesse mutters.

I elbow him, and he laughs under his breath.

"I wonder what they consider common areas," Savannah says.

I shrug. It had better include the library or I'm going to be breaking that rule.

Gideon continues, "No one is allowed to perform unsanctioned magic. No exceptions. All violators will be removed from the premises and barred from readmittance. Unsanctioned magic is any magic performed outside controlled settings or under the direct care and supervision of either a mentor or professor."

That one resonates with me. Being removed would also mean having memories erased. It's implied, but I know better than to think otherwise. Not after Lady Alene's explanation. I refuse to let something like that happen to me. The ramifications of having my memory erased could be deeper than anyone is willing to say. Especially with how much weight they put on that consequence.

I almost shudder at the thought of having my mind messed with. My memories have been what has kept me going for the better part of six years. On cold nights, shivering on the ground in the troll village, I relived my childhood with my dad. Sometimes, I would fantasize about breaking free for good, running so far away that not even the trolls would catch me. Ever.

To have someone invade my mind and wipe my memories would be catastrophic, and who's to say the right memories would be taken and not the ones that I hold so dear?

Nope. I'm good.

"Meal times," he says and pauses to make sure

everyone's attention is still on him, "are posted outside of the cafeteria. No excuses will be accepted for not making it to meal times promptly. Nor will special arrangements be made. Our cooks are busy and don't have time to prep a separate meal for anyone. Student or staff."

"Guess I better have my stash ready," Jesse says. "Don't worry, Wren. I'll share."

I switch my eyes to him and the way his eyes level on me I have to wonder what, exactly, is he going to share. Because it implied much more than just food.

"Everyone," Gideon says, "is expected to perform weekly chores. On that same note, student hygiene will be expected out of respect to yourself and your fellow students. This also leads me into sex and relationships…"

Jesse sits forward, seemingly eager to hear this one.

"No initiate may be involved with any student or faculty member during their time here. I don't want to go into details, but having already learned of the trials, I feel it's self-explanatory."

Savannah snorts. "Not likely."

I look at her, shocked that she would be one to

break a rule such as that. She smiles and shrugs like it's no big deal.

"Are you…" I ask.

She smiles and says, "Never kiss and tell."

I shake my head.

Jesse says, "When there is a will, there is most definitely a way. How 'bout it, Wren? Up for the challenge?"

I sigh, half-heartedly. I'm attracted to Jesse. No doubt about it. With his bad boy looks, piercing steel blue eyes, and killer smile—not to mention his equally sexy body—it's hard to ignore the way he teases. He narrows his eyes, with his lips parted again, and I'm ignited in desire once more.

Snap out of it, woman!

I clear my throat and say, "I would, but… no."

He smiles and says, "It's my personal goal to make you squirm."

I try to shrug him off, but it doesn't work.

"Challenge accepted," he whispers, and I put my focus on the untouchable headmaster, Gideon Storm.

"The use of magic without a conduit is a serious offense at this school and will be considered a willful act of insubordination which will be dealt with accordingly. Please don't do it. You really don't want to know what will happen."

"Worse than a mind wipe?" I hear myself ask.

But the question goes unanswered as the final rule is delivered.

"Lastly," Gideon says. "Thievery will be punished in accordance to school law, following a thorough investigation. Should you be found guilty, you will be expelled."

Ugh. His voice makes all these horrible things sound like paradise.

I'm hopeless.

"I just have one last announcement before we eat," Gideon says, turning toward us initiates. His eyes rest on mine and my cheeks warm. Pressure pools beneath my thighs, and before I can fall back into my dark desires, I pull my gaze away. "Initiates, you will, at sunrise, report to the main courtyard for training preparation for your trials. Each of you will be given an elite mentor. They will help you through your trials and make sure that you are at your best for when they begin. They are your life-line of sorts. Use them well. Absorb what you can."

He pauses for a brief moment and asks, "Any questions? No? Good. Let's eat."

Our meals appear on our plates and the smell is simply mouthwatering. The chicken is covered with buttery herbs and crispy skin. Next to those is a helping of red potatoes, a dinner roll, and asparagus.

"Talk about service," Jesse says and digs in with his fingers.

I decide to use my utensils and spear a potato wedge on my fork, blow off a little of the steam, and shove the bite into my mouth. The flavors burst along my tongue and I'm quite sure magic is the reason for this food tasting as amazing as it does.

Savannah gently elbows me to get my attention. I look to her expectantly and she nods in the direction of the headmaster. "Wanna know what I found out about him?" She smiles as she cuts a piece of chicken and places it into her mouth.

I hate to admit it, but I do. I want to know everything I can about him. "Sure," I say, trying to keep it casual.

"He first came to the school as a self-defense professor and is now the head of the school. He's mysterious, good looking for a slightly older man, and very respected in the mage community. He also happens to be the youngest headmaster in the history of Blackbriar."

Jesse leans back into his chair and looks toward the headmaster. "He's not *that* good looking."

"And your opinion counts, why?" I ask.

"Because I'm sizing up the competition. Best to fully understand what I'm up against, right?" he says as if it's just normal to be this damn competitive.

"He's a teacher, and more than that, the academy's headmaster, nothing is going to happen between him and his students," I say.

Jesse shakes his head and laughs under his breath as he toys with the asparagus on his plate. "You really don't get what you do to men, do you?"

Huh?

I stare at him blankly. What am I doing? Honestly. Far as I'm concerned, it's *them*. Not me. I shake my head and return my attention to Savannah.

"How do you know so much about him?" I ask. "Where do you get the time to fish for the information. I mean, you're right here and you suddenly know things about him like it was just placed in front of you."

She shrugs. "It sort of was. I'm sort of a telepathic empath. But it's more involved than that."

"So, you are psychic?" I ask.

"Not really. I don't have much control over it. I

just get glimpses." She shoves a spear of asparagus into her mouth and moans. "So good."

That could either be really good. Or really, really bad for me. "What did you see about me?"

"Nothing yet. At least, nothing bad, if that's what you're after," she winks as she takes a bite of potato.

That makes me feel a little better. But only a little. I don't want to know what she would do if she had the knowledge of me doing magic without a conduit. Especially now that the rules covered that, and it's apparently worse than murder here. At least, that's what it seems.

## CHAPTER ELEVEN

I finish my plate, and dessert appears shortly after. Red velvet cake. I devour it while Gideon announces a demonstration has been prepared from each house.

"First up is House of Phoenix." His voice booms as the lights in the room dim until we sit in darkness. Music echoes through the room, soft at first, gaining in crescendo as drumbeats pick up their pace until a loud bang of a cymbal slowly fades, leaving the room bathed in silence.

In the center of the arena, now void of all the tables and students, a small light appears, shining from somewhere above in the vast darkness of the unseen ceiling.

"Oh, I'm going to love this," Savannah says. I

laugh under my breath as she leans back in her chair and intently watches the show.

"Should be fun," I say and look to Jesse who seems on edge compared to his normal carefree self. "What's up?"

He shakes his head and says, "Shh… I'm trying to take a nap." A smile pulls on his lips as he sets his gaze on the show in front of us.

I shake my head. Such an enigma this one is. I wonder if, once the trials are over, he will still want to hang out. I'm sort of becoming fond of this guy.

A pillar of flame shoots up from the floor and takes the shape of a bird made of fire. It slowly flaps its wings as it hovers. Yellow eyes move over the audience before looking up to the sky and the creature dissolves into ash, collecting in a smoldering pile along the floor.

"Wow," I say and keep watching for something more to happen.

"And you know who belongs to that house?" Savannah asks, pointing her finger at the demonstration. It really wasn't a question.

I settle my attention on her. She winks, grinning from ear to ear. I shake my head. "He's got a long way to go for any of that."

"Besides," Jesse says, "Hard to give anyone else attention when I'm so fun to be around."

I playfully smack him on the arm.

"Don't damage the goods, woman." Jesse straightens his shirt sleeve and smooths his hand over his arm. "Precious cargo, you know."

A voice speaks, sounding like it comes from a speaker nearby, it's a deep, rich baritone. Part of me sighs in relief. I didn't want it to be Soren's voice, yet I kind of wish it was.

"The phoenix, born of fire, represents strength and courage. For only with strength and courage can one find a means to become what they are meant to be. That is what the House of Phoenix stands for. Do you have what it takes to be reborn from the very fires that claim you?"

Chanting, deep and melodic, echoes from around the room, coming from all directions, soft as a whisper. "Fire, death, rebirth, life."

I hold my breath and watch as a new phoenix is birthed from the ashes of the last one. The ashes start to ignite and burn. A small phoenix slowly emerges and flaps its wings, growing in size, until it hovers in one spot.

The demonstration tugs at me. I can see myself being part of the House of Phoenix. Their symbolism of death and rebirth resonates with me. I too have experienced a rebirth in a sense. From the death of my old life and being born into my new, fresh start with this opportunity.

All at once, the light is doused with the phoenix. Applause erupts, and I join in. It's hard not to with a demonstration like *that*.

Gideon's voice echoes through the room as he says, "Next, the House of Drakon."

I have to admit the first demonstration is going to be hard to follow. But I'm excited to see what is in store.

The light returns to the center of the arena and I hear the beat of giant wings and feel the wind pushing off of them before a large dragon comes into view. He lands and lets out a roar that reverberates throughout the room. His skin is the color of raw blue celestite, and he has four limbs, with his two front limbs connected to his wings. A row of spikes crown his head and stretches down his back, slowly shrinking across his tail which has a tip spiked like a flail.

He's gorgeous and fearsome, especially as he rises up on his hind legs and flaps his wings. As his mouth opens toward the sky, a torrent of fire blasts into the darkness of the ceiling. Anxiously, I peer at the dragon. I lean toward Jesse to get a better view of this magnificent creature, but goofy Jesse wraps an arm around my shoulders.

"I knew you liked me," he whispers in my ear, making my magic go wild. The warmth of his breath tingles along my skin, setting my nerves in a flurry.

I force the feeling away enough to narrow my eyes on him. "Are you serious?" My voice is low and deadly.

"In due time, you'll be mine, love."

His words and my magic give me the shivers.

Savannah chuckles at my reaction. I can't help but smile and return my attention to the demonstration.

I also feel like I could belong to this house as well.

A woman's voice echoes around us as she says, "Behold, Lord Drakon, king of the skies and all dragons. Mighty ruler of air. Bold fighter, yet merciful. This is what it means to belong to the House of Drakon, for it takes a bold, kind heart and swift resolve to conquer the air. Do you have what it takes to conquer the skies?"

Rushed whispers replace the woman's voice. As they move like the wind around us, I catch bits and pieces of the chant until I finally know what is being said. "Air is in you, and all around you."

The dragon flaps his wings again and floats in the middle of the room, hovering as his eyes roam over us sitting and observing him. With a loud roar, he blasts the ground with fire that grows brighter by the second. I feel the heat from the flames, and just as soon as it starts… it's over. Once again, we're cast in darkness. Another round of applause.

"What did you think of that one?" Savannah asks.

Honestly? I'm at a loss for words. Finally, one comes to me. "Amazing."

"I can't wait to see what comes next." Excitement is clear in her voice.

Once again, Gideon introduces the next house. "The House of Kraken."

The floor of the area starts to flood. Part of me wants to hold my breath, but I don't. As soon as the floor is completely covered in water, waves form and rush toward us, and a tentacle reaches out of the dark liquid. More of it is slowly revealed until what looks like a strange octopus emerges, slapping its tentacles along the water. Ocean sprays my face and I'm fascinated at how thorough this demonstration is.

Another voice speaks, this time male. "The mother of the sea, the Kraken, protects the depths and all her sea life. She does what is right, brings healing to those in need, and hope to the stormiest of seas. This is what it means to belong to the House of Kraken. Do you have what it takes to calm the stormy seas?"

Like the rush of ocean waves, whispers careen toward where I sit. "Power of the sea. So mote it be."

With each crash of the waves against the table, the whispers grow. As do the waves, until the water rushes high above me, forming a wall. The Kraken moves through the wall, illuminated by lightning behind it. The display is raw, awe-inspiring, and makes me wonder if this house would be a good fit.

A bright light flashes. Once the light fades, darkness is all that is left.

Following another round of applause, murmurs echo throughout the room. There seems to be a lot of excitement over this one. I brace myself for what's to come next.

"The last house demonstration for the evening is," Gideon says, "House of Winterwolf."

Crickets chirping replaces the dying murmurs. A light from above appears, silvery blue, like a moon. Growls take over the crickets. The hairs on my arms stand on end as I wonder what massive beast makes a sound like that.

I don't have to wait long as a silvery white paw steps into the light, followed by the rest of the body of a massive wolf. He's the size of a house at least. Once he stands completely under the light, he takes a seat and lets out a long, mournful howl. I notice a long black streak that starts at a point in the middle of his head and stretches to the tip of his tail. It looks like it was dipped in paint. In the light, the black glitters. I suck in a breath at the beauty of it all.

"Great Winterwolf," a woman says, her voice is sharp and commanding. Strong and proud. "Master of Earth, protects us and provides us with sustenance. His cunning is unmatched by any friend or foe. Mighty as the night. Do you have what it takes to run with the pack?"

As the wolf howls once more, chanting as rhythmic as a drum rises above it. Soft at first, but it becomes louder as the wolf sits and settles his moon-like eyes on us. "Run with the pack."

The drumming chant becomes so loud, I cover my ears. Drum, drum, drum, is all I hear until a final beat. The wolf and light disappear once more.

Thunderous applause takes over the silence, and

the lights from earlier appear again, growing from dim to bright enough to illuminate the tables and tapestries, which are all sitting where they were before the demonstrations.

The initiates around me stand with their applause, and I join them. Each member of the houses stand and bow in turn, and some of their bigger fans give out hoots and hollers. The applause slowly dies, and we initiates reclaim our seats.

Gideon stands and says, "Job well done on the demonstrations, Houses. Initiates, as you proceed through your trials, keep in mind which house you would like to belong to. Which mascot called to you the most? Before I release you to your rooms for the night, a reminder: tomorrow morning at sunrise, be prepared to meet your mentor. If you have any questions, ask them of your mentor. They are at your disposal for the length of your trials. Good luck, initiates, and goodnight."

All the initiates are prompted to stand and leave the room first, to give us time to make it back to our rooms before the halls become congested with students. As we move, I catch Soren's eye again. He's so stern and looks at me as though I've committed a murder. But he's so freaking hot. Such a shame.

I pull my gaze away as I follow Jesse out into the hall. Savannah skips to my side and slides her arm through mine.

"You know," she says, "I heard there is a special ceremony that you do with Lady Alene that places you in the house you fit into once the trials are over."

"Really?" I ask. "I wonder how that works?"

She shrugs. "I'm not sure, but word is, the students all represent the traits the houses represent."

"Huh, what would I do without you?" I ask. That little tidbit of information is interesting, but I have no idea where I would fit.

"Be totally lost," she bats her eye lashes and brushes off her shoulder. "Where do you think you fit, right now?"

"I don't know." I shrug. Truly, I don't.

"What about you, Jesse?" she asks and waits for him to respond.

He walks with his hands in his pockets as he chews on his bottom lip, looking up to the ceiling as if he's willing the answer to come to him. He pulls a hand from a pocket and snaps his fingers. "Winterwolf."

"I think I'm fitting into Kraken," she says. "Healing is my thing. It's part of what I can do."

I nod. "I haven't figured that stuff out yet, honestly. My main focus is just getting through the trials first." Without using magic sans conduit.

We walk the rest of the way to our rooms, which are on the same floor, talking about our favorite parts of the demonstrations while Jesse pretends to be a wolf.

CHAPTER TWELVE

I'm having such a good time that I almost didn't catch my name. It takes another time of hearing it before I realize I'm definitely being called. Turning around, I find Professor Lawrence leaning against the wall, waiting for me.

He waves me over. I hold up a finger and say to Savannah and Jesse, "I'll see you guys later."

Jesse tries to beg me to stay by dramatically falling to his knees and crawling after me, hamming it up really good, but I laugh and shake my head and continue to the man who gave me his only invitation to attend the trials.

Once I'm between Jesse and the professor, I use my senses to check in with my magic. There's nothing there. No reaction. Just like before. But then, I wasn't looking for one until it happened once I arrived here and met Jesse. Maybe that is something to note?

"What can I do for you, Professor Lawrence?" I ask as I stop in front of him. Still, no magical reaction to him. It definitely seems like Jesse, Soren, and Gideon are the lucky ones.

Interesting.

He walks into an empty classroom and holds the door open for me. "You need a new conduit. I brought several for you to choose from. It will come in handy during the trials."

I follow him to a desk with the top covered in different pieces ranging from rings, to things more extravagant like a diamond encrusted belt. Even a couple of wands lay on the top.

"Which would you like to try out first?" the professor asks.

I stare at the wands for a moment. One is made of black wood with silver vines wrapping around the length. Rubies are inlaid sporadically throughout, and it emanates a beautiful peace that calls to me, but the urgency in the call isn't for me.

It's too much, too needy, and the energy within the conduit makes me worry.

My father once told me that a conduit is a choice

not to be made lightly. "Choose wisely, for it will become an extension of you. You want it to flow with you, not through you or drag you down. If it feels just right, then that is the one for you."

I smile to myself. His voice sounds clear as day in my mind, and I realize just how much I truly miss him. And my mother.

I pass on that wand and move to the next. This one is made of blonde wood, and has leather wrapping around the handle, which holds an intricate silver medallion outlined in filigree. In the center is a dark blue stone. The blue is so deep it almost seems black within the facets that don't reflect the light.

But I don't feel much of a call to this one. If there is any at all, it's too soft. Too bad. This one is beautiful. However pretty, my father's words stay at the forefront of my mind. I frown.

"Take your time, Wren," the professor says. "It's a very delicate process. And don't worry if you can't find one tonight. If that happens, I'll simply bring some more for you to choose from. I take it the wands aren't to your liking?"

"No, they are quite beautiful. Just not… right." I chew on the corner of my lower lip, hoping that came across in the way I meant it to. Hearing the words out loud made it much more complicated than I meant it to be.

But if he had any issues with what I said, Professor Lawrence didn't so much as bat an eye.

So, I move on.

The next three are different rings. Not much to them. But pretty to look at.

The first is made of purple and silver stone—lepidolite, I think. The stone ring fits on my right middle finger, and it looks nice. However, I yawn. I feel a little dizzy. And the energy makes me more lethargic and sluggish. Not what I'm looking for. I slip it off and set it back in its place.

The next ring is made of stainless steel and holds a rectangular pink rhodonite stone. It too fits on my right middle finger, but its energy is too much, too fast, and I feel jittery and anxious. Magic sparks at my fingertips. This one is a definite no. I need to be in control of the conduit, not the other way around. I quickly slip that one off and set it back where I picked it up from.

The third ring is silver. Instead of trying it on, which didn't go so well the last two times, I just hover my hand over it and feel what it has to offer. The moonstone in the center, inlaid with ivy leaves in place of prongs, makes it a very beautiful ring.

Just hovering my hand over the item gives me a sensation of being enclosed in an airtight case. I can't breathe and it feels like the walls around me are closing in. This one is most certainly a no. I remove my hand and after a few moments of getting my breathing back to normal, I move on to the final two pieces left to choose from.

I frown again. I don't like how it's much more difficult to pick a conduit than it is to make one, but I don't exactly have the means or the time necessary to do so. The trials could very well start tomorrow and I'm not about to perform magic without a conduit. Breaking rules and outing myself before I'm accepted into the university would make this whole thing seem like a waste of time.

"Just two more pieces…" the professor's voice sounds patient, smooth. I look to him as he smiles. "Something tells me one of these is just right for you. The rings weren't suitable, right?"

I shake my head.

"Perhaps, one of the last two then?"

I hope so.

The last two pieces are an amulet and a wrist cuff.

The amulet is simple. With just a wrap of silver at the top for the hook on a leather rope. The color is earthy in the sense that it has reds, silver, brown, and a bit of orange. I don't recall what type of stone this one is, but when I hover a hand over it, it's almost as if the stone is repelling me.

Nope.

I sigh.

"Deep breath, Wren," the professor says. "Clear your mind and focus. Remember, I can show you more in the morning."

I nod and follow his simple instructions.

The wrist cuff seems simple enough. It's silver, and it has a line of small stones embedded into the surface. All of them are sunstones. Pretty in the false light of the room, but they will burn like tiny fires in the sunlight.

After I take another deep breath and refocus, I hover my hand over the final piece. Its energy is warm, soothing, inviting, and it seems to be at ease with me. Like it's cool for whatever. Completely relaxed.

This is it. This is what I need.

I pick up the cuff and slide it over my right wrist. Holding it up, I analyze it with my skin and how the light refracts from the stones. They glow a little and my magic feels... happy.

I smile.

"I think we have a winner." Professor Lawrence claps his hands, smiling, and goes to pick up the other items and slip them into a small black leather bag.

"I think so too," I say. "Thank you. I owe you big."

He shrugs it off and tells me, "If you insist on wanting to pay me back, pass the trials. That will be payment enough. I only want to see you enjoy your time here and know that you are safe and wanted."

I smile and nod. "Deal. And I love this place more than anywhere else I've ever been. It's an amazing opportunity that I don't want to waste."

"Off you go," he says as he seals the bag and stands straight. "Lights out in ten minutes."

I quickly turn and start to head for the door when he stops me.

"Wren?"

I turn and face him. "Yes, Professor Lawrence?"

"Make sure you get good sleep. The trials are brutal. I know you will make it through, but sleeping well is a necessary component of that."

I nod and head out the door for my room.

By the time I'm in my pajamas, I'm exhausted.

I crawl into my bed and shiver a little.

Jesse says, "If you're cold, we could always warm

ourselves with body heat. Naked is the preferred method."

I toss one of my pillows at him. "You wish," I finally push out between gasps of laughter.

"Can't blame me for trying, but thanks for the pillow. Smells like you." He snuggles up to it and sighs. "I shall sleep well tonight."

"You do that," I say and turn off the light next to my bed.

As I drift off to sleep, images of fiery phoenixes and gigantic winterwolves haunt my mind, almost as if calling to me. I wonder which house I will belong to in the end. They all seem magnetic in their own right and just as strong and powerful as the others. Soon, the trials will be over, and I'll be sorted into a house.

I just hope I can make it through the trials without my magic getting out of hand.

## CHAPTER THIRTEEN

Themorning is cold.

There is a chill in the air I can't shake. I wrap my arms around me to try to keep warm, but it's no use until the sun rises fully above the island. I wish for a jacket, but that does little good for me at the moment as we all stand in the courtyard, surrounded by stone walls that keep us from a steep drop to the ocean. We stand facing the body of the castle in its massive height, blocking out the sun, and thus, the warmth as we're all eclipsed in its shadow.

It doesn't help that my magic runs cool through my blood because I'm standing next to Jesse.

I shiver.

"It's not too late to let me keep you warm," Jesse says.

I shoot him a look. But it doesn't do any good. He shrugs it off and says, "You'll come around eventually."

"Dream on, Romeo," I say and force back the giggle that wants to bubble out of me. Right now, I need to focus, not get lost in flirting with Jesse. He's adorably hot, not to mention the muscles that curve and bulge along his body through the shirt he is wearing makes my imagination run wild, but I can't get caught up in that. My focus needs to be on the mentor, training, and then the trials.

Jesse sighs. "And what wonderful dreams they are." He looks to the sky and cocks his head slightly to the side as if he is pondering something. "Wonder if the real thing will measure up."

His gaze meets mine, and it's dark, brooding… smoldering sexy. I gulp and try not to think about what he was implying as that would take my mind to places too inappropriate for the company I'm currently in.

I clear my throat and tear my gaze away from his and say, "Guess you'll never know."

"That's what you think." He smiles.

"Relationship ban," I say and shake my head. He

just never takes the hint. Instead he finds a way to somehow keep the option open for him regardless.

"I have my workarounds. I'll give you a demonstration later." With that, he winks and becomes serious and focuses ahead.

That's fine by me. I don't really have a witty comeback. Just curiosity as to what workaround he thinks he has.

Speaking of workarounds, I need to figure out my magic. Sure, I have a conduit, but I know what I can do now, and no one can ever know of the true extent of my abilities. I have to research this more. Figure out a way around it, because if it's one thing I'm good at, it's figuring stuff out and adapting to situations.

Gideon Storm, headmaster of Blackbriar, appears at the top of a set of stairs that curve downward, along the side of the castle, toward the courtyard. Following him is his group of elites. And I'm not sure I should be surprised that Soren is among them. I am, however, shocked to see Anderson. That energy-sucking creep is the last one I would expect to even come close to being an elite. Compared to him, I prefer Soren.

Even in his six-foot whatever broodiness, he's fucking hot as hell. And the way my magic responds to him, there's more to figure out. I have no idea what it is about me that makes him hate me so much, but I want to figure it out and rectify that before he becomes a problem for me.

As Gideon passes in front of me, my magic buzzes, strengthens, and I feel like I'm ten-feet tall. Our eyes meet as he passes by. He gives a short nod. My cheeks rush with warmth as I'm thrown into all the dirty little thoughts that should be the furthest thing from my mind again.

Soren stays too far away for me to feel my magic react to him, and for that, I'm grateful. Jesse and Gideon are enough for one morning.

My eyes take in the men and women who will mentor us initiates, and I'm left staggered. They are all beautiful. The men are freaking gorgeous, and it suddenly feels unfair to be so talented and have all the looks too.

It's sort of… unrealistic, to be honest. But here they are.

"Initiates," Gideon says, walking in a path between us and his elites. "These men and women are my best and brightest students. My elites. Each of them will select one of you to mentor and train during your trials. Once you are housed, a new mentor may be selected at that time. Assuming you pass your trials, of course."

"Yes, Headmaster," we all say.

He nods. "I expect you to absorb all you can from your mentors. You will treat them with respect and honor. However, I understand not every match will work. This is why I give both mentor and initiate the opportunity to bring any grievances to me. I will give one hour to settle whatever disagreement is between you two. If a solution is not met, a new mentor can and will be assigned. Any questions?"

His eyes glance over every student. When he meets mine, his lips curve up ever so slightly. Almost undetectable. But I notice. I wonder what it is about this man, Gideon Storm, that has my hormones rushing with such naughty desires.

After a moment of no one volunteering a question, the headmaster nods. "Very well. Let's begin. Savannah Fey."

Immediately a blond, short-for-a-guy elite, steps forward and says, "I volunteer."

He's cute. But that wasn't the goal, now was it? Savannah certainly seems happy with the pairing.

"Guess I won't be needing to ask who will take on this initiate." Gideon chuckles. The rest of us let out a small laugh as he clears his throat. "Jesse Taylor."

Jesse winks at me with a half-cocked grin as he steps forward.

"Who shall mentor this initiate?" Gideon asks.

Another elite male, this with light brown hair steps forward. He crushes his knuckles and says. "I volunteer."

"Oh, this is going to be fun," Jesse says, and I worry for him. The guy doesn't look like he's going to make it easy, and Jesse is too much of a joker to take much of anything seriously.

I mean, the elite is cute. But the way this guy holds himself makes me think he and Soren could be best friends. All serious. And Jesse? Let's just say he has a knack for making everything a joke.

"Wren Blackwood," Gideon says, and the sound of my name kicks up the pace of my heartbeat.

I look to him, and he nods once. Letting out a deep breath, I step forward and catch Soren's gaze. And he's a bit too focused on me for my comfort. His lips are pressed into a thin line, and it looks like he's about to strongarm me and march me off the castle grounds. Probably would, if it were up to him.

Forcing back a shudder at the mental image

conjured, I wonder what the hell I did to this guy. All I can figure is I showed up. Maybe exist in the first place? That last one always seems like the popular vote for most people I encounter.

Hate and I sort of have a thing. Best buds until the bitter end.

"Who shall mentor the initiate?" Gideon asks.

So far, this whole thing feels like all pomp and show. A ritual. As far as I can tell, this school has shown they like those things. They abide by them and put a lot of importance in doing things in a ceremonial way.

My eyes flit between Soren and Anderson, and I find myself praying to anything out there that's listening that I don't get either of them.

Anderson smiles, his foot lifts from the ground. No sooner than he places that foot forward, Soren steps out. "I volunteer."

I'm beside myself. The man who hates me just volunteered to be my mentor. Don't get me wrong, I'm glad he beat Anderson to it, but why?

Anderson's clearly pissed off, so that's just icing on the proverbial cake for me. He stares daggers at Soren. I don't blame the guy on that at least. With Soren's charming personality and all. What's not to like?

But a weight forms in my stomach as the realization fully sets in. Soren chose me to mentor.

This can't be good.

Shoving my curiosities aside, I wait for the rest of the initiates to be assigned their mentors. And before long, everyone has been paired. I follow suit and join my mentor as we face Gideon Storm one more time.

My magic ignites with the burn of an inner fire as I stand close to Soren, and it's almost too much for me to wrap my mind around. I don't know what the hell is going on with me and Soren, much less my magic, but I need to figure it out soon.

Soren doesn't seem to notice anything different. At least, he's not showing a sign, if he does.

"Mentors, your duty is to your initiate. Train them well. For their success or failure will be measured against you," Gideon says, raking his gaze from mentor to mentor.

Oh.

Oh, no.

My success or failure will be held against Soren. So, if I crash and burn, that's going to reflect on him. I have the sneaking suspicion that this isn't his first rodeo. Which means, he knew damn well what he was doing when he took me on.

I just can't fathom that.

"Execute your training immediately. Dismissed." Gideon's words travel with the weight of a gavel and I'm suddenly weak in the knees and finding it hard to breathe.

Slowly, I drag my gaze up to Soren's who stares at me expectantly. After a moment, he shakes his head and huffs out, "Follow me."

Something about the way he said those words makes me think there is something sinister awaiting me wherever it is I'm following him to.

This makes everything just so much more fabulous.

Fun times.

## CHAPTER FOURTEEN

S oren is intense.

I can feel waves of suspicion pouring off him, and needless to say, it's freaking distracting and starting to piss me off.

He leads me to a secluded training area—apparently there are twenty of the fifty-foot radius circles on this island, all surrounding the castle, and ten of them with reservations for the mentor-initiate trainings—and we get the one farthest out. He demands I show him what I can do. But I can't focus for the life of me. With his heavy glares, and my magic's constant burning from being in proximity of him... I'm a confuddled mess.

Lucky me.

"What are you waiting for?" he demands.

"For you to stop looking at me like you're going to murder me and to give me some damn space so I can focus."

He takes a single step back and crosses his arms over his muscular chest. "You're not going to get time to 'focus' when you're in the trials. They all have time limits, Wren. You need to show me what you can do so I know how much work I *have* to do."

I sigh. "Fine."

"I'll step this down a little. Give me a ball of light."

I nod and square my shoulders and spread my feet a little wider. I place my hands in front of me, one over the other, with my abdomen resting in the center. Closing my eyes, I focus on my magic, and feel it pulsing, pooling in my hands. Slowly, I draw it out and focus my intention on creating a small ball of glowing light.

"Good," Soren says. "Now, release it."

I pull open one eye. "What?"

He runs a hand through his hair, frustrated. "Did you have any formal training whatsoever?"

"My father taught me everything I know," I mutter and bring my legs closer together. The ball of light sputters and sparks as it shrinks into nothing.

"That," he says pointing at where the light was just moments ago, "That is what I meant."

Oh. Now, I know.

"Your father taught you magic?" he asks.

I nod.

"How much?" He takes a stance in front of me and I wonder just where, exactly, he thinks he is going with this.

"Not enough, apparently. What are you doing?" I ask as he starts to take a position to cast.

"Did he teach you how to block attacks with your magic?" He continues his interrogation, avoiding my question.

Honestly, I don't remember. "Most of his lessons were the basics. You know, what to do and what not to do. Things like that."

"So, you don't know how to block?" A ball of light forms at his center and I'm nearly frozen in place.

The only thing I can think of is he really is trying to kill me.

"Quickly, Wren," he says. "Can you defend yourself?"

"Uh… with magic?" I shake my head but it's too late.

He shoots the burning ball of energy toward me

and I have little options available to me. I do the only thing I can think of and dodge, tossing myself to the ground and rolling into a standing position, all in one motion. The ball of light flies past me, hitting an invisible wall that domes over us, highlighting in beams of white light above us as the energy gets absorbed into the shield.

I watch in wonder as that happens, and I'm impressed. That is a really clever idea.

"I'll take that as a no." Soren's voice is flat and disappointed which pulls my attention to him. He narrows his amber eyes on me. "Why come here?"

"What do you mean?" I ask.

"I mean, why come to Blackbriar? Why not another academy? You know this place is for those who have the potential to be among the greatest mages alive. You clearly are in over your head."

I raise an eyebrow. "Oh really?"

He thrusts his hands out to the side. "Uh, yeah."

"Professor Lawrence doesn't share that opinion of me. He's the one who brought me here. But that's not *your* concern, is it?" I point at him. "Let's move on to whatever you have planned next."

He looks down his nose at me and huffs. "Fine. Attack me."

"With pleasure," I say and take my casting position again, but he stops me.

"No. Not like that." He pinches the bridge of his nose as one hand rests on his hip. He's clearly restraining himself and I can't understand why. "Hand-to-hand."

Oh. Well, if you insist...

I take a position in front of him, fists at eye level. I move to land a punch to the gut. He expertly knocks my hand out of the way with a block, instantly attacking with a strike to my throat using the side of his hand. I block, front kick, and get blocked.

"Good."

"Did that hurt?" I ask, shocked he complimented me. Generic, sure. But still. Coming from a guy like Soren, who seems to hate my very existence, a compliment had to be difficult.

"Focus." He gets a little dirtier with his attacks. I keep up. Mostly. And then his questions continue. "Where did you live before coming here?"

I throw a side kick as he side-steps out of the way. I throw my elbow back, hoping to land in his nose, but he's too good and too quick. "Trolls. I lived with a village of trolls in Idaho."

He stops. "Bullshit."

Panting, I shake my head. He's not even breathing hard. Not fair. "Wanna bet?"

He shakes his head, pacing in front of me. "Nope. Don't buy it."

"Well, I don't know what to tell you," I say and take a seat on the grass as my breathing slowly returns to normal. "Are we done with the interrogation or are you still convinced I'm hiding some dire, terrible secret that could undo the fabric of reality?"

"Stop being dramatic."

I shrug. "Says the person who is pacing and hates me for no reason."

"I… I don't trust you. There's a difference," he says.

"Perhaps you should be on the receiving end of your attitude, because I know the difference between hate and distrust. You happen to have both. Why?" I have a feeling this question, like the others, will go unanswered, but eventually he will answer them. Or I'll find a new mentor.

"Get up. We need to continue."

I sigh and stand. He watches me, and when I catch his gaze I shrug. "Now what?"

"Show me you can attack with magic." He goes to stand about five feet in front of me.

At first, I stare at him like he grew two heads

right in front of me. But then, I wonder how often I can take advantage of an invitation like this. If this guy wants to see what I can do. Who am I to stop him?

So, what the hell? Why not?

"I'm going to show you the proper way to defend yourself with magic," he says.

"I can defend myself with magic. A lot of the time it's second-nature. Not terminology and step-by-step, like you are asking for."

"Attack me." His voice is firmer this time.

"Don't forget you asked." I smile as I take my casting stance. Once the light is formed, I shoot it out from me. He stands there and starts to perform a spell, moving almost like a dance in front of him. But the light veers to the left and nearly takes off his arm, at least it would've if he wasn't so damn good at avoiding hits. The ball of light hits the tree that is apparently on this side of the shield and cracks a thick branch, forcing it to fall to the ground.

"Jesus, you're going to get us all killed," he mutters.

I open my mouth to ask what he means by that when he beats me to the punch.

"I want you here, in this training circle every day an hour before sunrise. You will train until breakfast. Then you will also be here following dinner every night and will train until I'm satisfied by your progress or when it's curfew. Got it?"

"No," I say and cross my arms over my chest.

"No?" he asks, voice deeper and threatening. It's as if he can't believe I defied a direct order.

"That's what I mean. No. I won't train that much with you. Not until you give me answers." I stand my ground. But I wonder if maybe he's about to implode as his face starts to turn red and his hands ignite in magic fire.

"You came to this school, agreed to go through the trials, and as such, receive a mentor who is trying to help you pass them, never mind that I don't think you deserve to be in a school like this, and you are going to stand there and tell *me* no?"

I crack in my resolve a little. "I want answers too. It can't be one way all the time."

He stands a little closer, and damn my magic, it burns even hotter. His smell is... intoxicating. Whatever soap he uses, it works for him. It's delicious.

He keeps his voice dangerously low, as he growls, "You want to be a part of this academy, correct?"

I nod. Because if I try to form words, my tongue

will get tripped up. Seeing as how my body is in a tug-of-war with itself, it's the safer bet.

"You want to pass the trials, right?" he growls again.

Again, I nod. I'm starting to get a little light-headed and I can't be entirely sure, but I feel like it's him.

"Then you will do whatever it takes to do that."

It wasn't a question, but I still nod.

"In order for that to happen, you need to train. I'm trying to do that. As your mentor, that is my recommendation. If you want to pass the trials, be here. If not, don't bother wasting another minute of my time and request your immediate withdrawal from the trials. Understand?"

I bite the corner of my bottom lip and nod, dropping my arms and taking a step back.

"Good. Be prepared to train hard. I can't afford you killing anyone in the academy, and you had better come prepared."

I half-ass salute him. Just to spite him. The distance, the air between us, helped to clear the fog from my mind. But still, my magic burns.

For a moment, he looks like he's about to rip me a new one. But then he just runs a hand through his hair and shakes his head before telling me to take a break.

As he walks away, I groan. The magic dulls, leaving me chilled from the constant warmth coursing through my body, and I want to kick something. Training with him at the level he demands will leave me all too little time to research my magic in the library.

Fan-freaking-tastic.

The only silver lining so far is that he's willing to help. It's his duty. Because if I fail, that reflects on him and he strikes me as someone who hates to lose or have a black mark on his reputation.

Shit.

At least I still have the option to ask for a new mentor if he continues to be too much of an asshole. I have a feeling I may end up using that option before too much longer.

I reclaim my spot on the grass and lay back against it. Holding up my hands, I stare at them. I can get this magic under control. I can learn some stuff and apply it. I'm a quick learner, so I know this constant training thing isn't going to be forever. Hell, maybe Soren will see I'm not a threat and stop being such an ass.

Doubtful, but a girl could dream.

I hear Soren's name get called and I turn my head to find Gideon standing outside of the training circle. He and Soren have a short chat. Soren gestures toward me, rather forcefully, and I sit up and watch the interaction, wishing I was closer so I could hear what is being said.

They're best friends, I get it. But that could also mean Soren could persuade the headmaster to get rid of me. That's something I can't stand for.

Just as I stand up and dust myself free of the little blades of grass sticking to me, Soren turns and starts walking toward me.

As soon as he is within hearing range, he says, "Training is over. Use this time wisely to practice. I'll see you here tonight."

I go to salute him, and he stops me. "Don't. Just don't. A simple answer will suffice."

"Okay." I roll my eyes.

I watch him rejoin the headmaster and they walk off together before I make my way back to my shared room to shower and change. There's a library calling my name, and I'm sure I can squeeze in a good half hour of research before I'm called on again.

My mind is occupied with where to look next as I mindlessly move through the halls and stairways toward my shared room. As soon as I make it to the front of the castle, where the stairway to my room is, I hear a voice I would much rather forget.

"You looked really good out there. Shame Soren beat me to you."

I turn my attention to the sound of the voice and look into the cold grey eyes of Anderson Stone. I groan. "What do you want?"

He shrugs. "Only a little of your time."

"Oh, is that all? Or would you like to take more of what *doesn't* belong to you?"

He smiles and leans against the wall with his hands in his pockets. "Whatever do you mean?"

I raise an eyebrow. "Leave me alone. I mean it."

As I start to walk away, I hear footsteps whisper behind me, stepping in sync with my own. I stop, look behind me, and groan. "Why are you following me?"

He shrugs, boyish smile plastered to his face. "I'm going in this direction as well. But if you want, I can walk with you instead of behind you. Mind you, I rather like the view."

Ew. I roll out my shoulders to cover up me forcing back a shiver of disgust and stop mid-step, quickly stepping to the side to keep him from bumping into me. I don't know how this stealing energy thing goes, so I don't want to take the risk of him touching me again.

"I would prefer it if you didn't follow me or walk with me. I would prefer it if you left me alone completely." I wait for him to move.

"Aww, I'm just wanting to be a friend. Nothing more. No strings attached." He smiles.

My lips curl as a thick ball forms in my throat. Stomach acid burns through my stomach. If he doesn't stop, I may just vomit all over him. I suck in a deep breath and let it out slowly to calm my nerves and ease my upset tummy. However, it's done nothing good for my rising anger.

"Not. Interested. I'm too busy for friends and I need to go, so please, move it. I don't want you following me." My voice is starting to raise and carry down the hall, and though I try to keep my temper in check, it's getting very difficult to do. I scan the hall behind Anderson to see if anyone is coming, and it's deserted. The other side doesn't look favorable for me either.

Damn. Something has got to get this guy to give up and move on. I'm not freaking interested.

"You're cute when you are angry. I get it, though. One of Soren's talents is bringing out the beast in everyone." He gestures for me to continue walking.

I don't move. I cross my arms over my chest and wait for him to go.

He smiles, chuckling under his breath. "How about you let me take you to lunch. Maybe a coffee? We can talk about what he did and maybe form a bond over a shared hatred."

"I have plans," I say. This man is infuriating. It's like my turndowns are motivating him to continue. Nothing I say fazes him. I don't get it, but I'm tired of standing here, waiting for him to leave me alone. I start to walk off as I sigh heavily, nearing a groan.

"Come now." He steps closer and reaches toward me.

I skirt out of the way of his hand and snap, "Don't touch me."

He sighs, clearly feigning disappointment. I don't buy it though. "All right. But I will keep asking until you give in. Because you will give in. Eventually." He gestures to himself. "I'm not the bad guy, Wren. I just want to be a friend. Offer a reliable shoulder and listening ear. Maybe a little more someday. But not immediately. I'm around, if you change your mind."

He walks off with his hands in his pockets and his head lowered.

Damn he's good.

But not good enough. I can see straight through that act and I'm far from having forgotten what he did to me. Taking my energy without my permission is the very last thing I will forgive of anyone. As far as I'm concerned, my coming around eventually is wishful thinking. Something he'll have to square with someday.

Perhaps I should give up on the library and spend the rest of the day in my room. But then, I can't let a guy like Anderson Stone get the best of me. Finding out more about my magic is top priority if I'm going to survive here at Blackbriar Academy.

## CHAPTER FIFTEEN

I peel myself from my bed as my muscles scream at me.

After the hunt, the fight with the trolls, and training with Soren, I'm freaking *sore*.

Groaning, I force my legs over the side of the bed. At the very moment my toes touch the carpet, Jesse walks out of the bathroom working a towel through his head and brushing his teeth. The froth of the paste encircles his mouth. I force back a chuckle at the sight. He's just so darned cute.

The upper half of his body is bare, exposing his deliciously tanned arms, abs, and pecs. Only a towel covers his lower half. Even though my body protests the very movement, I look him up and down. My mind wanders and I imagine running my fingers through his long, wavy hair before trailing the tips of my nails along the curves of his sculptured body.

He smiles and bobs his eyebrows, clearly catching me in the act of checking him out. I blush and quickly look away. The motion makes me groan again.

"Did you get the license plate of that truck that hit me?" I ask.

Jesse holds up a finger and makes his way back to the bathroom. I hear him spit into the sink and the sound of rushing water. The knobs squeak as he twists them to turn off the water and he reappears within seconds.

For a moment, I think he's actually going to write down a license plate number.

He says, "I have just the thing for you. It will help ease the ache in your muscles."

"What is it?" I ask, a little wary. Not that I don't trust Jesse, I just think he would take the opportunity to prank me given the opportunity.

"Let me get dressed and I'll show you." He starts to walk away, but stops mid-step, and points at me. "You may want to change too. We have to go to the kitchens."

I throw myself onto the bed. "Oh man! Do I have

to?" in my most kid-like, whiney voice. But I already know I have to. I have to meet Soren for training. Again.

Once dressed, we walk to the kitchens and Jesse works his charm with one of the lady workers. She blushes and grabs what he requested. I didn't pay attention to what he said, I was too caught up in her reaction and the sheer size of the massive kitchen.

Five ovens and stoves seem a bit excessive on a normal day, but this place is far from normal and it makes sense with how many people probably live in this castle. I can't even process everything I see before a steaming cup of an herbal potion sits in front of me. It's a dark, murky green color and far too thick for any regular potion I've ever heard of. I look at Jesse with a raised eyebrow.

"Trust me," he says with that devilish smile of his. "I promise you'll feel better."

I sigh and pick up the cup, still not convinced, but he's never given me a reason to not trust him. And that is saying a lot considering we share the same room and he just loves to mess with me in all the right ways.

I'll never tell him that, but still.

I breathe in the smell and almost gag. "You're trying to kill me."

"Good medicine doesn't taste great, love. Drink." He pushes on the bottom of the cup, forcing it to my lips, and I hold my breath as I gulp the steaming liquid.

It's… not that bad. Just smells horrible. A bit earthy and minty.

I chug down the last of it, and I can already feel the tension and ache in my body fade. Setting the cup on the counter in front of me, I face Jesse and say, "Thank you."

Yeah, he's not so bad of a guy.

"Oh, you owe me one for that. Payment is due at time of service." He presses a finger on his cheeks and leans forward.

I shake my head and smile. My magic's reaction to him works through me, further soothing my body. Combined with the warm potion in my belly, it's a pleasant mix of hot and cold. Like a hot summer day with the right amount of cool breeze.

He laughs, drops his hand, and shrugs. "Hey, can't blame me for trying."

"True," I reply. "I can't." I gently slap him on the shoulder and say, "Better luck next time, eh?" I wink then turn and walk away.

He groans and I giggle to myself. That was fun. I'm gonna have to do that more.

As I head out of the kitchen, I have about an hour before I have to meet Soren for more of his 'So Fun, I Just Can't Get Enough' training. But before that, I have to brush my hair and teeth. Especially after that potion.

Once that's finished, a knock raps on the door and I answer it to find two men dressed in formal all black with a burgundy sash over one shoulder. Each of them has a different house symbol on them. One Winterwolf, and one Kraken.

The first one with light brown hair and blue eyes and the Winterwolf emblem says, "Wren Blackwood, you are called to the first trial."

The second one has the same color hair but light brown eyes. He says, "How do you answer?"

Sheesh. So much formality.

"How am I supposed to respond? Just a simple yes?"

They nod and say, "Follow us."

Oh. Okay. Guess I will see Soren later.

But if I'm honest, I'm not really bothered by that. I mean, he's hot as hell, sure. Just leaves a lot to be desired when he hates the very fact I'm me.

I step out of my room and shut the door behind me. They do an about-face and walk in time down the hall. I follow them as I try to ignore the curious onlookers, and the nervous anxiety rushing through me.

This is it. No turning back now. And I certainly won't be going back to the trolls. Do or die, I will pass these trials.

Well, not *die*. But the gist of it is there. After all, I will either keep my spot here and go on, or I lose my memories of this place and lose everything I have gained.

"Don't be nervous," the Winterwolf guy says.

The Kraken guy snorts. "Says the one that nearly fainted when the escorts came."

"Point is," Winterwolf guy says as he gives his partner a disparaging look, "we were all nervous for our first trial. It's all downhill from here."

I nod, not that they can see it. "Good to know."

I become lost in my thoughts, following the two men like a drone until the garden comes into view and Lady Alene stands, waiting for me with a smile on her white marble face.

"It's lovely to see you, Wren Blackwood," Lady Alene says.

The two men step out of the way just before the entrance of the garden, standing at either side of the walkway to allow me to move forward. "It's lovely to see you as well, Lady."

"Are you ready for your first trial?"

"I am." I try to stand still, to keep from wringing my fingers together, but it's difficult. Nearly impossible.

"Nervous?" she asks as her eyes take in my obvious anxiety.

"A little," I admit.

She softly laughs. "Don't be. This is an easy trial based on your knowledge. You already have what it takes to apply your magic in any situation. And in the three scenarios you will go through, you will be able to demonstrate that application."

I nod.

"Be warned, dear one, there is a limitation of time. The quicker you act, the better."

Awesome. No pressure at all. "Thank you, Lady Alene."

She bows her head and says, "Just do your best. I will see you again soon." The Lady nods to the men behind me (I assume). A blindfold is placed over my eyes, and they lead me to a location that seems like it's miles away.

Birds chirp and things I can only guess at move through the trees around us. Before long, the stone path softens into dirt and little bits of rock pushes against the bottom of my shoes as we walk.

I try to keep track of the direction we walk in, but after a couple of turns and some stairs, I'm lost. But that's probably the point, right?

Right.

Finally, we stop, and the blindfold is removed. I blink away the blinding light and the blur of the scenery around me. Before long, I stand before a small stone building that reminds me of a mausoleum. But this one is built into the cliff face.

A breeze wraps around me and I look around to find myself alone. I suck in a slow breath and let go of it as I face the door. Reaching out a steady hand, I open the door and step inside the room. The door shuts behind me and the only light I have to see by seeps in through the cracks around the door. I see four sconces in the corners of the room, but the shadows seem to move between them like ink. I can't see where I'm going, where I'm supposed to go, much less know what I'm supposed to do.

If this is a test of knowledge, I'm going to fail without light to see by. I don't have a lot of time, despite not really knowing how much I have to begin with.

I take a casting position and pull on the light around me. My hands glow with magic, my conduit illuminating as well. The light starts to warm, and I know within moments I can light the sconces and have light to see by.

In moments, the heat is strong, and I touch each sconce with the magic. They burn to life. Slowly, the wall across from the door I entered through absorbs the light and another door takes shape. A puzzle forms. A symbol that looks like a maze of sorts.

Underneath it reads:

*Whether you go high or low, magic is the purest flow.*
*Beautiful, yes, but deadly too, for its potential is up*
*to you.*
*What is taken, must be given.*
*To find your way, you must pay.*

A memory pulls at the back of my mind, where my father taught me everything I thought there was to know about magic. The days when life was simple, innocent, and sweet. We did fun little activities to teach me the rules of magic.

A demonstration of all magic coming with a cost. To make a flower grow, I had to give it life by spending my energy. By giving a part of myself, I was able to give life to something new.

"All magic comes with a cost," I say out loud.

Nothing happens. I stare at the symbol on the

door and wonder if I'm supposed to do something with it to make the door open. Biting the corner of my bottom lip, I press my right hand over it. I slowly let my magic bleed into the shape, filling all the crevices.

"The cost is my energy."

Once done, I stand back and the magic seeps into the shape and the seal around the door breaks. Wind blasts into the room, dousing the sconces. Before long, the next room is open to me and I step through.

Water rushes underneath me, but I can't see the bottom of the cavern below. Beams of sunlight shine into the room, pouring light onto the bridge stretched out in front of me. At the end, I know is another door.

I blow out a raspberry and analyze the bridge in front of me, but I need to be careful and not spend too much time figuring this out. Not knowing how much time I have really sucks. The bridge is just a long platform. No sides. And with the breeze flowing into it, I'm sure it could blast me over the side and into the pit below. If I stabilize my legs and balance, I will slow down. That is the cost. To get across, I have to sacrifice time. Or fall.

My choice is simple, but risky. Because, again, I

don't know how much time I have, how much has passed, and that could create a problem. But to be safe, I need to get across without falling off.

I cast a stabilization spell, and my legs feel heavy, glued to the ground, but I can move. And with the clock ticking, I make my way across the bridge. My hair blows in front of my face. I tuck the strands behind my ear and wobble. Thanks to the spell I cast on myself, I don't fall.

As soon as I reach the door, there is another riddle to solve.

*Raw power, fiery flame, must be shaped and must be tamed.*
*Not by force of will, nor by hand, but through an object of the land.*
*Take special care without this.*
*Darker than shadows your soul will twist.*

My heart drums harder. I know what this is. This is the very thing I'm trying to figure out while I can.

"All magic must be cast with a conduit." My words echo and a handle appears on the door.

Simple enough.

I grip the knob and twist, but the door doesn't move.

Maybe it's not as simple as I thought.

To get through the last door, I had to use magic. That must be how to get through this one. As I call on my magic again, my conduit starts to glow, and I try once again.

The knob gives way, the door opens, revealing a tunnel that looks as though it goes underneath the castle. It's arched, and there are small gutters on the side of the path for run-off.

This is it. The last room. I just have to get through this room without running out of time, and the first trial will be done.

I already know what this is going to cover. The first two were the first two main rules of magic.

There's just one more left.

"Okay, Wren. Let's go. Time's a wasting." My voice carries through the tunnel and I know that not all is as it seems. But maybe it is. I can't overthink it though. Not this close to being done.

I step forward, bracing myself for anything to happen.

Every step I take echoes through the tunnel and it's hard to tell if I'm going the right way. I let my intuition guide me. If getting back to the castle or out of the tunnels is the goal, I need to keep my ears open for signs that I'm coming to an end.

I arrive at a "T" intersection and strain to hear a difference between the directions. Movement in my periphery draws my attention. A gnome, working diligently on whatever it is they do, is running off to my right and I figure, they are throughout the castle. Why not go in that direction?

It's a gamble, but nothing else is really sticking out to me.

The tunnel eventually curves to the left and angles up. Once I reach another intersection, to my right is a dead end lit with two torches spaced close to the corners. As I reach the wall, like I expected there to be, is another riddle.

*Brightest day meets darkest night.*
*Beauty born and deathly might.*
*Those who tread between the two are those who wield the power true.*
*Brightest day meets darkest night.*
*From the deepest pit, the mage takes flight.*
*To command powerful energy, one must uphold magic's symmetry.*

Of course.

"The third rule of magic is, magic must have balance and harmony."

The three rules tie together into a perfect circle. Just like the points of the triskele on my wrist and the rule of three.

Once again, I conjure my magic. And this time, I draw my triskele. The bricks within the wall fold in on themselves and reveal the arena. Applause ushers me forward and I take in Soren McCallister, Deacon Lawrence, Gideon Storm, and Lady Alene.

I smile, a little beside myself because I started off the trial feeling utterly unprepared, and practically bluffed my way through the last part.

A cacophony of congratulations surrounds me as I fully step out of the tunnel.

Professor Lawrence steps forward and says, "Well done, Miss Blackwood."

"Thank you," I say and try to ignore the heat burning through me from being so close to Soren. I look toward him. He simply nods. Scowl and all. I nod and return my attention to the professor.

"I wonder, if you would mind meeting me in my office for a quick talk?" he asks.

I look around wondering why he couldn't just talk to me here and he says, "It's a confidential meeting I have to hold with my initiate following the first trial."

I nod. Well that makes sense. "Sure. When?"

"Just as soon as you can step away." With that, he walks off.

Okay… Nothing weird about that.

## CHAPTER SIXTEEN

There is something not quite right about Deacon Lawrence.

And I need to find out what that is, soon.

After meeting him at his door, he invites me into his office and has me take a seat. This feels a lot like a "sorry, but you're not working out," sort of conversation instead of checking in on me following the first trial. But hey, what do I know?

I'm distracted by the number of curious things inside this room. I want to marvel at the mini-statues of various figures, the taxidermy owl frozen in mid-flight, and the large wall of books that line the shelves taking up the back of his desk. There's a door that probably leads to a closet on the left and one on the right that has a strange lock on it.

Though I want to stare at all these wonderful things, I keep my attention on the professor.

"So, not bad for your first few days here, huh?" he starts.

It's so casual that I almost want to drop my guard. But I don't. Instead, I smile. "It's amazing here. Definitely a far cry from the troll village."

"Indeed," he says and takes a seat in his chair. The leather groans against his weight as he settles his forearms on the surface of the desk, adorned with even more interesting items. "Are you liking Blackbriar so far?"

"Yes, I am. Very much," I say and wonder if there is more of a point to this.

He nods and sits back in the chair, completely relaxed and acting like we're playing catchup like long lost friends. "Tell me a little more about your past."

"Like what?" A pinch forms in the center of my forehead.

"Like how you came to live with your aunt," he says, and there's something in his eyes that lets me know he's searching for something. Something he's not willing to share, but is asking questions to dig for that information. His stare is unrelenting, as if he's trying to reach inside me for answers.

I don't like it.

Part of me wants to question him on why it's so important to know, but I keep in mind that he gave me his only invitation to the school. He has a lot riding on my success, and maybe he's just trying to be nice about getting to know me so he can rest assured he made the right decision.

Maybe.

Either way, I owe him big time for taking a chance on me. And the answers he wants are simple enough. Still… I can't help but wonder what he's looking for.

"When I was fourteen, my mother was killed in an accident. Two weeks later, my father disappeared. No one knows what happened to him or where he went. Only that he was on his way home from a grocery run." A slight smile tugs at the corner of my lips at the memory. "He insisted on picking up some ice cream for us to share while we watched our weekly movie together. It was a ritual of ours, and we desperately wanted to get back to as close to normal as we could. But he never made it home."

The professor nods as he stares at something on his desk. He picks up a pen and writes something down on a piece of paper I can't see, and I wonder what he's doing. Before I can find out, he asks, "So, you went to live with your aunt after that?"

"Yes." I wipe my hands on my skirt and continue, "It was less than one month when I was taken by the trolls in the middle of the night."

"One thing I have always wondered," he says as he holds the pen to his chin. "Why trolls?"

I shrug. "I don't know."

He nods. "Well, I was able to get a letter to your aunt regarding your stay with us. She's currently overseas. She'll be gone for two weeks. She assured me as soon as she is back in the States, she will reach out for a reunion with you."

The idea that I will soon be reunited with my family again fills me with immense joy and hope. I'm instantly filled with questions that I want to ask her. Like, how long did she look for me before giving up? Did she give up? Will she want me home over breaks? But first, I have to actually make it into the academy. I need to focus on the trials.

"I appreciate you reaching out to her. I can't wait to see her, but won't the trials be over by then?" I ask. "Not to sound like I'm not grateful, because I am. But if I don't pass, I will have nowhere to go."

"I figured that into everything. Either way, you

and your aunt will be reunited. Whether that is here or at her estate."

I nod. "Thank you so much. Means the world to me."

"Of course. Now, you say your father disappeared. He hasn't tried to contact you since then?"

I shake my head. "How could he? There was no way he would have been able to find me. I mean, the trolls aren't exactly in a place to receive mail."

A shadow crosses over his eyes and I wonder if he knows more than he is letting on. The questions are too specific, considering the excuse he gave me for this little meeting in the first place.

"What was your father working on when he disappeared? Do you know?"

Why would that matter? "No. Why?"

He shrugs. "Just wondering what would cause a man to disappear like that. Leaving his young daughter at home, subjecting her to the life she has lived up to now."

"I assume he's dead," I answer.

"Do you?" There's something about the way he said those words that makes me believe he knows a hell of a lot more about my father and my past than I do.

I shrug and shake my head, honestly unsure with what he wants as a response.

"So, you haven't heard from him? At all?" he asks one more time.

"I already told you I haven't."

"Hmm. That's too bad." He taps his pen on the surface of his desk a few times. "Well, what did you think of your first trial?"

"It was eye-opening. Is there anything else you want to ask me? I would like to get something to eat before I train."

He narrows his eyes. I can almost see the gears turning in his head. He is definitely up to something.

"Do be careful, Wren. I would hate for any unnecessary harm to come to you."

His words... they are dark, with hidden implications that make my intuitions flare. If he wants me to trust him, he's going about it in all the wrong ways. Still, I stand and say, "Thanks, Professor Lawrence. I appreciate your concern. I'll be careful."

"Please do," he says and gestures toward the door.

As soon as I'm out of the office I release a heavy sigh. Something is definitely not right. The sooner I can figure this out, the better. Because, I have a feeling that he suspects I know more than I do, and I really don't know what he will do next to get those answers. I'm sure his little 'unnecessary harm' bit probably has something to do with it.

Even though I'm hungry, I lied when I said I wanted to eat. What I really want is to get some research in. I have to figure out my magic and fast. I can't risk going dark. My plan is set. First, research. Second, figure out what Professor Lawrence is up to. This one may take some time. A little digging, even. Preferably when he is otherwise busy. He's hiding something, and I need to find out what.

Time for step one: find a way to stop from going dark.

## CHAPTER SEVENTEEN

I'm on a ladder, stretching up on my tiptoes close to the highest prong and I still can't reach this book. I barely graze the spine with the tips of my fingers. If I continue to try, I'm probably going to lose my balance and fall off. And I don't dare climb any higher.

My magic starts to react, and it tingles through my body like tiny snowflakes falling on my skin.

"Need some help?" a tenor voice asks, and I nearly jump out of my skin.

Below me is the cutest man ever. He's blond, wearing glasses, and as he smiles at me, I'm dazzled. I realize now that my magic is reacting to *him*. Rushing through my veins with a tingling sensation and igniting my senses.

Interesting. Now there are four. Four men who are hotter than hell and have a knack for making my magic run *wild*.

"Sorry for startling you," he says.

"You're fine. I wasn't expecting anyone else to be here. But yes, I would love help," I finally say and smile. Carefully, I descend the ladder and let him take my place.

"This one right here?" He points to the very book.

"Yes, that's it." I glance at his very nice ass, and I'm thrown into dirty places in my mind involving him and me and a whole lot of skin.

Good God, Woman.

I shake my head to clear the fog in my mind and take in a deep breath. He slips his finger expertly over the spine and tilts the book back before pulling it completely from the shelf. He holds it down toward me as he descends the ladder. As soon as I can reach it, I take the book. "Thank you. I really appreciate it."

He runs a hand through his hair and smiles so bashfully, it's like he doesn't even know how freaking hot he is. "You're welcome. Didn't look like you were going to get the book without falling. So, I had to offer."

"I'm glad you did. You're like my hero now." I smile.

He chuckles under his breath. "It was my pleasure."

He stands in front of me and he is about half a foot taller than I am, looking down at me with those stunning brown eyes. I feel like I could fall into them forever and be quite happy. I want to reach up and pull his mouth to mine and explore his mouth.

I blink away and clear my throat. Holding out my hand I say, "I'm Wren Blackwood."

"Milo Moreau," he says, taking my hand.

Holy hell, his hands are soft, warm, and his name is *perfect*. I try to keep my mind from going full-tilt into sexual scenarios, but it's hard.

So. *Hard*.

There is something about him that takes control of me and I realize I don't want this encounter of ours to end. Not yet.

"Wanna join me, Milo?" I ask, still holding his hand.

He chuckles. "Sure. But can I have my hand back?"

"No. I'm keeping it forever." I laugh, genuinely belly laugh, and release his hand.

This guy is something else. I can feel so much through my magic. And it's all because of him.

Oh my.

He follows me to a table as he asks, "So are you researching the trials too?"

"No." I take my seat. "I hadn't thought of that, actually. I'm looking into something a little different."

"Maybe we can help each other out?" he suggests.

I bite the corner of my lower lip. "How about we sit together. I don't know what help I would be, not to mention how you could help with my problem."

"You'll be surprised at what I can help with. Libraries are sort of my super power," he says.

I chuckle. "Good to know."

He opens his book and I follow suit. This is a very different feeling, sitting with Milo. It's calm, peaceful. I truly enjoy this time with him. It's so easy to be with him. I just *have* to know more about him. It's like some deep-seated desire I can't shake.

To be honest, I really don't want to.

"So, Milo…" My God, I love the feel of his name in my mouth. "Where are you from?"

"Quebec. You?"

My eyebrows raise in wide arches on my forehead as his last name makes sudden sense. "Idaho."

I leave it at that. He doesn't need to know more. Not yet.

He pushes his glasses up the bridge of his nose. "What brings you to Blackbriar?"

"I was invited to the trials by Professor Lawrence. How about you?" I've pretty much forgotten all about my book. I'm having too much fun with Milo. I like getting to know him.

"I've studied my whole life to get into a top academy. You should see my parents. They don't stop talking about it. Sometimes I think they're more excited about it than I am, though I won't complain. I'm lucky to be here."

"I bet. It sounds like they're really proud." I say, cocking my head to the side and I'm unable to remove the smile that stretches my life.

He shrugs. "As proud as any parents, I suppose. Aren't yours?"

My smile fades. "I wouldn't know. My parents died when I was fourteen." I start flipping through the pages as emotion overwhelms me. It's almost too much for me to handle. The story I flip to is much like the others. Just a mage battling a shadow mage, and the defeat of said shadow mage. Nothing about the shadow mage's side. About what he had done, or what made him dark.

This is getting frustrating. I have such limited time. Surely, I can't be the first.

Can I?

"Oh, I'm so sorry," Milo says, placing his hand gently over mine.

I turn my attention to him. There's so much warmth, understanding, and empathy within his eyes, I can't help but feel like I can be truly open with him and he wouldn't mind. He's so gentle and kind.

"It's okay." I shrug. "Happened a long time ago. Not the worst thing that I've been through."

His eyebrows knit together, darkening the shadows on his face just a little. "There's something worse than losing your family?"

"Trust me," I say as I use my free hand to flip through the pages of the book, skimming key words like dark, shadow, and mage. "There are a lot of worse things I don't wish even my worst enemy to go through."

"Wow." He pulls his hand away as he sits back in his chair and I frown, wishing he would cover mine again. "If you ever want to talk about it, I have a great listening ear."

I meet his gaze again and get lost in the warmth within them. I'm overcome with the desire to kiss him again. It's hard to pull my eyes away, but I do. Briefly. "Thanks, Milo. I'll take you up on that someday."

"Please do." He seems serious about his offer. I wrestle a little with telling him about the trolls, but I don't want to scare him away. Besides, nobody believes me. Trolls are so secretive. They prefer to be among the legends of blurry images of Bigfoot and Nessie.

But I promise myself that someday I will. I'll share all my horrors with him, and he can help me be free of them. But for now, I prefer learning more about who the amazing Milo Moreau truly is.

I wonder…

Maybe he could help me. Not with specifics, because that wouldn't go well. No one needs to know why I'm researching going dark. But, he looks like the bookish type who has an idea of where to look for the generalized topic of going dark.

"Hey, you still wanna help?" I ask.

He puts his book down and levels his gaze on me. "I'm glad you asked. What can I find for you?"

Excellent. "I'm looking into shadow mage

history. What made them dark. Their backstories, if you will."

His eyes widen and I regret asking for his help. His expression changes to that of confusion, and I feel him pull farther away from the table. It's such a small movement that he probably didn't even notice that he shifted. But I did. And I worry I jumped ahead of myself too soon.

"Shadow mage history?" he asks, voice dark with a hint of suspicion.

I shrug and try to play it off as much as possible. "Yeah, just a mere curiosity. Notes on what not to do. Stuff like that."

He narrows his eyes on me and damn the sexiness of it all. "Curiosity and learning?"

"That and I just had my first trial. It made me realize that I have to be prepared for all possibilities. I'm guessing at some point, there will be a test against the darkness, and I need to know how best to handle that."

"What all happened in the trial?" Milo asks.

"Now, Milo, you know I can't tell you. I don't even know if what I have already told you breaks the rule. I take it you haven't had your first yet?"

"Not yet," he says through a sigh. "I hope soon though."

"I'm sure it will be." Though I really hope it's not too soon. There is a flicker of doubt in his eyes. "Are you nervous?"

"A little." He chuckles under his breath. "My parents would be so disappointed if I failed. That's why I'm here. To study the trials as well."

"So, are you willing to help out?"

His eyes light up with a smile and he says, "I think I know of a few books that could help."

I sigh in relief. "Thank you."

For some reason, I trust him. I feel like I can open up to him completely and not have to worry about the backlash of it all going wrong. Now, that doesn't mean I'm willing to open up just yet. I still want to be one-hundred percent sure I could place that trust in him. For now, I'll keep my real motives to myself.

"Milo Moreau," a man with a deep, gravelly voice speaks from the door of the library.

Milo snaps his attention in that direction and stands. "Yes?"

"You are called to your first trial. How do you answer?" the man says.

I slouch back in my chair, slightly deflated. They are taking Milo from me.

"I accept," he says and looks at me. A smile pulls

on his lips and I almost get caught in his eyes again. "It was a pleasure to meet you, Wren. I hope we can talk again soon."

I smile, floored as excited energy pulses through me. It takes everything to keep my giddy self from popping out and dancing in my chair. "Likewise, Milo. Good luck."

He nods and walks to join the man at the door that called him away to his trial. The magic in me soothes slightly until evening out and returning to its normal state. But it feels slightly sluggish. Like it hated him leaving as much as I do.

I wonder what I can learn about my magic and the reason why it reacts to four incredibly hot guys. Albeit one is an asshole, but still. In an island full of mages, these four have to be special in some way. There's no other logical explanation for it.

The godfather clock in the far corner of the library strikes four. It will be dinner soon, and then more training with Captain Serious.

I look at the spot where Milo last stood and sigh wistfully. There's no doubt about it, I would rather spend an evening pouring over books and research than training with a man who seems to hate me for no damn good reason.

God, I hope Milo passes.

## CHAPTER EIGHTEEN

The sunsets here are beyond magical.

The way the colors blend and melt toward the horizon is spectacular. It's like a vivid painting of light and wonder, and I love the sight of the day blending seamlessly into the night, all right over my head.

Though the sight is beautiful and all, I should be training. However, Soren isn't here. At first, I figured he was just running late. But he hates me. So, perhaps he decided I'm not worth the effort?

I've been here for over an hour and he still has yet to show. And that pisses me off.

Figuring he is done with me, I'm okay with being done with him. Yes, my magic reacts to him. Yes, I'm annoyingly attracted to him. Yes, I need the training. But I refuse to be treated like this. I have better things to do with my time than wait around on a man like Soren.

Headmaster Storm said we could elect to have a new mentor if the one we have doesn't work out. Well, I have just reached my breaking point and won't wait around for Soren any longer. I don't care what his reason or excuse is. I'm getting a new mentor, and he can kiss my ass if he doesn't like it.

Besides, waiting on a man who hates me is not only cruel punishment but also sours my enjoyment of the majestic sunset.

I slap my hands together, dusting them off from the wait, and make my way toward the headmaster's office.

Once inside, I read the signs that indicate where Headmaster Storm is and follow them through the maze of halls and stairways to a dead-end wall covered with a painting of a window overlooking scenes that magically change. The entire painting takes up the entire wall, and I stare in awe as the movement seems real.

*Feels* real.

The burgundy curtains blow in the breeze from the sea. The sun shines its warmth in a wedge of light that folds over the window sill. A pot of flowers rests on a table to the right and the pink petals soak up the breeze and sun, dancing as though it has a life of its own.

Something large and massive flies in front of the window, startling the ever-loving crap out of me. I fall on my butt as the realization dawns on me. It's a dragon.

Working to catch my breath, I stare in awe as the image changes. The window is gone. In its place is a meadow with long blades of grass and bright, glowing purple wildflowers growing from the floor. Trees line the side, angling toward the middle of the painting. As the leaves fall, they glow in a pinkish color, collecting on the ground.

I stand and walk toward the image, reaching a hand to touch the wall as the scene changes again.

This one is of a ship. One that looks like an old pirate ship. But this one has billowing white sails fully extended, and on the bow, as the boat floats closer, a wooden image of a beautiful woman wrapped in a loose tunic dress, barely covering her breasts. She turns her head toward me as she passes by and waves. I slowly wave back as the ship presses onward, past my view.

The image changes again, but this time, I hear

arguing behind the wall. It's muffled, but one voice stands out.

Soren's.

He spits out my name, and I'm suddenly acutely aware that he is arguing with someone about me. I step closer to the wall and press my ear to it, to hear their conversation better.

"I know you have seen her soul, Gideon. Her true nature. But that is not the point. Souls can change. And I don't trust her," Soren says. His words are forceful and full of rage.

Interesting. Gideon can see a person's soul. I wonder if that's what helped him climb the ranks so much quicker than others. Being able to tell if someone is corrupt or predisposed toward light or dark, can be a useful gift for someone like Gideon.

This is a development that needs further looking into. I wonder just how much he can see and not see.

"Not only that," Soren continues, "but it seems recently you have been having some troubles with that gift of yours, correct?"

"True," Gideon says. "There are a few individuals within these walls whose souls I cannot see. However, it isn't a flaw of my power, it's a block. They are somehow preventing me from seeing them. I'm doing my due diligence by keeping a close eye on them in hopes of finding out how and why they are blocking me. A flaw in my power would have shown itself before now, Soren." his voice seems even. Tried on patience maybe, but even.

Well, at least Gideon Storm is willing to give me the benefit of a doubt. I still don't understand why Soren hates me so much. It doesn't make sense. I've done absolutely nothing to him. But maybe I can find out why now?

"You know how I feel, dammit," Soren says. "We've been through this before. She shouldn't be here."

"She's different," Gideon says. "I have seen her soul. She is pure. Powerful, yes. But if she was prone to dark magic, I would've seen it. Trust me, brother. As you have done for so many years."

Oh, so I may be on the right track with that soul reading thing, and it looks like he can tell who is more susceptible to dark and light magic. It still doesn't answer Soren's penchant for hating me.

"A lot of people died then, Gideon. Too many. She is a risk we should *not* be taking. I have no idea what Deacon was thinking when he brought her here. She should be forced to leave."

And have my memories messed with? No thank you. Soren, you asshole, what the hell is your deal?

"Why did you volunteer to train the girl then?" Gideon asks.

At first, there's nothing. I press myself closer to the wall in case they moved deeper into the room, but I still can't hear anything.

"I can keep an eye on her," Soren says. "She's waiting for me now. I should get going."

Oh, no I'm not. I gave up on that.

I don't wait to listen to their goodbyes. Instead, I run down the hall and wait for Soren to be out of earshot and out of view before going back to the headmaster's office. Now, more than ever, I want answers, and I certainly don't want or need Soren as my personal babysitter.

Ducking into a doorway in the intersecting hall, I press myself against the corner as far as I can go. Soren rushes by, a concentrated expression on his face. But I don't have time to worry about him. I need to get to Headmaster Storm's office, and he has another thing coming if he thinks I'm going to leave without a new mentor. Especially after what I just heard.

Not that I will reveal that part, but I will if I have to.

I poke my head around the doorway and watch as Soren turns completely out of sight. He's gone. Time to go.

As I make it back to the office, Gideon is outside of his door. The wall of shifting, moving paintings are gone, leaving the smooth ivory colored wall and the dark cherry door and trim. He turns as I make it half-way down the hall.

His eyes widen and my magic buzzes through me. I freeze in place for a moment and watch as his eyes light up and a smile pulls on his lips.

"Miss Blackwood," he says. "Is there something you need?"

I blink away the spell I was under, refocus on the reason I'm here. "I need to speak with you about getting a new mentor."

His smile falters a little and he nods. Turning to face the door, he unlocks the handle and opens the door. "Please, come in."

The closer to him I get, the more my magic buzzes, strength pulsates through me. I feel stronger, unstoppable. And it's all frustratingly unclear.

That frustration becomes replaced with instant awe. His office is huge. Impossibly larger than what it seems on the other side of the door. Bookshelves line the walls, except the one where a fireplace takes residence. A small table with two large, cushy leather chairs sits in front of the fireplace.

The wall across from the entry has a large window with a desk in front of it and a couple over-stuffed chairs in front of that.

The whole room has a smell of firewood, cinnamon, and clove. There's a sweeter scent under all of that I can't place.

I look up, and the ceiling is a reflection of the sky with a chandelier seemingly hovering in the air directly above me.

"Wow," I say.

"I'm glad you like it," Gideon says, pulling my attention back to him. He sits at his desk and when I settle my gaze on him, and he gestures to one of the chairs in front of him. "Please, sit."

I smile and take a seat.

"Why do you want a new mentor?" he starts.

"Does 'he's an asshole' work as a good excuse?" I ask and wish my mind didn't suddenly become lost in the idea of fucking him on the desk. It's a bitter sweet image in my mind because he is the headmaster and I'm an initiate. No relationships.

But a girl can dream.

Gideon chuckles. "He can be, yes. Particularly

with things he feels strongly about. Why don't you explain what he has done so that I have more background?"

I nod. "Well, he threatens me, treats me like I'm an idiot, acts like I'm an unruly child, and hints that I'm evil. He hates me for no reason. I've done nothing to him. And just tonight, I waited for over an hour for him to show up to our training he demanded I do."

"Forgive his tardiness. He was with me. That wasn't his fault," Gideon says. "Soren is a good friend of mine and has been for many years. Though his methods are a bit harsh—"

"A bit?" I ask.

He nods. "A bit, yes. My point is, he's only trying to do what he thinks is best. It's nothing personal toward you, specifically. It's more situational. Try to see past that and just do the best you can."

I narrow my eyes on him. "So, you won't give me a new mentor?"

He holds up his hands in defense as he leans back in his chair. "I didn't say that at all. Consider this a learning curve for the both of you. He needs to learn to be gentler with his methods, and you need to learn to hone your skills, so you don't hurt yourself or others and pass the trials."

I shake my head. "Still sounds like a no."

"Look at it this way," he says, "it's more of a second chance. Allow him to see he has nothing to fear with you. He'll come around."

"How can you be so sure?" I ask. "Seems like he's more of an obligated, glorified babysitter than a mentor."

He chuckles.

And I get a little wetter between my thighs.

Everything about this man is sexy and threatens to undo every thread of my self-control. He's very pleasant to top it off, and I still remember what his touch did to me during the welcome ceremony.

I bite the corner of my lower lip and cross my legs to keep the pressure from building any more than it already has.

As much as I hate to admit it, I want to agree to a second chance for Soren. Just because he asked me, I want to do whatever it takes to keep me on his good side. It's deeper than that though. Maybe more like I want to please him and oblige his request because it's hard not to.

Gideon says, "He's the best we have in this school and I trust him to take care of you when the need arises."

"He has a pretty crappy way of showing that."

"That may be very true. Tell you what…" He points a finger at me and sits up in his chair. "I'll let you in on a little secret. But you have to keep it between you and me."

I sit forward, make a gesture like I'm locking my lips closed and ask, "What?"

"He's harder on himself than he is on anyone else," he says.

"That's hard to believe," I mutter, sitting back in the chair. A man like Soren doesn't strike me as the type.

"So, will you do that for me, please?" His voice is soft, and his eyes pull me in like an embrace. "Give him another chance. If he still belittles you, I'll find you another mentor."

Ah, dammit. He asked so sweetly. And that need to do as he requests is just too much to ignore. I nod.

"Thank you," he says.

"Oh, believe me, there will be changes. I'm not going to be snapped at and treated like an idiotic child. If he wants to train me, he can also show me a little respect."

He chuckles again and says, "You are quite head-strong, aren't you?"

I chuckle with him and shake my head. "Maybe a

little."

"I have no doubt that you will do great things, Wren." The way he says my name is so... *erotic*. "Not only here at Blackbriar, but in the world as well."

The fact that this is my moment to find out more about his power doesn't escape me, and as soon as I can speak, I ask, "How can you be so sure?"

Damn. My voice shook. I wonder if he noticed it.

He smiles like he knows damn well what he does to me, and I can tell once I'm accepted into the academy, he's going to have fun with me like this until I completely implode.

"I have gifts of my own. Let's just leave it at that for now, shall we?"

Reluctantly, I nod.

"I want you to place your trust in me. Any time you need anything or just want to have a place to hang out for a while, come here. My door is always open to you." He waves his hand toward the door and the area surrounding the wall glows with golden light for a moment. It's gone as quickly as it appeared.

I return my gaze to him. Flattered and so freaking turned *on*. I was just given an open invitation. That may be my downfall. "Thank you, Headmaster."

"Call me Gideon," he says. "Is there anything else I can help you with?"

Well… we could release this increasing ache between my legs.

"Nothing that I can think of," I say.

"Very well," he says and stands.

I stand with him and he leads me toward the door with his hand gently pressed on the small of my back. My body erupts in unhinged desire.

Yup. He definitely knows what he does to me.

Bastard.

I really need to figure this out. But I have to get a handle on my magic before I can tackle why my magic reacts so much to the four men that have come into my life. I don't know if I can face Soren right now. My body's flux of emotions are a bit to handle for the current moment.

"Actually, will you do me one favor?" I ask.

"Of course," he says.

"I need to clear my head and think. Will you tell Soren I'm not well and I'll see him in the morning?"

We step through the door and he removes his hand from my back.

He nods. "Just this once. But it's best for you to

be as open and honest with Soren as much as you can. It will benefit your relationship with him more than you know."

I nod and say, "Thanks for your help, Gideon. Have a good night."

"Sleep well, Wren." He smiles and I swear I caught a wink. But it was too quick, I can't be sure.

We turn in opposite directions at the intersecting hall and I nearly run into Professor Lawrence.

"What are you up to over here, Miss Blackwood?" he asks.

I shrug. "I just had a question I needed to ask the headmaster. That's all."

He levels his stone blue eyes on me and says, "Miss Blackwood, I insist you come to me from now on. Not the headmaster of the entire academy. He's a busy man, and until you are a student here, I'm the best person to come to. Come to me only. Always."

I nod. But, honestly, I'm not so sure. On one hand, he did grant me his only invitation to go through the trials for admission to Blackbriar. On the other hand, he clearly has motives he hasn't shared with me. Not to mention, is *willing* to share. And this conversation isn't helping that. It's almost as though he doesn't want me going to the head-master for anything. I'm sure the man is busy, but if he didn't have the time to help me out, Gideon would have said so. He seemed very willing to help me.

Something is off about the professor's request to only come to him. I clearly need to find out more about him before I find myself in a situation I can't back out of.

He smiles, and again it doesn't reach his eyes. "Good. Have a good evening, Miss Blackwood."

"Thank you, and same to you," I say and continue heading back to my room.

## CHAPTER NINETEEN

S oren is pissed.

I can practically see the waves of rage pouring off him as he stands in the training court assigned to us. But I won't let him demean me any longer. Squaring my shoulders, I approach him. As I near, my magic starts to burn and I'm reminded that for some reason, my magic reacts to him. With Milo, Jesse, and Gideon, I don't really mind. But him? I'm freaking perplexed.

Once I'm within two-feet of him, he digs into his speech.

"Where were you last night?" he asks, spittle shooting from his mouth at the last syllable of night.

"Where were *you*?" I ask folding my arms over my chest. "Or is it just a part of your amazing training to keep your student waiting on you for over an hour before she gives up and goes to bed?"

"I gave you an order," he says.

"You're good at giving those. Bravo. Just so we're clear, I was here exactly when you *ordered* me to be. Again, where the hell were you?"

He positions himself for an attack. This suits me just fine. If he wants to spar, who am I to stand in the way? But I'm not holding back.

I position myself and my hand glows with light. As soon as his gaze moves to my hand, I release it, shooting it toward him. He dodges, much to my disappointment. I was really hoping it would hit him. Knock him on his ass, maybe pound some sense into him, at the very least.

"I don't have to answer to you." He paces in front of me. "You answer to me because—"

"Yeah, I get that. But if you want to make sure I don't kill anyone, then you can do so by treating me with respect and not like an ant you can torture with the sun and a magnifying glass." My hand glows again with another ball of powerful light. This one is stronger, larger, but I don't release it just yet.

"You are dangerous, Wren." His gaze travels from my power-lit hands to my face. "You have power. Too much power. Have you ever considered that it's unnatural?"

The heat that burns through me grows, and my magic pools in my arms, building in pressure as my hands clench into tight fists, causing the magic to erratically swirl around my fingers. But I know I can't lose control, so I let the powerful energy disperse and fade. "You will either be civil, or I will find a new mentor. I haven't done a damn thing to you, and I will not stand for being ridiculed or snapped at anymore."

I step closer to him and swing a fist at his face. It connects in a satisfying pop. I swing my other fist, but he blocks the attack. His expression changed from the serious, angry face to one of being impressed. Maybe he's not accustomed to people getting so close to hitting him. I don't care. I'm going to do it again, eventually.

He smiles a little, and that only pisses me off more. This isn't cute or funny. He says, "I will not allow you to have another mentor. I'm going to keep a close eye on you, and nothing you say will keep me from that. Not even Headmaster Storm or your precious Deacon Lawrence."

I lift an eyebrow and swing. If he wanted to fight

with me, insinuating that I'm unnatural, then so be it.

He takes the hit, grabs my wrist, pulling me close, as he narrows his beautiful amber eyes on me, full of burning fury. I swing with my left and he catches my fist, forcing it behind me and twisting me so that my back is pressed against his firm muscles.

His breath blows hot over my neck as he says, "Nice try, but you will have to do better than that."

I try to ignore the way the warmth tingles in all the right ways or how his voice sounds dangerous and pleased at the same time. I throw my head back, nailing him in the jaw. He grunts but doesn't let go.

"Try harder," he says.

I roll my eyes and hate the way my body is responding to him right now. I'm pissed, and my body wants to screw him more now than ever.

Not freaking fair.

"You asked for it," I say, stomp on his foot, and use his weight to throw him over my back and to the ground.

That worked.

And the look on his face is a mix of shock and, dare I say, thrill…

"You're an asshole, Soren. You wouldn't know

kindness if it slapped you in the face." I pant as I walk in an arc around him. "I'm not the problem here, you are. Don't you think I want to succeed here? I want to pass the trials, and I'm willing to prove myself. Isn't that enough?"

He flips himself to his feet and there is something about him that seems slightly different. Not much, but still there. His eyes are softer even.

"Now we are getting somewhere." He smiles and that distracts me.

What the hell is he smiling at? And it's a damn nice one at that.

But that's what he wanted. A distraction.

Before I realize it, I'm on my back on the ground. Somehow, he cushioned my fall. My head rests on the grass and I look up at him, narrowing my gaze. I swing.

Again, he catches my flying fists and pins them to either side of my head. He lowers himself. "I wish I had known that getting you to focus on the fight required pissing you off first."

His voice is soft and it's almost like a complete one-eighty.

"What the hell has gotten into you?" I ask.

He shrugs. "Never had an initiate stand up to me before. It's refreshing."

"It was provoked," I growl as I try to free my hands.

He forces my hands back down and says, "And do you think your enemies are going to actually fight fair against you?"

"Let me go," I growl out.

"Make me," he whispers while he levels his eyes on mine.

Yeah… something happened, and I'm lost as to what. It couldn't be the fact I stood up to him… did he actually get laid?

That thought sent my stomach plummeting lower. I don't know why, but I don't like the idea of him being with another woman. Which is just ridiculous.

"Come on, Wren. You'd be dead by now if this were a real fight."

I lift an eyebrow. My magic lights up my right hand. His eyes flit to the ball of light rapidly forming. He rolls off of me just as I release my magic. It shoots against the barrier on the other side of the training court, absorbing into the invisible shield with purple and pink tiny lightning bolts that fizzle and sizzle until they're fully absorbed.

Soren is already on his feet and I roll to mine and face him. "Feel better provoking a girl?"

"You're not just a girl. Are you?" He smiles.

"What the hell is that supposed to mean?" I ask through a laugh. I wish he'd lighten up a little more like this. This is nice. I may actually end up tolerating him...and dare I say, liking him.

"Come at me and find out." He beckons me to him.

I shake my head. He's toying with me. And I don't know how to feel about that. "All because I stood up to you?"

He shrugs. "Maybe. I still don't trust you yet."

"The feeling is mutual. Believe that," I say.

I don't know what happened, but this is more like it. If it's one thing I know, it's not to look a gift horse in the mouth. He's obliging my request, and that's all I asked for. Now, I get to absorb this training. Although I'm not sure what tonight's training is going to look like, for now, I'm good with this slight change.

## CHAPTER TWENTY

The strange change in Soren stayed on my mind for the rest of the day. Jesse tried to drag it out of me, but I wouldn't let him. Eventually, we both fell asleep. Except, at some point, I'm transported out of my bed toward a steep cliff overlooking the ocean with sharp, jagged rocks jutting out of the water at the base of the island, reflecting the moon's light.

The air is cold, making me grateful I had put on warm pajamas before I laid down. The chill of the ocean seeps through me as the wind picks up, urging me toward a dark path within the woods. I wrap my arms around me and try to keep as warm as possible.

I have no idea where I am, except, I'm clearly

still on the island. Without any idea as to where I'm supposed to go, I walk along the path. The trees creak and moan and I keep my eyes peeled on the moving shadows in case this is some attempt to catch me off guard. The trolls were really good at that.

Eventually, I find flickering lights up ahead and as I step closer, I notice there are torches on either side of the pathway, and in front of me is the Lady Alene patiently awaiting my arrival. I smile as I approach. She's always been so pleasant to me. But despite how nice it is to see her, I realize this is my next trial.

"Good evening, Wren," she says.

"Hello, Lady." I marvel at how the light dances along her stone features. I wonder what she looked like in life. The detail of the statue is amazing, but it still leaves some questions to fill in. Like what color was her hair, her eyes, and skin?

"Do you know why you are standing in front of me right now?" she asks.

I nod. "My next trial."

She nods, clasping her hands in front of her. "Indeed. Sometimes, a mage's aid is called upon in the most inconvenient of times. You must demonstrate your ability to perform magic with little sleep and while ill-prepared. This is a demonstration of your physical strength."

I nod in understanding. Soren had canceled our evening training session, telling me I deserved the break for a job well-done, but I wonder if there wasn't more behind it. If maybe he knew that my trial would happen tonight. I used the free time in the library to research my magic more and with hopes of seeing Milo again, but to my disappointment, he wasn't there.

"Your task is to make your way back to the castle. The path is wrought with danger, and for that reason, you must only travel by the light of the moon." She points to a path that appears. Bushes and trees move out of the way, the lower branches forming an arch. "Good luck, Wren and farewell."

Lady Alene steps to the side and I settle my focus on the path ahead. I take a few deep breaths, shaking away the last of the sleep beckoning me back to my bed, as I approach the path. I have no idea where this is leading and I'm not quite sure what type of trial this is. *Get back to the castle using only the light of the moon, because the path is dangerous.*

That leaves a lot to my imagination, and after the things I've seen in my life, this unsettles me.

I glance over my shoulder at Lady Alene. She

nods once with a soft smile on her stone face. I return the nod and face the path again.

Ready or not, here I go.

As I move along the path, it becomes darker and more difficult to see. It's like the shadows have a life of their own, seeping into every possible space and claiming darkness over as much as possible. Things around me move, and I keep a look out for anything coming for me. Just ahead of me is a bend in the path, and I slow down. There is more to this trial than what meets the eye. I know I have to be careful.

I was told this is a dangerous path. So far, it only seems that way. But Lady Alene wouldn't warn me of the dangers if there weren't actual dangers to be careful of. With that in mind, and the mysterious time limit ticking away as the seconds roll by, I pause and take stock of my surroundings.

My eyes have adjusted to the dark now. On either side of me are bushes of dull, greyish looking flowers that are probably white in the daylight. These flowers are tiny and appear delicate. This sends a thread of warning through me. That could mean they are poisonous or have some other kind of undesired effect.

"Better avoid those," I tell myself and continue on, albeit a little more cautiously.

One step forward and the light of the moon reflects off something in front of me, closer to the ground, that makes me think of a trip wire.

Awesome.

This trial is turning out to be something that feels more like it was designed solely for the purpose of making an initiate fail. Maybe that's the purpose? Only the best of the best gets in here and that means you have to not only know your stuff, but you have to be clever and efficient.

Makes much more sense.

As I approach the line, it fades into the shadows, blending into the dark and making it incredibly much more difficult to see. This is going to take some work.

I can't use anything but the light of the moon to see by, but that didn't mean I couldn't use magic. Carefully, I push out my feet, one at a time, and as soon as I feel the thread for the trap, I bring my foot back a fraction of an inch, so I don't trip it.

Lowering myself to the ground, I gently drag my hand along the wire to what the trap triggers. At my level, moonlight glints off of a pipe sticking out from the ground. I stand and inspect the pipe more, touching it. I pull my hand away to find my fingers covered in soot. That means it shoots fire. A lot of it, judging by the size of the opening.

I'll have to be careful to not get my body caught inside that. I would step over the trap, but something tells me I need to disarm it, even if that triggers the fire, so that I can show my resourcefulness. But I'm not positive. The first trial was challenging in the sense of solving riddles and finding clever ways to make it from door to door. I had to use my magic to help me.

Since these are trials to help with my admission to the academy, it would make sense that I would have to be both clever and talented with magic.

Very well. I move a few feet back and aim my hand toward where the trip wire is. My hand warms with fire. I aim a concentrated stream toward the trap. The wire gives way.

The pipe clicks and the smell of gas fills the air just before igniting. A torrent of flames shoots across the path, making it completely impossible. The plants on the other side start to wilt and I know I have to act quickly before whatever danger Lady Alene warned me of comes in search of roasted Wren.

I hold my hands out to the side and they start to

glow radiant blue. Wind blows against my back, passing me and blowing into the fire. Soon, the wind fills with moisture, and before long, the fire eventually sputters out.

One trap down… and I have no idea how many more to go.

I make it to the bend and follow it around. Branches from the trees above me reach for the ground like spiny fingers.

Great. That's probably another dangerous thing to avoid. I don't want to even think about what that could mean, but I know I have to be careful. Army crawling will zap too much of my energy. But I can't just walk straight through either.

I sigh. "Won't this be fun."

To my left is the sound of rushing water. It sounds like it's pretty far down, which lets me know there is a cliff to avoid. To my right, snaps of twigs, moving bushes, and dark groans echo toward me.

Whatever is making the noise seems to be getting closer to me, and I certainly don't want to find out what it is.

This is going to take some effort, but I have to get through quickly and as carefully as possible.

Now the sound is coming behind me and I'm out of time to figure a way through. I start moving, lowering myself, bending, and twisting to avoid the branches. One catches on the sleeve of my pajama shirt and tears a hole, leaving a burning cut in my arm. Before long, the pain throbs through my whole shoulder.

I don't slow down as I continue to move, extra careful to keep from getting scratched by the branches again. Judging by the sounds of the creature behind me, I've gained some distance, but it's not enough.

Another bend and the ground inclines before leveling out. The path ends in a large drop where the ocean water rushes through. I narrow my eyes as the rope bridge looks like it flaps against the other side.

Great.

I can't jump that far, and I certainly can't float over there. But I have no choice. I have to use my magic.

But exhaustion is setting in. I'm running on pure adrenaline. Already my endurance has been tried and my energy is rapidly depleting from the lack of sleep.

As I look over the top of the gap, the castle towers stretch into the sky with lights shining through some of the windows. I know I'm almost there, and that thought alone helps keep me going.

I use my magic to pull the ropes toward me, beckoning them to me. It's a risk, because of the glow in my hand, but there's no other way across.

That creature is catching up, judging by the sounds echoing behind me, and I know I'm running out of time. I will either have to get across this expanse or fight off something I probably have never seen before.

Not a pleasant idea. But it's what my choices have come to.

"Come to me," I beg of the bridge, using my magic to pull the bridge to me. There's give to the bridge and as it slowly raises toward me, I feel the tug of the wind that blows it and the weight of the material itself fighting against me.

Finally, the rope reaches me, and I struggle to grip it and tie it to the post next to me. I pull on a plank to bring the other side to me and tie it as well. I add an enchantment to the rope to keep it from coming loose as I cross, even though I know nothing will be in place to stop the creature from following me.

Still, with no time left to get moving, I move across the bridge on my hands and knees, keeping the other side in my sight. When the wind blows through me, I grip the planks and hold on for dear life.

Half-way across, the bridge drops a little. I look behind me to see the ropes slowly coming free.

Shit.

I move quicker, but still being careful not to lose my balance. I have less than a quarter of the bridge left to get across, and I hold my breath.

Once I'm on land again, I release the breath I have and quickly fall to my rump to watch the bridge give way completely and fall back down to slam against the side of the cliff.

The sky lightens more as the sun starts to rise over the horizon. But the light does nothing for the shadows around me.

After a few moments to catch my breath, I climb to my feet and continue on. The shadows move more violently on this side, but nothing hangs over the path here. I can see the sky as it lightens, and before long, torches light the way.

I make the final turn, reaching one of the paths that leads through the garden behind the castle. I half-run the rest of the way back, until I'm met with two figures dressed in burgundy cloaks. I can't see their features, shrouded by the hoods.

"Follow us," one says in a whisper.

They lead me back to my room. As they gesture to the door, one says, "Dress quickly. Your next trial is only moments away." Although the words are spoken in a whisper again, I know it's the other person that speaks. The pitch is slightly different.

I nod and quickly dash through the door, closing it behind me.

Jesse is sitting on the edge of his bed and he looks like he's been through hell.

"Are you okay?" I ask.

"Where have you been?" he asks. He clears his throat and adds, "I was worried."

"Trial." I pull a fresh set of clothes from the closet and dash into the bathroom to get ready.

Jesse is at the door, and he taps on it lightly before he asks, "They do trials in the middle of the night?"

I sigh. "Apparently so."

"Brutal."

"That's one word for it." I don't say anymore as I finish peeling off my pajamas and slip into a pair of jeans and a t-shirt. I don't know what this next trial has in store, and I don't want to be in the academy's uniform in case it's anything close to what the last one was.

I analyze my arm and hiss as I touch it. Quickly, I grab a rag and soak it in cool water before gently dabbing the cut on my arm to clear out the debris. Once I finish, I run a brush through my hair and pull it back, so my hair doesn't get snagged.

"Are you okay?" he asks through the door, and I feel my magic surge with that cool sensation I get when I'm near him.

"I'm fine. Tired. But I'll be okay." I toss open the door to find him leaning against the wall opposite of the bathroom door, and I'm caught off guard. Heart hammering in my chest because I wasn't expecting him to be so freaking close.

Damn him for being hot on top of it.

"I have to go to another one. I'll see you later," I say.

He smiles. "Promise?"

I laugh under my breath. "Promise."

I turn to walk out, and he says, "Damn woman, I love watching you leave."

I roll my eyes, but I can't help but smile. Jesse just does that to me.

# CHAPTER TWENTY-ONE

I'm led to the arena. I know the way well, but the escorts, who haven't said a word to me since leading me to my room, seem very focused on taking their time and making the trip last longer. Which doesn't bode well for my already exhausted self. I just want to get this trial done.

The doors open as we finally reach the arena. The two escorts turn and nod to me as they gesture for me to walk in.

I do. The moment the doors shut, the lights in the room cut off. In the center of the room, directly in front of me, a light turns on, shining down from the endless expanse of darkness above on Lady Alene.

"Come to me, Wren," she says. And I slowly step forward.

I don't know what to expect, but since this to be my third trial, anything is possible. Especially if the first two are anything to judge by.

As I stop right in front of the statue, she looks to me and smiles. "This is your third trial, Wren. A test of your mental strength. However, it doesn't reflect the knowledge you hold. It's a bit deeper."

I sigh heavily and say, "All right, I'm ready. What do I have to do?"

"Give me your hand," she says. I lift my left hand and she shakes her head. "The other one."

I place the palm of my right hand over hers, and my conduit turns to dust. A gasp rushes from my lips, echoing into the depths of the ink-filled room. My stomach churns as I realize that I'd have to beat this third trial without my conduit. Does someone know the truth about me? Is this meant to expose me?

"Why did you do that?" I ask, meeting Lady Alene's gaze. I force myself to remain calm despite feeling my heart pound in my chest.

"Fears must be faced," she states matter-of-factly. "And I see yours…"

She disappears, leaving me in the room alone.

I'm starting to panic. I can't do a trial without magic so far, and I have no idea who is watching, if anyone. If I do magic without a conduit…

My thoughts are interrupted by a series of loud clicks and pops.

Whispers soon replace the other sounds as I'm surrounded by rushing images. They rapidly swirl around me. My breaths come short and my palms sweat as my magic pulses through me. I'm in fight or flight mode, and I don't know what to do.

The image stills, settling on a young girl, no older than I am now, and she is using magic without a conduit. Power flares from her hands as she manipulates the world around her. The more she does it, the more seductive it becomes, and she cannot stop. As she finishes her work, a thin black cloud surrounds her. The image fades. Soon, more shuffle around me in an endless sea of blurring shapes and colors.

Once again, the image settles on the same girl. But now she is older, and the black cloud has grown around her. It's much larger and much darker. The color in her eyes has dulled. She's trying to do magic again. As she casts, something happens to her that I can't see. She cringes and doubles over as though she is in an immense amount of pain. She cries out, though I can't hear her.

I stand helpless, watching as the last of the light within her disappears and she stands soulless. I nearly tremble when her face takes on a semblance to my own, warning me that this could be my fate.

"This is what it means to be a shadow mage," a voice speaks from the dark, seeming as though it comes from all directions. It's deep, and foreboding.

I shake my head. "That's not me."

The image shifts to the girl. She causes destruction and leaves everything she touches in ruins. People flee her presence in fear, but she doesn't seem to care, almost as if she doesn't have a heart anymore.

The voice speaks again, "Shadow mages aren't suffered to live."

The image changes to show the girl being cornered by a group of other mages. She screams and tries to fight them off, but in the end, she is killed.

"No," I mutter, shaking my head and trying to step back from the image. But no matter how far away I try to get from the image, it follows me.

"They are too dangerous and unhinged..." the voice grows louder.

"That is not me!" I shout to the darkness. "This won't be me…" my voice comes out softer.

"Their magic is corruptive and raw, burning away the soul to leave a shell of who they used to be."

That voice is even louder now, and it surrounds me, pressing on me, weighing me down. My legs shake, and I struggle to stay on my feet.

"I don't want to cause pain," I say. "I have endured pain most of my life, and that is the last thing I want to inflict on everyone around me."

A dark, whispering voice, much like my own says into my ear, "But they deserve it…"

"No!" My voice reverberates around me.

A scene unfolds before me—the trolls beating me and robbing me of my freedom, laughing at my pain as they land blows. Anger and humiliation rise within me at the sight. The scene fades and a group of mages, led by Anderson, corner me. Their hands are ablaze with magic and their intent is clear in their expressions. "It's either you or them…they deserve it," the voice affirms.

It then shows me a scene where I fight back against my assailants, without a conduit. I kick their asses, reducing them to ashes.

I know I wouldn't hesitate to defend myself, but

unleashing my magic without a conduit is not the way. "No, not like that."

"Yes!" my twisted voice whispers into my other ear.

My arms and legs tremble as my stomach twists into knots. The heavy weight of the voices' accusations increases, and I refuse to fall to my knees. I won't give in and I damn sure will not give up. "I don't care. I won't go dark."

"You are dark," voices, surrounding me, chant around me. "You are dark."

"No, I am not!" My hands start to glow.

But the voices continue.

I won't give them the satisfaction. Regardless of what the voices say. I know in my heart, there is an explanation for me being able to use magic without a conduit. I will find it.

I have to.

Despite my resolve, the voices continue. I simply shake my head and say, "You're wrong."

The images and voices cease all at once. The door opens, shining a wedge of light into the darkened room. Gideon steps into view and approaches me. My heart sinks into my stomach and my lungs fail to take in air as he levels his gaze on me and approaches with smooth steady steps.

The worst possible outcomes run through my mind in a torrent of thoughts. Because I know, as the headmaster, he is going to lock me away.

I look around him and wonder if I can make it to the edge of the island before getting caught. Because right now, despite how my magic surges stronger with each step he makes toward me, it's about self-preservation.

Gideon's expression changes from complacent to concerned. He holds up his hands, and I flinch.

"Relax, Wren. I'm not going to hurt you."

I've heard that before. The trolls were great at that. Fill me up with false hope only to shatter that for their kicks.

"I know you aren't going dark. There will be thousands who will disagree with us, but I've seen your heart and know beyond a doubt you are the furthest thing from a shadow mage."

His words start to register, which creates a large sense of questioning in me. I don't know what to say. Instead, I just stare at him like he's grown a second head.

"Keep this secret from everyone. I will do the same. Once you are through the trials, I will help you learn to control it. We will find a way, Wren. You don't have to worry."

I stare into his beautiful bright blue-green eyes and see all the truth that is there. He really does want to help me. The breath caught in my lungs is released in a loud whoosh as I throw my arms around him. My body implodes with arousal and I fight that back as the buzzing sensation wars with my relief.

"Thank you," I whisper.

Gideon wraps his arms around me and holds me close to him. It's gentle and sweet, and I feel safe for the first time in forever, it seems.

The realization that we are standing in the middle of the arena, where anyone could happen upon us, dawns on me and I pull away. Gideon's arms refuse to let me go completely as his eyes search mine for something. My gaze drifts to his lips and that seems to be all the invitation that is needed. He presses his mouth to mine and squeezes me to him.

Heat pulsates through my core and my body is overcome with desire. His mouth tastes like sweet mint and I relish in the way it feels to kiss him. We slowly break away from the kiss, panting. I feel the thickness of his erection pressed against my waist and fight myself to not go further.

"I've wanted to do that since I first laid eyes on you," he says, voice deep and almost slurred.

I smile. Because words are not a strong suit for this moment, and I would just end up tripping over them anyway.

He plants a single kiss to the top of my head before releasing me. "Go get some sleep. I'll see what I can find and let you know as soon as I have something solid."

I nod, lightheaded.

He smiles, making my knees weak. Damn him.

"Sleep well, Wren."

"Thank you." I sigh softly and pull away from him, though my body screams at me to let him hold me for just a little while longer.

I'm in a daze as I traverse the halls lost in my thoughts. Not only does Lady Alene know of my ability to use magic without a conduit, but so does Gideon. And wow, that man can freaking kiss!

I stifle a giggle as my thoughts return to what happened in the trial. Gideon is going to help me with what he can, but that doesn't mean I can't do my part and research in the library.

Before long, I'm back in my room. Jesse looks up and he seems puzzled. But I ignore the look long enough to see that my conduit rests on my pillow. I grab it and slip it on.

"Holy shit, Wren. You went through a trial without a conduit?" he asks.

I settle my gaze on him. He can't know. Not yet. Maybe not ever. But definitely not right now.

He persists though. "How did you do it?"

I really don't know what to tell him. But I can't ignore him either. We live together, and Jesse has proven to me he will never leave well enough alone. Then I recall the rule of the trials for initiates.

"We're not supposed to talk about that, remember?" I lay down on the bed and I'm barely able to keep my eyes open any longer.

"Right," he says. But the look in his eyes is a mix of awe and wariness. That look cuts into me. I don't want to lose him. He's grown on me in the time I've been here. Though I have never been one to form attachments, I know deep, *deep* down, I'm quickly becoming attached to him.

But the look he just gave has me feeling like things are going to change between us.

I huff out a breath through my nose and close my eyes, shoving the pain in my chest deep, deep down so I can sleep and move on in life.

Because that's what I do. I don't let pain take over me. I deal with it and move on.

There isn't any other choice.

My only comfort is that at least Gideon knows and accepts me.

CHAPTER TWENTY-TWO

I n the training circle, underneath the evening sky, I can't help but notice that something is... different... with Soren.

Though I can't quite place how. He seems—dare I say—kinder.

Not by much, mind you. He's still an ass.

The energy between us buzzes with sexual need, and my magic burns through me with being so close to him. It's a lot to handle, and I struggle to maintain my focus through a multitude of thoughts of his body intertwined with mine. The tension between us, fueled by my sexual fantasizing, is stronger. So much so that I wonder if he can feel it too. Or does he shove the idea down so far that the sensation is only a fleeting moment, if anything at all?

Before today, I wouldn't have thought that possible. I would chalk it up to a girl with an overdose of pheromones and call it a day. But now? I feel a bit thrown off.

Regardless, none of this makes sense. For the most part, he is rather pleasant to be around—so far. He's not hateful toward me unless I try to take his arm off with a stray blast of magic. Then he's fuming and staring daggers again, slinging insults. It's almost as if he can tolerate me now.

I wonder if Gideon had another chat with him, or maybe after we had our more pleasant training session, he's decided to ease up. Whatever it is, something has changed. And it seems like for the most part, things have turned in a better direction for us.

We just finished with some magic drills and are moving onto sparring. As he presses his body against me, I become lightheaded. His body is so very close to mine and *warm*, and his smell is *intoxicating*.

Though I didn't think it was possible to attack within such a narrow opening, he does. I block his attack. But just barely.

"Very good. You're a quick learner," he says. "You're progressing much faster than I originally thought you would."

I smile. "Thanks... I think."

He quirks an eyebrow. "You think?"

I smack him on his arm as we share in a chuckle. Not bad for a guy that would kill me soon as he looked at me less than a week ago.

We share chemistry, sure. And my magic definitely reacts to him. But he has acted like the last thing he wants is to be near me since the day I met him, and now... now the training is *intense*. Electric. It's a puzzling thing for me to figure out. This is a sudden and new change in things between us. Not that I'm complaining. I rather like this side of him.

"Let's work on your balance." He breaks away from me and squats into a horse stance about five feet away with both his arms squared with his knees and his hands held palm out toward me. "Firm stance means you will be harder to take down, like so." He gestures with a nod and I lower myself into what I feel is the same position.

"Good. Think I can knock you over?" he asks.

I shrug. But I also think, with him... he probably could knock me over as he seems to have a knack at pointing out my weaker abilities. And I don't mind finding those out and making them stronger myself. So, I level my gaze on his, forcing myself not to get caught up in the sea of light amber eyes that make me feel like he can see right into my soul, see my darkest secrets, and see my deepest desires.

His lips quirk up into a dangerous grin. "Care to make a wager?" he leaves the horse stance and approaches me.

"Do I have a choice?" I ask.

He pauses and, after a brief moment, nods to himself. "Good point. If I can push you over, you have to answer one question of mine. If I can't, I'll answer one of yours."

He doesn't give me a chance to respond. He firmly presses on my shoulders. I'm knocked off balance. My ass no sooner hits the ground and he is already diving into his first question.

"What happened to your parents?"

I stare up at the giant pillow-like clouds hovering in the evening sky. They darken to a steel grey color in areas, which promises rain within the next couple of days. The sight is a welcome distraction. Honestly, I don't want to answer that question. It's painful to talk about. However, I also don't want to ruin this chance at keeping Soren talking to me like I'm an actual human being.

After climbing to my feet, I re-enter my horse stance. "First of all, I never agreed to this wager. Second of all, this is a painful subject. Act like an ass, and I'm done."

He nods. Albeit not before a flash of thoughts rush behind his eyes, darkening their color. But like most things in this place, it's so quick, I almost question the fact it happened at all.

"My mother died when I was fourteen. My dad disappeared shortly after."

"Then you went to live with the trolls?" he asks.

"Ha! You didn't—"

He firmly presses on one shoulder this time, from my right. I catch myself mid-fall. "Counts."

I narrow my eyes at him. "What if I didn't fall?"

He shrugs. "I knew you would. Answer the question."

"Nope. I feel like that was a cheat and earns me my own question." My thighs start to burn, and I lift up out of my stance for a moment. This one, I refuse to back down on. He cheated. Fair is fair.

"Return to your stance," he says, looking away from me.

I shake my head. "Nope. Not until you give me one question."

"I knocked you over," he said pointing a finger at me.

I arch an eyebrow. "After you asked your second question."

"But I did make you lose your balance." He faces me, and dammit, I love the sight of him. All that brooding sexiness.

I shake my head. "Doesn't count if you asked the question before hand."

He laughs, although it looks like he's trying to keep himself from doing so, twisting away and covering his mouth. But his shoulders shake. And that's all the tell I need.

"You're laughing at me?" It comes out flat, and though I want it to be an accusation, it comes out more curious than accusing.

Facing me again, he says, "Fine. One question."

I nod. "Good. How long have you been at this school?"

He shakes his head, and he is genuinely smiling. "That's it? That's your burning question?"

I shrug. "Sort of. Figured that was the safer one of the thousands running through my head."

"I'm entering my last year."

Huh. He's going to be leaving soon then. Bummer.

"Now, answer my question."

"Seriously?"

He nods, lips pressed into a firm line.

I groan. "No. I went to live with my aunt. The trolls came after that."

Once again, I go into a horse stance, and before he can shove me, I adjust, placing my right foot slightly farther back and bending less at the knees.

He circles behind me and shoves me on my shoulders again. I don't fall this time, but I stumble. I roll my eyes. He's going to count this as a win for him.

"When did the trolls come then?" he asks.

Called it.

I sigh. "They kidnapped me in the middle of the night not long after I went to stay with my aunt. I think it was less than a month."

He walks in front of me with a perplexed expression knitting his eyebrows together. "Trolls kidnapped you?"

"You didn't knock me over, but yes."

I can see what he is doing. He's trying to find that reason to keep being an ass to me. He's desperate to find something to hate me for. And I can tell he's finding it difficult to do.

"Fair enough." He pushes me.

I start to fall back. He grabs my arm before I hit the ground and pulls me to him. I'm pinned to his body as mine quakes with unhinged desire. I bite the corner of my bottom lip and look him in the eyes. Those beautiful, intense, amber eyes.

He's searching my eyes for something I can only guess at, but I assume it's to see if I'm lying. Yet, I can't help but feel like there is more than that. He's cautious, sure, but the way his eyes brighten just a fraction, the depth and searching within them, I know there's something happening between us.

Keeping me pinned to him with one arm, he uses his free hand to wipe a strand of copper-red hair from my face.

I can break free from his grip now. But frankly, I don't want to.

There should be a law against how good this feels.

Completely criminal.

He clears his throat and blinks away his gaze, releasing me to the colder world around me, even with the heat of my magic coursing through me. "Let's try some more defensive offense tactics with your magic." His voice is commanding with a hard edge. He must have seen something in my eyes for this one-eighty in mood.

I lift an eyebrow at the sudden change but prepare to do as he asks.

"I'm going to shoot magic at you. I want you to avoid it by either using a shield, dodging, or both. If you do both, I want you to also counter attack me."

I nod and conjure my magic, feeling it pool into my hands. Once I'm ready, I nod again.

He fires off a flame, stretching toward me like a whip. I block the snap by forming my magic into a small shield and dodge-roll to my right. As I come up to my feet, I launch a ball of light toward him.

"Very good. Truly, that was impressive."

I gawk at him for a moment. That's two. This one sounded more genuine than stemmed in surprise.

Well color me shocked.

The last two times we trained together, there was a change. I could see it. But it seems like the more time we spend together, the more his seeming impenetrable wall chips away. I don't understand why, considering he was extremely adamant about hating me.

The exercise is repeated several times. And the more we go through it, the more distracted I become by everything.

When I shoot off my ball of light in my counter attack, I graze Soren's arm.

"What the hell, woman? You had this down pat." His voice is sharp and right back to the cold tone he has used with me before. He shakes his head. "Do we need to start this over? How many times do I have to tell you to pay attention and be careful!"

Then again, maybe his sexy, suave, softness was all in my head.

Jesus, woman. Take cold showers from now on.

With my magic and the way it reacts to him and the other three, I'm a ball of raging lust. And I cannot afford to keep getting distracted.

"I'm sorry, Soren," I say as he paces in front of me.

He looks to me and makes a double-take before stopping and facing me with his arms across his chest. "I accept your apology."

He still sounds angry. But that's an improvement from before.

His eyes scan the sky above us and the growing shadows around us and he says, "Let's call it for the night. You did well."

"Okay, thank you."

He nods once as he passes by me and I spin to watch him walk away. I marvel at the way my magic urges me forward, to stay closer to him. But the warmth dwindles and so does the need. Once he is fully out of sight, I head inside. I had just been given some extra time, and there is an issue I've been needing to check up on.

I just hope Professor Lawrence isn't there when I show up.

# CHAPTER TWENTY-THREE

I don't have much time. Soon, the halls will be clear of traffic and that will make for sneaking through them a bit more difficult. Because I'm used to sneaking through trees and using the shadows to my advantage. Empty hallways with nothing to use as cover makes being hidden much, much more difficult.

But I make it to Professor Lawrence's office and am standing outside the door. I strain to hear anything behind the door and tap on it just in case he's in there. There's no answer. Carefully, I twist the knob and push the door in just a few inches, enough to peek inside and glimpse all the curious things in the room.

As I open the door a bit wider, I see the room is

empty and, as quickly and quietly as I can, step inside and close the door behind me.

I run through a couple of excuses in my mind, just in case he shows up and catches me here. But if I'm quick enough, he will never know I was here.

His hiding something from me about my family is obvious. Whether he feels he's sparing me from some type of pain or if he has sinister intentions, I deserve to know the truth, whatever it may be. And in my experience, when someone conceals the truth, more than likely, they have bad intentions.

I have no idea what I'm looking for specifically in his office, but I know I want—*need*—to find out more about this man that gave me his only invitation to participate in the trials for admission into Blackbriar Academy. I know an answer is here. I just have to find it.

I scan the books on the bookshelves and then move to the extremely organized desk. There's a locked drawer, with no key in sight, and I wonder what could be in there and wish I had some semblance of lockpicking skills. Still, that doesn't stop me from grabbing a couple of paperclips and unbending them to try.

The lock doesn't even budge.

I chew on the corner of my bottom lip and

desperately try to figure out what I'm missing. It dawns on me.

The closets.

I go to the one on the left, but it's just used for storage of boxes filled with random files on previous students, including their transcripts, classes, photos, and samples of work. There's nothing in here that is useful to me, so I move on to the other door, the one with the strange lock, and I can't open it.

This piques my curiosity.

I know he has something behind this door, and I want to not only find out what, but why it's locked away. What's worth keeping locked up within a school? He lives here, as do the other professors and staff… but this isn't a bedroom. Though I can't be sure how, I feel it deep down inside me.

So far, this trip has been a whole lot of nothing in terms of evidence to support my suspicions, but this is only the first time. I plan to come back, again and again, until I find something of use. Especially, to get inside this door. Whatever I'm looking for, I have a feeling that it rests on the other side.

Some shuffling and popping sounds come from the other side and I know that if I don't hide, right now, I'm as good as caught, and I'm not the best at lying about why I'm in his office.

I quickly duck under the desk and wait as my heart pounds hard against my chest.

The door opens and closes a short moment later.

I hold my breath, praying to whoever is listening that the professor doesn't decide to come and sit at his desk. Because I would be caught, and it would be a lot harder to explain why I'm hiding under his desk more than it would be to explain away me loitering in his office.

The lower half of the professor comes into view, and he seems to just stand there for a moment.

Panic starts to course through my veins.

The only thought in my mind is I'm caught, and now I have to worry about what is going to happen next. The only way this could end is poorly. I may get expelled, have my memories toyed with, or any other number of things that could have disastrous results.

My lungs ache for breath. Burning to exhale and bring in another inhale. Tingling fills my limbs and my ears fill with the pounding of my heart. So loud, drowning out all other sounds.

Finally, Professor Lawrence turns around and leaves my view.

Before long, the office door clicks open and closed. The lock is engaged, and I settle under the desk, poking my head around the edge of the desk to see if it's really clear. A dark rim lines my vision as I strain to check the rest of the room.

As soon as I see that I'm alone, I let out my breath and gasp for oxygen.

That was close.

Too close.

I rush to the door and wait a few moments before slowly twisting the lock. I don't want to make a sound in case someone is out in the hall. Most of all, Deacon. There's a small grinding sound as the lock disengages. I roll my eyes and pause to listen for any signs of someone in the hall waiting to catch me.

There's nothing but calm silence.

Turning the knob, I repeat the same motions as I did when I came in by inching the door open enough to peak into the hall. Empty. Good.

I step into the hall and carefully close the door before making it back to my room. And as soon as I'm on the other side of the door, I lean against it and work on catching my breath.

Jesse takes a seat on the side of his bed and plasters on his devilish smile. He quirks an eyebrow and says, "Well, well. Look at what the cat dragged in. What sort of mischief have you been up to, kitten? More importantly, why wasn't I invited?"

I level my gaze on him. "What are you talking about?"

"I'm talking about what you were just up to before you came in here looking like you did some rule breaking." His voice is gravelly and deep.

"Nope," I say. My heart is just now starting to settle, and I absorb the cooling effect my magic takes on while around Jesse.

His smile widens and he says, "I still owe you a demonstration. Shall I begin now?"

"What?" It comes out flat. I can't help but wonder what he means.

He leans back on his elbows. "Come now, darlin'. I have a specific skill set that could come in handy. All you have to do is ask."

I shake my head and make my way to my own bed, taking a seat and tucking my legs under me. "Why would I do that?"

He shrugs. "Curiosity killed the cat. However, I'm told that satisfaction brought him back."

There is a dangerous glint to his eyes and it's not frightening but alluring. I can't help it, I'm curious.

My cheeks warm, despite the cooling effects he has on my magic.

This guy is just too much sometimes. I shake my head, trying to hide the smile on my face, but it's no use.

"So, how about it? Wanna find out exactly what I can do?" he asks, as he stares at me through partially-closed eyelids, alluring and captivating.

I take a moment to try and find a reason not to, but honestly, I don't. "Sure."

He sits up and levels his unwavering gaze on me.

There is a shimmering haze that fills my vision before clearing slightly, and he stands and walks to me. He stops right in front of me and holds out a hand to me. My gaze moves between his hand and his eyes. He nods. I don't know what he is going to do or why, but something within me wants to throw caution to the wind and enjoy the moment with careless abandon. I don't fully know him, or really have complete trust in him, but I have no reason to believe that he will do anything to jeopardize our budding relationship.

So, I take his hand.

He pulls me into him, brushes my hair from my face, allowing the warm softness of his skin to seep into mine as he brushes the back of his fingers across my cheek.

I'm caught in his eyes, wondering what is going on in his mind and marveling at the sharp angles of his jaw covered in stubble. His lips are inviting and promise to be just as delicious as they look, and I'm overcome with the desire to kiss him.

As if sensing my need, he slips his hand to the back of my head and lowers his mouth to mine.

The kiss is soft at first, slowly increasing in speed and passion until I'm out of breath.

I snap back with a jump.

A pinch forms in my forehead as I try to figure out what the hell just happened.

I'm sitting in the same position I was in before and Jesse looks like he's never moved but has a shit-eating grin stretching his lips.

"What the…"

He says, "That's my gift." His eyes widen and he makes a grand gesture in front of him. "The power of illusion."

"Wait," I say, breathless, "that was all in my head?"

He bows as he sits on his bed, acting like a magician on a stage who just finished his performance.

I laugh. "Wow."

"I aim to please," he says, leaning back on the bed on an elbow and bending a knee to rest a single foot on the bed. "Now, what were you up to, you sneaky little devil?"

I arch an eyebrow and shake my head. Some things are better kept as secrets. But somehow, in the midst of it all, two things have become clear to me. One: Jesse isn't going anywhere, and two: everything is somehow going to end up okay.

"I can drag it out of you," he says, voice full of challenge.

"Good luck with that." I stand from the bed and grab a fresh set of pajamas. "I'm going to go shower. Behave yourself."

He places a hand on his chest and makes an undignified expression. "I'm a perfect little angel."

I chuckle as I make my way to the bathroom. "Uh-huh. Sure, you are."

I lock the door behind me in case that 'perfect little angel' decides to show his horns. Bringing the tips of my fingers to my lips, I think about the kiss and how real it felt. The way the coolness of his mouth danced with mine was expert level heat.

Everything about the kiss seemed real. I shake the sensations and the left-over imagery from my mind and turn the shower to full-blast cold. That ought to clear my mind enough to get some sleep.

Still, that was a neat little look into his power and the things he can do.

Well played, Jesse Taylor.

Well. Played.

## CHAPTER TWENTY-FOUR

There he is.

I felt him before I saw him. That icy tingling that burns as much as it cools.

Milo Moreau. The sexy book worm I have missed since our last encounter. I smile to myself as he keeps his focus on his book, head cocked to the side, dangling strands of blond hair over the side of his glasses.

After my morning training session with Soren, I need some time in the beautiful library, but I wasn't expecting to see him. I hoped I would. But I didn't expect it.

He doesn't seem to feel me. At least, not like I can *feel* him. If he does, he's too pulled into his book to notice.

I smile as I watch him a moment longer before walking over and sitting at the desk.

He finally looks up, and as soon as his eyes connect with mine, he smiles. I damn near melt.

"Wren, I thought I wouldn't see you again," he says, casting his book to the side.

I giggle. "Why did you think that?"

He shrugs and pushes his glasses up on his nose. "I, uh, haven't seen you here. Thought maybe I scared you off?"

"Oh, no! I have been busy with the trials and training with my mentor. That's all. I'm actually really happy to see you." I smile.

"Really?" He smiles, cheeks reddening a little as he runs a hand through his hair and shifts in his seat.

He's so freaking cute. I really don't think he knows that about himself.

"Yeah. So, how have you been?" I ask.

"I'm okay. You?"

"Good."

We are caught within each other's gazes for a very long moment. But it's not an impatient time, it's more peaceful. Blissful. Incredibly sweet.

A sound echoes through the room, and though I don't know what made that sound, it reminds me of a book falling onto a floor. But I'm not sure. Still, it was enough to break the spell we were under.

Milo smiles bashfully and says, "I know what you have been looking for."

My smile fades. "What do you mean? The research on shadow mages?"

He shakes his head. "You say research, but I cheated and saw your notes."

A weight settles in my stomach.

This isn't good.

He reaches for me. I jump back. Slowly, he pulls his hand back and says, "Relax, Wren. I'm not going to tell."

"It was an accident," I say barely above a whisper.

"Do you want to talk about it?" Milo asks, his voice soft, sweet, caring.

My heart feels like it's shattering into a thousand pieces, each shard turning into a weight that makes my center heavy and my body can't move.

I try to stop the words from bleeding out, but it was no use. My mind and body operated on their own terms.

"I was fighting off a lamia... My conduit was broken." My voice remains barely above a whisper.

"I didn't intend for anything to happen. It just… did."

Milo shakes his head as I rub the blur from my eyes. "Wren, there is a simple explanation to it. Yes, there have been mages who have used magic that way in the past, but they aren't talked about. Not in books, not in whispers."

"I thought…" I couldn't finish the sentence.

"What? That I was going to turn you in? Wren, no. We are in this together, okay?"

I blankly stare at him. I almost don't believe him. "I don't understand."

He nods and holds his hand up. "Although those types of mages aren't talked about in books, they are talked about in homes. Mine included."

"Wait. What?" I lean forward, keeping my voice low.

"Long ago, an ancestor of mine had done magic without a conduit and was later put to death. One of the reasons my parents are so bent on me succeeding here is because they want the prestige and boosted reputation to make up for that tarnish on our family name."

"I'm so sorry," I say and reach across the table to cover his hand with mine. His skin is so freaking smooth.

I smile, and the relief that runs through my body is instantaneous. My body sinks into the chair and I release a breath. "Thank you, Milo. I don't deserve it, but thank you."

"But you do. You don't deserve to be condemned for saving your own life." Milo smiles. The warmth of it flows through me, sinking lower until it settles in between my thighs.

And just like that, I'm aroused.

I'm just a mess of emotions and hormones.

"I appreciate your kindness, Milo. Truly. It's not something I'm used to getting."

"That's a shame."

My eyes focus on his lips and I wonder what they taste like. I'm compelled to find out but grip the side of the table and try to focus on something else other than how nice it would be to have his lips on any part of my body.

Relationships with initiates are banned. And I don't need one more way to get into trouble. I already have enough on my plate.

"Thank you. For everything."

"You are very welcome." He sits forward. "Don't worry. I won't tell anyone."

"I appreciate that. I seriously owe you one."

I'm astounded he is taking things so smoothly.

That sort of worries me, but this is Milo. He has never given me a reason to doubt him so far. I hope this isn't a warning. At this point in the game, though, I might as well go for broke.

I need a way to get into the professor's office and that secret room he keeps locked. I can't risk being caught again. Milo is book savvy. He probably knows what I need to help get the job done.

"Hey, so, do you know of anything that may help with stealth?"

"I might know of something." He playfully places a finger on his chin and looks to the ceiling. He shifts his eyes to me. I giggle. He adds, "What sort of time limit are you needing? What is the task?"

"That's necessary for a stealth spell?"

"I'm an alchemist."

I study him for just a moment. He's stellar with book knowledge, a bit nerdy. Alchemy is based in philosophy as well as experiments aimed for specific results. I nod. It's so easy to see the two things coincide with each other. "That actually makes perfect sense."

"So…" He drags out the word, eyes focused on me, pulling me into those brown depths.

I clear my throat and shrug. "As long as I can, with as little as possible, I suppose."

He nods. Pulls out a book, flips a pages, and runs his fingers along a paragraph. He taps the spot. "Got it. It will make you seem invisible for about two hours. Is that enough?"

"Should be," I say. Though I don't know. I may need more time. But this is a start.

"It's an illusion. The problem is someone will need to cast it for you. I can do that."

"No. You are risking enough as it is. I would hate for you to get caught and risk your place here."

He waves my concern away. "We won't get caught. That's the beauty of this spell. It doesn't leave much of a residue if at all."

"Huh. That's good to know."

"So, my lovely Wren," he says with a smile, and I try not to swoon. "I insist."

"All right, since you insist." I hold out my hand and we shake on the deal.

He marks his page with a ribbon from the spine and sets the book aside. "What do you need the spell for?"

Somehow, I knew I would have to tell him. He's in this with me now. With just as much to lose as I do when it comes to the Academy. Might as well tell him the reason.

"Something is off about Professor Lawrence. I

need to find out what that is and why he is so focused on me."

Milo's eyes darken to nearly black as his lips form a tight, thin line. He nods once. The movement is stiff and insinuates he has carried the same suspicions, which only encourages me further.

"I take it you're not too fond of him either?" I ask.

"Let's just say I've had my own unpleasant run-ins with him, and leave it at that for now." He leans forward on the table and I join him, almost like we're sharing dark secrets, or exchanging devotions to each other in a quiet manner.

I like that last thought best.

"We need a plan," I say.

"The best time for the spell to go off without a hitch is when there will be no distractions. That means everyone else needs to be occupied," he says.

That makes one time in particular the best. And it's soon, which makes it even better. "The ceremony for the end of the trials."

He points at me. "I like that. Everyone in the academy will be there. It's prime time for additional coverage. Even Deacon will be there. No one will notice us gone."

"Right," I agree. "The ceremony isn't over until

midnight. We can meet at my room at nine. That gives us an hour to prep, cast, and get me going. You can hang out there while I'm gone. I'll come back when the time is close to being out. So, when the spell is over, it will look like I never left."

"Wow," he says, leaning back in his chair with a smile. "I'm impressed. Looks like we have a plan then."

"Yes. Thank you again." I cover my hand with his this time, and he sucks in a breath. But it's such a quick movement I almost question if I only thought it happened. He tightens his fingers around mine with a dazzling smile.

My heart skips a beat.

This beautiful man just doesn't know what his smile does to me.

"See you at nine?"

I wink. "It's a date. See you at the ceremony."

I stand and gather my things. Milo stands as well, and as I face him, I smile again. He runs his hand through his hair while the other is tucked into the pocket of his slacks. I close the gap between us, breathing in the scent of his delicious cologne and lift on my toes to place a kiss on his cheek, which is soft and warm.

As I pull away, there is need in his eyes that doesn't escape my notice. "Bye," I say.

"Bye," he repeats, voice low and deep.

As I leave the library to take my things back to my room, I realize there are two men, whom my magic reacts to, that know my secret and still don't want to hurt me. Two of the four men that want to stay by my side.

It's almost too much to comprehend, but the feeling inside me is one of hope. True hope. Not just a dream of it. And I know, deep down, the connection between the men and my magic isn't coincidence. There's more behind it. Now that I'm a step closer to figuring out what Professor Lawrence truly wants with me, and I'm a little closer to figuring out my magic, I can allow myself to entertain the idea of these men of mine.

## CHAPTER TWENTY-FIVE

S he's quite vulgar for a girl. But *funny*.

I laugh at Savannah's joke. The sound echoes down the hall and bubbles away as I walk with her toward the garden to sit and enjoy some sunlight following our lunch.

"Where do you learn this stuff?" I ask.

"When you have four older brothers, you come across things naturally," she says, slipping her arm through mine. "Do you have any siblings?"

"Nope. I'm an only child."

"No wonder you're so out of the know," she shakes her head and laughs.

"Hold on, I do know some stuff other girls don't. In fact, most people don't."

"What's that?" she asks as we turn a corner.

But instead of her being with me and getting my vague reply, she's gone—the academy is gone—and I stand in a dark forest alone.

It dawns on me this is my fourth trial.

Crap. What's in store for me *this* time?

One thing is for sure, since this is the last trial, it's not going to be easy.

A path stretches in front of me and I follow it, knowing full and well there is a time limit I'm not allowed to know specifics on. Regardless, I move forward until I arrive at a fork. Either direction I pick, I know one thing is for certain... it's darker here. The blackness is so thick, I can barely see the outline of my hand directly in front of my face.

In order to go forward, I have to use light. But the deathly quiet that surrounds me warns to not draw unwanted attention to myself. However, if I don't make some sort of light to see by, I could fall over the edge of some ravine.

Either is a gamble.

But time is not on my side.

So, I take the somewhat safer bet, and make a small ball of yellow light in my hand. I hold it up, so that the light cascades down in a shower of light bright enough to see by, but hopefully dim enough for me to go mostly unnoticed for whatever unpleasant things lurk in the intense, endless shadow around me.

I take one step forward into the path to gauge a direction in which to go when the ground starts to quake. At first, I wonder if I made a mistake with producing the light and consider dousing it when hedges shoot up from the ground in all directions around me. Soon, the trembling stops, and I look around me to figure out what just happened.

The path behind me is now blocked. A wall of green surrounds me on all sides but one. With no other choice, I move forward to a turn on my right. From there, the path opens to the right again but seems to remain a solid wall of green on my left.

This is a labyrinth.

And what does one do with a labyrinth?

Find the center.

In essence, it seems pretty clear what I need to do. So, I cautiously continue forward. As I move, about every fifteen feet or so, an unlit torch glints in my dim light. I turn right and left until I come up to a dead end.

Crap.

This isn't going very well. There has to be more to this trial than traversing a labyrinth. Like this school, not everything is as it seems. Still, I turn and try to find my way back, but come up against another dead end.

But this doesn't make sense.

I know I turned here not long before, but where there was an opening, it's now closed.

Well, if it wasn't hard enough to get through a labyrinth with nothing but dim light to see by, I have to do it with moving walls.

"You have got to be kidding me," I say under my breath. There's no way I can do this without more light.

I walk back toward the direction I came from once more, finding the same dead end.

"This is ridiculous." I'm frustrated. I can't really see much, and I have *no* idea what I am doing.

With the time ticking, I know I have to make a move, and soon. I'm so close to completing the trials and being accepted into the academy. I can't fail now. I won't. I'll be damned if this is the end.

Finally, I do the only thing I figure will help me in this situation. I give up on being anonymous and make my light brighter until its heat pulsates through my hands. I hold the flame up to a torch and it lights up.

No sooner than my eyes become adjusted to the

light, the remaining torches around me light up and the wall blocking my path lifts.

I have unlocked a new path through the labyrinth. Something tells me this part is going to be harder.

Moving through, able to see where I'm going now, as the torches that line the hedges are lit with the crackling glow of the fire I used, I traverse through the paths in front of me. The darkness above me moves slightly, revealing a colorful view of the universe above, complete with fuchsia and purple nebulas, and more stars than I have ever seen, all set against a deep navy-blue backdrop.

I'm in awe.

The sight gives me hope and I'm encouraged even more to continue.

The tightly woven leaves on the tall hedges begin to dance with a light breeze that cools my skin. It's the first time I realize I'm sweating as I focus on the paths in front of me, working my way through each twist and turn toward the center, where I'm positive will be the greatest challenge I will face with the trials.

But as I make one final left around the corner of a hedge, I stop. The path just... ends.

"Shit." My voice, though low, still carries through the air.

A chasm stretches before me, and it seems like an impossible feat. There is no hint to what I'm supposed to do other than get across.

But how?

A breeze blows around me. Gentle, comforting, cooling. It feels good, uplifting, and replenishes my energy.

I pause.

The torches. When I first entered the labyrinth, they were unlit. It wasn't until I lit them that the whole thing changes and opens up to allow me into the next section. Just as I was approaching this chasm, I notice the air blowing through.

What if…

"I have to use the elements." My voice shakes a little with nervous excitement. I had been given clues this whole time and it just now came to me.

Fire, air, earth, and water.

Those are the elements that are the pinnacle of all magic. The houses in Blackbriar also symbolize that. Phoenix for fire, Winterwolf for earth, Kraken for water, and Drakon for air.

I smile.

Nothing can stop me now.

Though the problem of getting across the open space still exists, I know what I need to do.

In magic, intention is *everything*.

Every spell, every ounce of energy, every thread of focus all comes down to the first basic step of any magic performed.

And my intention is to get to the other side of this expanse.

Magic glows through my hands, pulsating, waiting, willing to do my bidding.

"Not yet…" I whisper.

I close my eyes and will the winds to swirl around me as I take concentrated steps backward until my back comes up against the wall of a hedge. My eyes open. The path I had taken to get this far is sealed off by the greenery. That motivates me, because I know I'm on the right track.

Taking in steady breaths, I allow the magic to flow through and around me, strengthening my body. The air swirls around me as well, promising to keep me protected.

Good.

With a smile, I kick myself forward, pumping my legs as fast as they go. And as soon as I reach the ledge, I push off.

My heart pounds, my breaths still, as I float weightlessly through the air.

Though I don't know how far down the chasm goes, I know it will only end in a very bad sudden stop.

The other side of the labyrinth comes into view. The air around me propels me forward in short bursts.

But all too soon, I realize I'm coming up short.

I don't know exactly how short, but *short* is not a good thing. Using my magic, I urge the air to push me harder.

I'm descending, and there is about six feet before I reach the other side.

No! I... I can't die. Not now. Not this close. I will not fail. I can't. I have to find a way through this!

One last push from air is all I get before I slam into the other side with a heavy grunt. The air is forced from my lungs as my hands fumble to catch a grip of anything that will keep me from falling into the pit.

I grab hold of a root that barely supports my weight.

Without wasting a single moment, I pull myself up, willing the root to keep hold of the ground long enough to get myself over the edge and on land.

Finally, I'm on the other side, crawling a few feet from the edge of the cavern. I roll to my back and lay there a few moments to catch my breath and let my heart return to its normal pace.

That was *way* too close for comfort.

Though figuring out what I had to do was simple enough, the follow through was a lot harder than I expected. And underestimating the force needed to get across was a near grave mistake.

Once my breathing and heart rate level out, I climb back to my feet and face what is left of the labyrinth. Two elements down, and two to go.

And something tells me, these next two will be the hardest yet.

As I let out a deep breath, I move forward.

Unlike the last two parts, this one has no turns. Just a straight shot.

At first, I wonder if maybe I failed because, this feels too easy. But then, my feet start to get wet, and the hedges change from vivid, living green, to stone.

"Oh, come on!"

Obviously, I will need to use water, but how?

I try my best to keep my worries pushed to the back of my mind, but honestly, it's more difficult than I would like. I have no idea what to expect, what I will need to do, and the idea that I know I'm getting closer to the middle, makes me nervous. Anything could be waiting for me.

All of the unknowns within this trial, this is the most nerve-racking of all. I wish I had been able to speak to Lady Alene beforehand. She would've been a great help in knowing what to expect with this.

But I suppose that could be seen as cheating.

Regardless, the farther I go, the deeper the water.

Up ahead, rising into the sky—which has become even more vibrant as the glowing sliver of the moon appears—is what looks like a large arched door. I withhold any speculations of what that could mean as I've learned quite a few times things are not what they seem here in Blackbriar Academy.

The stone walls now surround me, but lower into the ground as though giving way to the marsh-like ground that pulls my feet, sinking several inches with every step in the ankle-high water.

This slows me down way too much. Still, I persevere.

Because I have to.

A bridge soon reveals itself not too far in front of me. And the water underneath it angrily churns. The rush of the flowing liquid hits my ears and a strange high-pitched call echoes to me every few moments. It's an eerie sound that causes the hairs on my arms and the back of my neck to rise. My body wills me to run the other way, but I won't back down.

Not now.

Not ever.

I reach the bridge as the sound of the water grows almost deafening. Once I'm in the middle, I take a moment to catch my breath and give my legs rest, also giving myself the chance to look around. Because, though this looks like a wide, dangerous river with violent currents, simply crossing isn't going to be enough.

The door on the other side of the bridge and river is as tall as the doors to the castle. It sits bordered by black mirrors that twist and distort its reflection. It makes for a terrifying view of what lies in wait in the water, hungry for whatever flesh it can take.

Above me, the sky shines in the same vibrant colors of fuchsia and pink, and purple now blends in with pale blue. And with the silver crescent moon glinting on something metallic about fifty feet above me, I see what it is I need to do in order to continue.

Get the key.

A creature jumps up from the water. I gasp and can hardly believe my eyes.

It's humanoid, with fins on the side of its face and arms, and it has a fish tail. I know the lore, but I never knew I would see one in my life.

Mermaids, unlike their human-told tales, are very dangerous, and very hungry, creatures. The knowledge I have warns against looking into their eyes, for if anyone meets their black as night gaze, they will come under their enchantment. Mermaids will make them believe in an illusion of beautiful things. Amazing things.

Right up to the grizzly end where they are stripping the flesh away from bone, bit by delicious bit.

But that's not the only way they can ensnare their prey. They like the thrill of the hunt from time to time. And they are *fast*. So, to fall victim while adrenaline is coursing through the veins makes the meal all the more delicious. I've read it's somewhat like a drug to them.

Few ever get away. Some lucky bastards managed to strike deals with the creatures. Such is humans' more favorable tales of the creatures.

And as I stand on the bridge, there's not just one of these creatures, but dozens.

I know I have to use water to get the key

dangling above me. But I have to do it without falling prey to the meat-eating mermaids.

The rushing river swells, pushing against the bottom of the bridge, and the small stone square I'm standing on, gives way, lifting just enough to let me know that the time-limit is not only ticking itself closer to zero, but this bridge isn't going to last much longer.

With some quick thinking, I decide to use my magic and the power of the water to swell and lift me toward the key. The problem? A mermaid can be trapped underneath the stone and get extra hungry for my flesh.

I'm virtually gift-wrapped for these creatures.

Silver platter and all.

Squaring my shoulders, I focus on the four-square foot of stone and feel my magic course through me. I have to do this slowly or I will most certainly fall into the hands of the mermaids like a pizza delivery.

But I'm not dinner.

For *any* creature.

I position my hands palms down and let the magic course through me. Calling upon the water, I command it to lift me higher. It rushes too quickly, and I nearly lose my balance. But I can't stop to figure out another way. I'm running out of time, and I need to get that key without being faced with what would surely be a disastrous and incredibly painful death. Because, unlike piranhas, mermaids like to take their time and enjoy their meal.

The water pulses again. And I realize that it's not me pushing my magic too far too quick, but a creature hitting the bottom of the stone, trying to knock me off balance.

So far, I've made it about five feet. I have about forty-five more to go, and this is going a lot more poorly than I thought it would. I look over the edge of my platform and see that not only is the bridge in pieces, floating like debris, but a circle of hungry mermaids is also waiting for me to fall.

Another thump, and I lose my balance. I manage to fall to my knees and grip the sides of the stone square, much to the displeasure of the creatures below me who all shriek in that same eerie sound I heard before.

"Shit, shit, shit!" I say trying to keep my focus on my magic and not fall over the edge at the same time.

My foot slips, and instantly pain ripples through my calf. When I pull it back up, blood runs from four deep gashes on the inside of my leg. The thumping continues, more intense and quicker than before. The creature has caught the scent, and likely taste, of my blood. It is hungry for more.

Absolutely fan-freaking-tastic.

There's no time to waste. Come what may, I have to get the key. I push all the force I can to close the last of the space between me and the key. Once I grip it, I lose my focus. The stone I'm kneeling on starts to fall.

Straining, I try to make the water lead me toward the door. Toward my way out of this area. The shrill screams of the creatures stab my ears and my vision starts to blur. It's painful, and my head feels like it's about to explode. Heart pounding, I manage to make it nearly the entire way before I realize I'm low enough to be captured. Claws snatch at my clothing and tear at my skin. Fire burns through the gashes covering my body and a black rim lines my vision.

Just before I'm taken under and feasted on, I'm on land. And the calls rupture through my mind.

Dizzy, bleeding, and weak from the attacks, I fumble with the key in my hands.

A loud ticking sound booms through the air, and I know I'm almost out of time. I pick up the key, barely get it into the lock, give it a twist, and silence falls.

The door inches open.

I stumble through the opening, collapsing on the ground, panting for air I can't seem to get enough of.

If I thought almost falling down a chasm was too close for comfort, nearly being eaten alive by mermaids creates a new level I never want to experience again.

And it's not over yet. There is still one more element to go through. One more step to this process, and I'm not sure I want to guess at what waits for me.

## CHAPTER TWENTY-SIX

"Come, child," a voice speaks from somewhere in front of me, and I wonder if I'm hearing things. The voice seems familiar, but I can't place how.

I pull myself up from the ground, and I find myself within a hall that leads to a circular room. The center of the labyrinth. The brilliantly beautiful night sky is no longer above me. Just a plain white cciling that tops the ivory walls and dark walnut colored wainscoting panels that line the lower half of the walls. Ahead of me, I see a brown leather couch, bookshelves, portraits, paintings, and a large map of the world.

"Don't make me wait longer." There was warning in the voice this time. I assume there is a need for the rush, so I do my best to walk without limping toward the room. After all, I'm still in the middle of my trial. And this one is to cover the element of earth. As I move forward, I can see more of the layout.

The room sits as a perfect circle with a domed roof. A couple of chairs come into view, matching the couch. And a person dressed in a red cloak stands in front of a desk. His back faces me, and as I enter the room, a click sounds behind me. I turn to face the way I came, but there is only wall. There is no longer a way in or *out* of this room.

The figure in the cloak turns toward me, but the hood conceals his face. "Finally. It's good to see you, Wren."

Again, the voice is familiar, tugging at my most buried memories, but no matter what I do, I can't recall where I know this voice from.

"Who…" I shake my head and narrow my eyes on the figure. "Who are you?"

"Do you not know my voice?" he asks.

"Your voice only sounds familiar to me. I just can't think of why."

The more this man talks, the more my memories unlock, and I'm closer to figuring out who this person is.

"Come now, Little Bird," the voice says, and I instantly know who this person is.

My father once told me a story of when my mother found out she was pregnant with me. A little wren would visit the house and perch on the window sill, singing its little tune. At first, she thought nothing of it, but the bird continued to visit.

Soon, my mom started to experience signs of my growth and movement in the womb.

Throughout her pregnancy, the wren visited daily. Always cheerful and singing the sweet tune she fell in love with. Once I was born, the wren no longer visited, and thus I was given the name.

Only my father called me his little bird. It was a nickname special to him. My mom had the gift of the visit, while my father got the gift of my nickname.

"Daddy?" I say, hardly believing my own eyes.

"I'm disappointed it took you this long to figure it out," he says and removes the hood of the cloak. He looks exactly the same as when I last saw him. Not aging a day. Not a single ounce of gray in his hair as I would expect a man his age would have. Not a single wrinkle marred his smooth features, and it's as if the man standing before me simply walked out of my memories, manifesting as a version of my father.

Deep down, I know something isn't right, but I'm overcome with joy at seeing my father again after so long. Ignoring my injuries, I run to him and wrap my arms around him in a hug I've longed to give him for many years. My body aches and screams with every movement, but I don't care.

I don't even care that he doesn't hug me back. I've missed him. "What are you doing here?" I ask, taking a step back, releasing him from my hold.

"Celebrating your success of completing the trials. Come, let's sit." He gestures to the couch. But the movement is off. Stilted. Stiff. Wrong.

More warnings sound off in my mind. I pay more attention to them, and cautiously take a seat on the couch next to him.

"Where have you been all these years?" I ask, curious to know more about the gap in time and filling in the pieces of the puzzle that led up to his disappearance. I look into his brown eyes that match mine and the way there is no light in them. I worry the warnings in my mind are wanting me to acknowledge this really isn't him, but I also consider that there is a very good reason he wasn't with me for the last six years of my life, and those events have taken the light of hope from him.

But they are so dark and lifeless. My magic pulsates through me with warning, and I play into the conversation. I need to know what's going on. I have to figure out if this man truly is my father, or some twisted joke for the sake of the trial.

"I am sorry for not being around. Frankly, I wasn't sure I would be able to face you now. I couldn't stand being around you. You look so much like your mother. It was like a constant reminder, seeing you. I left you that day, because I couldn't take the reminder anymore."

I gape. His words sting worse than the numerous gashes covering my body. There is no way this is my father. I don't believe it. I can't. There is another reason for this. I just don't know what yet, but I'm going to figure it out.

Squaring my shoulders, I angle myself toward the man that wears the skin of my father and say, "You're a coward. Giving up on a little girl who just lost her mother and leaving her alone in this world? And now, you decide to make an appearance for the sake of my trials?" I shake my head. "You should have stayed gone."

He nods as he levels his dark gaze on mine. "You

don't understand. I didn't just come to celebrate you passing the trials. I came to stop you."

I stand up, shaking my head and breathing through the rage that boils through me. "Stop me from what? Passing?"

"Stop you from living." He pushes himself from the couch, launching himself at me. In mid-air, I watch him pull a dagger, aiming it at my chest.

Using the training Soren drilled into my head over the days of training for hours twice a day, I instantly step into my horse stance and produce a magic shield around me with my left arm in front of me. In my right hand, a ball of fire grows white hot.

My dad's imposter slams against the shield. I stumble slightly back, not quite getting the stance right, and as soon as he bounces off, I launch my ball of fire at him.

He dodges the blow, and the flames are sent to the bookshelf to my left, igniting them like fuel.

I ignore the pain in my chest, the feeling of my heart shattering, because it's do or die now. It's him or me, and I refuse to be the one to die. Besides, it's not like this is my father. I know this now. But the fact that the trial is using my father to trip me up is disheartening.

There has to be a good reason for this. I just don't know what yet.

"You shouldn't exist, Wren. I should have taken care of my mistakes long ago."

The words don't faze me. I know this isn't my father. This is the academy's attempt to pull out all stops. Testing my will to the last fiber of my being. How far can I be pushed before I cave?

I shake my head. "You are not my father."

"No?" he says and attacks again, this time with a bolt of lightning.

I barely bring up my shield in time to block it. The power of the hit knocks me back a few feet. I lose my balance as I shuffle my feet to regain my pose. I don't get a chance to see what happened to the bolt of lightning. I hear it crash somewhere behind him, but that's all. He attacks again and again, knocking me back one step at a time until I'm up against the wall with nowhere else to go.

He charges. I push him back with a front kick, followed by a right hook and jab. "You could never be my father. I don't know who or what you are, but he would never say such hurtful, mean things to me."

"Well," he says, regaining his posture as I take a break from my attacks, now that I'm no longer backed against the wall. "not until you killed your mother."

"I what?" I say, momentarily distracted.

No. That's not possible. I wasn't there when Mom died. I had nothing to do with her death. She wasn't even home when she died, and it was considered an accident. But now, I'm not so sure. There's more behind her death. There has to be. And none of which is my doing.

My distraction was all that was needed to get a good, swift slice of the blade across my chest. "Yes!" he says.

I quickly throw up my shield and form a spear of lightning in my hands. The energy cracks purple and blue along my knuckles and arcs up my arm.

"Answer me," I demand.

"You killed your mother because you were a needy little brat. You drove her mad, pushed her over the edge of her will and *you* killed her!"

"She died in an accident!" I cry out, tossing the spear of lighting at him. He deflects, it hits me, sending me flying back against the wall. My shield disappears, and I don't have time to clear my focus and pull another one up before he is back on me. He pins me to the ground with the point of the dagger just two inches above my heart. I hold him back with my arms folded on my chest, one on top of the other, but it does no good. He uses his weight to press down on them, crushing my ribs and making it harder to breathe.

I have to defeat this thing. I can't die. Not now.

My hands glow yellow. Using what is left of my strength, I push him back, and just like with the lamia, a bright flash takes over my view. A searing heat escapes my hands. But instead of finding ashes falling to the ground, I find a figure of mud and clay. Nothing is recognizable about this thing. Just that it has a shape that loosely resembles a human body.

The whole event suddenly makes so much more sense. This was the last element. Earth. Golems are made using earth magic. They are virtually mindless and act in accordance with the goal they were created for.

As I catch my breath, the figure melts into a puddle. I stand and watch the goop used to create a doppelganger of my father solidify into dirt.

Relief floods through me. This was not my father. But it doesn't excuse the academy for forcing me into a scenario like this. Relief turns into sadness which then turns into anger. I can't shake the feeling of having been played. This whole trial has been horrible and damn near impossible to get through.

I understand now why we aren't allowed to talk about the trials. Nothing could have prepared me for this. Not that I had the same trials as the other initiates, but if my experience was anything to go off of, I believe a number of initiates would have quit before they reached this final one.

No one should be faced with what I had just seen.

Then again, not everyone is going to play nice with magic. Perhaps this was the point. Some mages, and that includes shadow mages, will try to trick me.

Smart play, Blackbriar. Well played too.

As the room shifts, revealing a door out of this nightmare, I realize that from now on, I will have to keep my guard up and be clever and smart about my methods. Each step is going to need careful consideration to the consequences, and I need to be able to account for *anything*. What I do from this day forward is going to be carefully thought out.

I step through the door and I'm in the hallway across from my room. Taking that as a sign, I walk through the door. The room is empty, and resting on my bed are some bandages, pain killer, and a bottle of healing elixir. A note that holds instructions sits tented next to everything. Before reading any of it though, I sit on my bed and reflect on the last part of the trial.

I know my father is out there somewhere. I feel it deep within me. And I refuse to believe otherwise. Now that I have passed my final trial, I'm going to devote every last second of free time I have to finding him. I will discover what really happened, and if there was foul play involved, I will make those responsible pay for their actions.

Come hell or high water, they will wish they never messed with me and my family.

## CHAPTER TWENTY-SEVEN

Of the ten initiates invited to attend the trials for acceptance into the academy, only six made it through.

Jesse, Milo, and Savannah all made it through. We stand together silent, lost in thought, with the final trial darkening our expressions. None of us want to speak, and I'm not particularly fond of celebrating either. In fact, were it not required to make an appearance at this celebration, I probably wouldn't be here right now. There's also the plan I have with Milo, which I refuse to miss. I'm finally going to get answers about the mystery surrounding Deacon Lawrence.

My injuries are gone, leaving my skin without a trace of what happened to me during the trial.

Though I attribute my improved physical appearance to the vial of elixir that was left on my bed, I'm still left with the haunting memory of the things I faced.

However, we now stand as proud students of Blackbriar Academy, officially. And we're bombarded with endless congratulatory handshakes and smiles from all members of the staff.

Every student in the academy is in the arena which was transformed in honor of those of us who have passed the trials. Our images are plastered onto large banners, lining the far wall of the room, while the other side has a long table full of goodies. Practically every finger-food imaginable lay spread on the table. The wall to the right of the room holds a mural of a fountain with colorful lights and trees standing in front of a backdrop of the castle with the amazing view of the universe that only works to remind me of the last trial.

A small table, big enough to accommodate the six of us remaining initiates, sits in front of that. And between us and that, are smaller round tables situated with centerpieces and reserved seats for everyone else.

It's truly a beautiful sight, and I do enjoy the

view, but I can't shake the horror from the last trial just yet.

As soon as the greetings are over with, we are escorted to our table, where we sit and wait for Headmaster Storm to give his official speech welcoming us as students to the academy.

It bothers me that Savannah is not her usual bubbly self, and as soon as this night is over, I plan to talk with her about the trials until we are blue in the face. She had to have seen something as horrible as I have to make her seemingly permanent smile fade. I hope, in time, this will become a distant memory and we can all return to our normal demeanors.

Even Jesse is less of a jokester. Though my magic still reacts the same.

As we wait for the opening speech, I search for Milo. I feel him near me, especially with the way my magic reacts. Between him and Jesse, it's a pleasant sensation that reminds me of fall. He's two seats to my right. Jesse is in the seat next to me, and Savannah is on my left, with the other two on her other side.

"You okay?" I ask, overcome with worry that my friend is in such a somber mood.

She meets my gaze and smiles. It reaches her

eyes, but there is still a sad light within them. "Oh, yeah. I'm good. Just still trying to recover."

"I hear you on that one. It was awful," I say.

Jesse says, "Let's hope that is the worst of what we have to face here."

I reach over and grip his hand resting on the table and give it a soft, reassuring squeeze. His eyes meet mine and there is a glint to them that makes me smile.

There's my Jesse.

"Milo," I say, leaning forward.

He snaps his attention to me, half-smiles and says, "Oh, hey Wren. Glad to see you made it."

I nod. "You okay over there?"

He nods. "Yeah. I'm okay. You?"

"I'm in one piece at least."

An announcement echoes through the room. "Students and faculty, please take your seats."

Good. We're about to get started. Because the sooner we start, the sooner I can meet with Milo and get that spell I need to snoop around Professor Lawrence's office again, and the sooner this night can be over with.

Before long, Gideon Storm stands next to us, causing my magic to create a flux between the three of the four men it reacts to. It's electric, the way it buzzes through me.

He says, "For hundreds of years, our academy has held the tradition of the trials for acceptance into this academy. In my time as Headmaster, I have seen many initiates pass the trials, graduate, and become outstanding members of the mage community. This year, I'm astounded by the talent, the passion, and the strength these initiates have shown during their trials, and I have to say these individuals," he gestures to us, "are the most promising group of young mages that have been accepted into the academy under my lead."

A round of applause rushes through the room with a mix of hoots and hollers.

"Tonight," Gideon's voice booms, "we celebrate not only their passing of the trials, but welcome additions to our family of mages. I give to you, our new apprentice mages."

Waves of people stand and applaud. Soon, everyone in the room is giving us a standing ovation.

"Celebrate your victory, apprentices," Gideon says. "You have earned it."

Gideon walks away, and most of the night flies by quickly. Dinner went by in a blur. The apprentices mingled with some of the others, talking to heads of houses that they most want to be a part of. Except me. I stand off to the side, relatively alone, watching everyone enjoy themselves.

I'm not used to so many people, and I prefer to avoid all unnecessary banter.

Professor Lawrence approaches my side with two drinks in his hand. He offers me one and says, "Well, what did you think about the trials?"

At first, I'm at a loss for words. I take the drink from him, fully not intending to drink it, and say the first thing that comes to mind. "Definitely different than what I expected."

He chuckles. "Yes, they most certainly always surprise initiates. How does it feel to be accepted?"

"It feels good." I pretend to take a sip of the drink. "Hard won."

He raises his drink. "And hard earned. To a rewarding education."

I lift my drink and gently clink it to his, repeating "to a rewarding education." I take another fake sip.

"If I may," the professor says, all charm and suave, like he has no care in the world, "what would you say was the best part of the trial?"

I shrug as I keep my eyes on the crowd,

searching for Milo. "Learning what my limits are and how to push those limits further, I suppose."

"And," he begins, but pauses a short moment before adding, "the worst part?"

"The final trial. Hands down." I pretend to take another sip, and I know he will catch on soon if he doesn't leave me be. But I smile, determined to fake it till I make it.

The professor angles himself toward me and he cocks his head slightly to the side. "Somehow, I'm always surprised to hear that. Care to talk about it? I'm curious to know what yours was like."

I meet his gaze and there is a dangerous glint to them. Almost like he already knows what happened, and he wants me to confirm it. Instead, I swallow my suspicions for the moment and say, "I would rather not."

Though I'm desperate to ask him about my father.

"How disappointing," he says, but it doesn't seem like he is particularly upset, just curious.

I add, "Everything is still fresh and raw. I would prefer to wait until after things settle a bit."

He smiles. As always, never reaching his eyes. "Of course. Mine was particularly brutal. But it's different for each student."

I snap my gaze to him. "It is?"

"Oh yes, dear. All of the trials are different for every initiate. That's why you can't discuss them. Well, part of the reason."

I nod slowly. That makes perfect sense, actually. "Good to know."

"Well," he says, cupping my upper arm and giving it a squeeze, "I best be off to enjoy the celebrations. You enjoy the rest of your evening."

"Thank you," I say and fake another sip.

"Don't forget, I'm here if you need anything."

"I won't forget." I smile my best plastic smile and try not to outwardly roll my eyes. I swallow my suspicions and wait to reveal them when the moment is right, and I have evidence to back them with. "If I need anything at all, you will be the first to know."

"Perfect," he says with a bigger smile that almost reaches his eyes. Close, but not quite.

As he walks away, I watch him move like he has not a care in the world. A couple of apprentices approach him and they both look my way. At the same time. He's talking about me, and the funny weight in my stomach makes me feel like I won't like what is being said. But that's not the worst of it.

Their eyes remind me of that golem. They were life-less, almost like they have no real consciousness.

With that thought comes a curiosity of just how far and how deep his influence goes.

Depending on what I find tonight, I may have to play my cards extremely carefully from now on.

One thing has been made abundantly clear to me since first meeting Deacon Lawrence and accepting the invitation to attend the trials, and that is there is no denying he is up to something and I am somehow part of that plan.

In case he hasn't figured it out yet, I'm going to have to show him I'm not a pawn in anyone's game. It didn't work for the trolls, and it most certainly will not work for him.

I'm done waiting around. I'll give it a little longer, after the professor and his two goons disappear from sight before I go grab Milo to get this show on the road. I don't want to wait any longer. I need to find out what the professor is up to and I need to know *now*.

I turn to find the nearest trashcan for this drink that could be spiked with who knows what, and nearly bump into Anderson Stone. I narrow my eyes at his smile and my nerves are filled with such a sickening sensation I consider running to the trashcan to vomit.

"Go away," I say as rude as I possibly can. But it does no good. I can't seem to shake him off. If anything, just acknowledging Anderson has given him encouragement. He simply smiles and holds out another drink to me. I glance at it in disgust and side-step around him to throw the current cup I have in the trash.

I turn to go look for Milo, stopping short yet again to avoid bumping into Anderson.

"I brought you a drink, aren't you going to take it?" he asks with a smile.

That thing could be filled with any number of drugs or an enchantment, or even a combination. I don't trust this guy, and the last thing I would do is accept a drink from him I didn't watch get poured.

"Nope. Bye." I go to move around him, but he steps in front of me to stop me.

"Where's the rush?"

"I'm looking for someone." As his eyes light up, I add, "No, it's not you, and I'm busy. Leave me alone."

The longer this takes, the shorter of a window of opportunity I have for sneaking through Professor

Lawrence's office. And I refuse to let the chance pass me by.

I side-step around him only to have him block me again. I groan. This guy is freaking annoying. "What will it take for you to leave me the hell alone?"

"One dance," he says with a devious smile.

"Never."

He shrugs. "Suit yourself. You'll come around eventually."

"Good luck with that." I finally make it around him and beeline for any area not near him. I don't like how I feel when he is around, and I certainly haven't forgotten what he did the first time we met.

That man is dangerous.

But there is only so much avoiding I can do. We are both stuck on an island and it's only so big. I know we were bound to bump into each other every once in a while. But not anywhere near as often as it has been lately. From now on, I will have to be extremely careful around him. He seems to know how to corner me when no one else is around, and that is all kinds of bad.

I start to feel drained again. As I look over my shoulder, Anderson is directly behind me, evil glint in his eye and a hungry smile that tells me he knows

I know what he is doing, but he doesn't care because he can get away with it.

Just as I'm about to lay into his ass, Anderson's gaze moves to over my right shoulder.

My magic rushes through me and I know who is behind me. I turn and smile as my eyes settle on his deep browns. "Milo!"

"Hey, I've been looking for you." He looks over my shoulder at Anderson. "Are you ready?"

This man is my freaking hero. I'm so grateful that he came at just the right time, I lean in and plant a kiss on his cheek. Milo blushes a little and runs a hand through his hair. I return my attention to Anderson and say a curt, "Goodbye."

If looks could kill, Anderson would have murdered both me and Milo right where we stand. It takes everything inside me not to chuckle. Instead, I slip my arm through Milo's and walk off.

Once we pass the brooding Anderson, I lean in and whisper, "Thank you."

"No problem. Are you okay?"

I nod.

"Good."

We leave the arena and head straight for my room. But I keep my arm right where it is, because I want to. And I like how it makes Milo blush a little.

As soon as we walk through the door, I freeze.

Jesse is standing there, looking at us with a mix of confusion and curiosity.

At first, I think he's going to run off, but then he saunters to me, really hamming up his smoldering looks, he pulls me into him and lifts my chin for me to meet his gaze. "Whatever mischief you are up to, my darling, you'll have to include me. I refuse to let you do anything otherwise."

Well things just got a little more complicated.

"Um, Milo this is Jesse," I say gesturing between the two with a hand. "Jesse, this is Milo."

Jesse doesn't look at him but quickly nods. "I'm certainly not leaving you alone with this chap."

I pull away and turn my attention to Milo who shifts uncomfortably as his gaze roams around the room, resting everywhere but on me and Jesse.

I sigh and rub my temples. "I don't have *time* for this."

My magic churns and quakes, and I'm at a loss of what to do. I wouldn't put it past Jesse to stop me for not allowing him to come, and my window of opportunity is now. I can't wait. I don't see what other choice I have but to let him help. But my plan only accounted for one extra. Not two.

Damn it all to hell.

Milo says, "I have enough to cast on two. It will help if you have someone with you. I'll stay here and wait for you to get back."

Jesse stands straighter and faces Milo. "And if someone shows up asking about our whereabouts?"

He shrugs. "I'll tell them that you are at the celebration. I was invited here to find something Wren needed."

"You think someone is going to buy that as an excuse?" Jesse asks and turns to me. "What do you see in this guy?"

"Look, cast the spell on the both of us, we went to the kitchens for some drinks and snacks, we were going to play a board game as soon as Savannah got here. Good?" I look to both of them.

They nod.

"Good. Now, let's get this thing over with."

## CHAPTER TWENTY-EIGHT

With the spell cast on both Jesse and I, we make our way through the halls to Professor Lawrence's office.

As soon as we get there though, the professor is stepping in.

Crap. I didn't account for him being here during the festivities. I look to Jesse who is serious until his eyes meet mine. He shrugs with a smile, a dark, curly strand of hair falls into his face and he winks and nods toward the door.

He seems to think even with Professor Lawrence being in the room, it's worth the risk. While the spell is able to conceal us, keep us hidden, it can be broken. And in less than two hours, it will dwindle on its own. We must be quick, and careful.

I let out a deep breath and we move forward, stopping in front of the door. I lift a finger and press my ear against the door. It's quiet. No shuffling of papers, no footsteps, no whispered breathing. Everything is quiet. But I just saw him walk in.

That locked door has to be where he took off to. I wonder what's behind there.

"Can you pick a lock?" I ask Jesse.

He smiles. "Does your ass shake in the most hypnotic way when you walk?"

I stare at him. How the hell am I supposed to know?

He chuckles under his breath. "Of course, I can."

Well, there's two answers I have now. Apparently, I shake my butt when I walk, and Jesse can pick locks.

We walk to the door and I gesture for him to do his thing. He bows lavishly and I force back a chuckle. We can't be too loud, or it will disrupt the spell. And I can't have that. Not now.

Within moments, the lock is undone. He pushes on the door and allows me to step through first. Once he is in with me, the door closes and locks automatically. I use my magic to form a soft light and shine it on the door. Apparently, it's a one-way lock, and a long handle makes it easier to open from this side.

Well, at least we won't have an issue getting out. But the question is, where do we go from here. All this tiny room seems to be is just that. And empty. Nothing to show for in terms of where the professor had gone through.

As if taking my thoughts into consideration, Jesse starts pushing on walls. Nothing gives until he tries the one to the right of the door. It's a stairway that leads downward, lights shine from torches every few feet or so, making my magic useless and the opportunity for getting caught that much greater.

But I have come too far now to stop.

"Smart," I say. I'm truly impressed with how useful Jesse has been for this mission of mine, and I'm grateful he practically strong-armed me into bringing him.

"I aim to please." He holds the door open for me.

I slowly take the steps, testing them for squeaking before applying my entire weight on them.

The steps curve downward to a short corridor underneath the castle. No more than one-hundred feet in front of us is a room. There are no torches to light the way, so there is no telling if there are any traps to speak of. I don't dare use magic to light the way because I don't want to give away our position.

However, echoing toward me is the professor's voice snapping. Someone replies, but their voice is too hushed, almost too weak sounding, to travel far or make out what is being said. Jesse and I exchange glances and carefully move our way to the end, staying in the shadows.

The room is like a wine cellar. It's small, rectangular, with short archways opening up into smaller rooms where wine must have been stored at one point in time. Now, all the nifty little holes are either filled with candles, books and papers, or left empty. In the center of the room stands a large mirror with intricate designs in the frame bordering the glass.

And in the center stands...

Wait...

I rub my eyes and struggle to focus them.

My father, looking the worse for wear, paces in and out of view of the mirror talking to the professor.

"So," Professor Lawrence says, "what you're telling me is, you've failed. Not only has there been no progress, but you have stopped looking?"

My father appears in the reflection and lifts his hands, begging the professor to listen. "No. No. That's not what I'm saying. I have been looking, I just keep coming up with the same answer."

"That's not good enough!" the professor roars, slamming his hands on a table near him. He faces my father again. "I want the last piece found. You know what's at stake. I don't want to hurt that precious daughter of yours just to prove a point and keep your motivations going."

I gasp. It was quiet, thankfully, but uncontrolled. However, now I know more than ever there is more to this man. My instincts tell me to keep a safe distance, but Professor Lawrence was responsible for me coming here in the first place. I sort of owe him a little for this. But not enough to disregard my father somehow being held hostage. I need to take each step carefully from here on.

I share a look with Jesse, whose eyebrows are knitted together. He frowns, and I can see the questioning in his eyes.

I lean in closer and whisper in his ear, "That's my father, Michael Blackwood."

He moves, I quickly grab ahold of his arm. "Don't. It will only make things worse."

I pull away, and the look in Jesse's eyes tells me

he is now out for blood. I'm flattered, but that's not necessary. I'll deal with the professor when the time comes. What I don't understand is why he is willing to draw blood for me.

My father's hair is disheveled and now all over grey when it used to be brown. He stares at the professor with dark circles under his eyes and says, "Don't harm a hair on her head. I swear—"

"You swear what?" Deacon asks, sounding amused. "She's completely out of your reach. It was difficult narrowing down her location, but I managed. Now, if you ever need proof of the seriousness of the matter, all I have to do is show you. She will trust me completely soon. Mark my words."

No, I won't. I never trusted him. Trust has to be earned, and all he's done is make me feel indebted to him for his invitation to the school. A feeling which is quickly falling further to the back of my mind.

Because if it's one thing I know now, it's that I was brought here as bait. A means to keep my father in line.

"The Order isn't going to be happy with you when they find out you're keeping me locked here," my father growls.

"You don't know half of what the Order does. Find the meteorite." The professor's voice left no room for question. The demand came across loud and clear. Find the meteorite, or I will be hurt.

Something about all of this tugs at the back of my mind, calling to me to bring it forward.

And I'm flung into a memory.

I'm a little girl, about five years old, playing in the field behind my house, dancing with fireflies. Something bright, like a star, catches my attention as it falls from the sky. It shatters into pieces, exploding in the air, and a piece of it lands in the field.

Me, being the curious girl that I was—always searching for answers, always seeking new discoveries—I went in search of the piece.

I find it, burning bright, glowing like an ember. The ground around it isn't hot, the light itself doesn't even burn. To test it, I touch a tip of my shoe on it and poke at it with my finger. It's as cool as the night itself.

But when I touch the thing with my hand, it explodes into a bright flash.

The next thing I remember is waking up in my room the next day.

My father started to act weird after that. He

never seemed scared of anything until then, and I couldn't figure out why. He always taught me lessons on magic when he got the time, but from that moment on, it was more intense and much more often. It had become a second job for us both. Devoting every waking, free hour to my magical studies.

Seven years later, my mother died. And a couple weeks after that, my father disappeared. That's when Aunt Patricia took me in.

And well… the rest is history.

Jesse's hand tugs on my shoulder, urging me backward as I'm suddenly back to the present. The professor's voice sounds closer.

We don't wait around to hear his final threat to my father. Jesse and I have heard enough.

Quickly, we make our exit, rushing through the halls until we are almost to our room. I don't know how much time is left on the spell exactly, but I do know we have only minutes left. We have to be in that room before time runs out.

We step inside and I nearly collapse on the floor. I fall to my hands and knees, panting for breath, my mind swirling with everything Jesse and I just found out.

## CHAPTER TWENTY-NINE

I suck in a breath as my magic flurries with heat. Soren is here too?

Crap.

My magic is a torrent of different temperatures and pressures. Jesse, Milo, and now Soren are in close proximity of me and it's a cascade of sensations that blend into one. It's amazing, but neither sensation lasts for very long, it's like each one is put on a continuous loop of taking turns.

At first, it's hard to breathe, but soon it feels like I can *fly*. I can't seem to get enough of it.

"Explain yourself," Soren's voice commands. "Now."

I slowly lift my gaze to him. And man, does he look angry. He looks down his nose at me, standing in the middle of my room with his arms crossed over his chest.

"What were you just doing?" he asks.

My gaze switches between Jesse and Milo as I sit up on my knees. Milo doesn't meet my gaze as he sits on the foot of my bed. Jesse seems overly nonchalant as he pushes himself past Soren and lounges on his bed, hands behind his head. He meets my gaze and winks.

I shake my head, forcing back my smile.

Adorable idiot.

"I'm waiting," Soren says, pulling my attention back to him. His amber eyes are alight with fury and it only makes him hotter.

I shake my head to clear that idea from my mind. Getting caught in a torrent of hormones and sexual desires won't do right now. "I snuck into Deacon Lawrence's office."

His eyes widen, his face reddens, and I think he's about to implode. Though, I would hate to be the one to clean up the bits of brain matter and blood and skull fragments. So, I really, really hope he doesn't.

Not to mention it would be a waste of so much sexy. But, it's nice to know he's still an asshole.

"It's not as bad as it sounds," I say, trying to soothe his rage. "Not really."

"Oh? It sounds pretty bad, in fact, it sounds like grounds for expulsion. What were you thinking?"

"Dude," Jesse says, "Chillax, take a seat, we're all friends here."

Soren twists at the waist to set his fiery gaze on my Jesse, who doesn't cower or look the least intimidated. "We are *not* friends."

Jesse shrugs. "Suit yourself, but before you go throwing threats of expulsion, you may want to first hear our little Wren's story."

Jesse, you gorgeous idiot, don't get yourself killed for me.

Soren huffs as he returns his deadly gaze to me. "Well? I haven't got all night. I have other things I could be doing besides standing here waiting on you."

Oh, so we're back to treating me like a child? Okay then.

I square my shoulders and rise to my feet, standing as tall as possible. "I did what I had to…"

"You did what you had to." He looks up to the ceiling, shifting on his feet, chuckling under his breath. It has no humor, and I'm feeling a bit undignified by the action.

"It's not like you were any help. He was up to something, knew too much about my background—things only I could know. It worried me, so I did a little digging, and I'm glad I did."

He points at me. "You're glad you performed highly illegal, advanced alchemy spells, sneaking around the school, and dragged two of your fellow initiates into it as well?"

"I did the spell," Milo says, adjusting his glasses from my bed. "Wren didn't. Just so we're clear."

"Is that supposed to make it better?" Soren asks as he settles his glare on Milo.

I'm impressed. He doesn't shift or squirm. He meets Soren's gaze head on.

He's got a little badass in him after all.

Jesse says, "Hey man, shut up and listen. She's not done. Besides, I forced her into taking me."

Soren snorts. "Sure, you did."

I can't help it. I smile. Even though Soren can be such an ass, he pays attention. "Oh, I *let* him because I was on a time limit and I didn't want to spend half of what was left arguing about whether or not he could come."

Soren returns his attention to me with an arched eyebrow. "Is that so?"

"We knew what we were doing," Milo added. "I

wouldn't jeopardize my place here without due cause. I have my own suspicions about the professor myself."

Bless their hearts. I don't want them to fall prey to Soren's hatred. It's not fun.

For a moment, I don't know if Soren is going to throw punches in the room, spontaneously combust, or a dangerous possible number three that I don't dare give attention to. Before any of that can happen, I step forward, closing the gap between us. This way, if he throws a punch at someone, it will be me, and because, damn it all, he's fucking hot and my body reacts to him in layers of heat and passion.

Soren levels his furious gaze on me. With his full attention, I say, "I found my father."

His eyes seem to burrow into my soul, desperately looking for a tell that I'm lying. I told him my story. He knows my father went missing. His eyebrows knit together and he asks, "How?"

"In a mirror," Jesse said. "I saw the whole thing."

"A mirror?" He sounds like he doesn't believe us. I wouldn't either, if I was just told that. But I was there. I saw it too.

"There is a mirror in a hidden cellar under his office. Jesse followed me down there, and Professor Lawrence was angry about something." I touch his arm. "Soren, he's threatening to hurt me if my father doesn't find whatever it is he's looking for."

If I thought Soren was angry before now, I hadn't seen anything yet. Flames spark and flicker along his arms. I jump back, removing my hand as I watch him start to combust. "Are you sure it was your father and not a trick?"

I narrow my eyes on him as a pinch forms in my forehead. "I'm positive. My father looked... old. Older than what he should be. He seemed weak and barely able to stand."

He shakes his head. I can't be sure if that means he doesn't believe me or if he's finally coming around. Either way, I don't regret my actions one itty-bitty bit.

He sighs and faces Jesse. "You saw it too?"

"Would it matter?" Jesses asks. "I heard Lawrence threaten Wren to keep that man—father or not—in line. That's all that should count, right?"

Finally, Soren faces me again and says, "I knew that man was *trouble*. This confirms a few suspicions of my own. But it doesn't relieve you from fault of your actions."

"I know," I say. I don't push any buttons. In this mood, with that fire crawling over his skin, I know better. Any slip-up, and the whole room could catch fire.

"Tell Gideon. Now." Soren's flames react to his last word, increasing his point. There was little room for argument.

But I shake my head. "No. I need proof."

"Jesse," he says.

"It's just our word against his, even with Jesse seeing everything as well. I need something concrete. Something the professor can't refute. Something beyond the room and the mirror." I start to pace, wringing my fingers together and chewing on the corner of my lower lip.

"The room," Soren says.

I shake my head. "We barely made it out of there without being caught. I really, really need proof. Something physical. Hard evidence. I need time to get that. I still need to know more. I have to find out where my father is."

"Gideon can help," Soren says. "I'll give you some time to think about it, but the sooner you tell him, the better."

I nod. "I agree."

"For now," he says, a little calmer, but it's like a scary clam. "Don't speak a word about this to anyone."

He switches his gaze between the three of us and we all nod.

He approaches me and the way his eyes drink me in makes me a little weak in the knees. "Please don't do anything else reckless."

I nod, unable to speak. As he passes me, his hand brushes against mine, igniting my body in all kinds of pretty and lusty thoughts. I bite my lip and watch as the flames covering his skin die off before he steps through the door.

Once the door is shut, my magic recedes into a pattern that switches between rushing and coolness pulsating through me. I face Milo and Jesse. "Well, that was fun."

"He's hardly what I would call fun," Milo says.

"Come on now," Jesse says. "A little competition never hurt anyone."

Milo levels his gaze on Jesse. "I'm not competing with anyone." He turns toward me. "Though I have had a long day, and as much as I hate to end our time together, I need rest. I have a feeling our task of uncovering the professor's secrets is just beginning."

I nod and wrap him in a hug. "I understand. Thanks for the help. Get some good sleep."

I breathe in deep his intoxicating smell and

damn near give into my desires. He always smells *delicious*.

"You are very welcome. I'm glad to have been able to help." He hugs me back and the feeling makes me melt into him a little. He pulls away, all too soon and smiles at me.

"Goodnight, Milo," I say, smiling back at him.

"Goodnight, Wren," he says and turns to Jesse, "It was nice meeting you."

"Oh, I'm sure we'll be seeing each other again real soon," Jesse says wagging his fingers.

I narrow my eyes on Jesse and wonder what the hell he means by that. For the moment, I ignore that exchange and walk Milo to the door. Once he steps out into the hall, I shut the door and lean against it.

"So, what now, cupcake?" Jesse asks. "Want a little repeat of what I can do?"

I shake my head and smile, because this man just doesn't quit, and I'm starting to like it.

"Bed." I make my move toward my mattress and fall on top of it. I'm exhausted. The day has been long and hard, and I want to put it behind me.

## CHAPTER THIRTY

All of us remaining initiates gather around the statue of Lady Alene. The spirit of the academy has been a crucial part for me in the process of the trials. I don't think I would've been able to do it without her.

I have relied on her wisdom and she has never judged me. So, as I face her once again, I feel as though I have a true friend standing in front of me.

And today, she's going to help me be sorted into the house I will belong to in the Academy. I'm both nervous and excited. I know, though, Lady Alene has my back.

I trust her.

"Are you ready?" Lady Alene asks.

I smile. "Yes."

We walk side-by-side through the garden. The stone path glitters in the warm sun light, and the stroll is taken at a leisurely pace. It's pleasant, and with the gentle breeze to cool my skin from the warm day, I'm in bliss.

The garden path leads into a small orchard. Blooms of every color create a portrait of a place too beautiful to be on Earth. But it's here, and so am I.

I smile, feeling like I belong for the first time in as long as I can remember. For the first time since home.

"Congratulations on completing your trials, Wren," the lady says. "I do hope there are no hard feelings about your third trial."

"No, not at all," I say, shaking my head and waving the concern away. "I knew it was only a matter of time before someone figured me out."

She smiles. "Not everything in our world is black and white. There are instances, events, and even people that stretch the boundaries of what is considered acceptable. This is how we grow as a race and build our world. Change in the way we think is inevitable."

I nod. "Makes sense."

We become shaded from the sun as we pass under the canopy of the tress. The blooms start to shimmer and change colors from pastel to white, and to deeper, bolder colors before returning to pastel again. Almost like fiber optics.

"This place is so freaking awesome!" I smile.

The lady chuckles. "I agree."

For such an important ceremony, this is very relaxing. I hope I can have more walks with the lady without cause. Just because.

We fall silent. Both of us enjoying the beauty that surrounds us and listening to the life of the faeries hiding in the trees, bunnies hopping across the path, and chipmunks chittering to each other.

As we approach a fork in the path, I ask, "Is it possible to stay here forever?"

"You love it that much?" Lady Alene asks.

I nod. "It's as close to being home I've felt in a very long time."

"Good," she says. "That is my wish for all those who attend here. It's meant to be considered a home. Even if that means a home away from home."

We slow to a stop as we reach the fork. But the sidewalk ends on either side no more than five feet ahead. I know there is a decision to make, but I have no idea which is the right way to go. I imagined Lady Alene had an idea of where to go, but instead, she waits patiently. Quietly.

"Where to?" I ask.

She nods toward me and says, "What does your heart tell you?"

I shake my head. I've never been asked that before. I know in my heart that I'm good. But to rely on my heart to make a decision? I can't be sure.

She smiles and says, "You have to learn to quiet your mind and follow your heart's desires. If you sit in quiet reflection, you often find what matters most to you. Difficult choices are made clearer, and it's almost as though the path you *should* take opens up to you."

Ah. I get it. It's another test of sorts, but instead of danger lurking around every corner, I have to let my heart guide me to the house I'm supposed to belong to. I slowly exhale a breath of sea mixed with the woods and floral scents and close my eyes.

I don't know which path to take, nor do I know where the paths lead. But as I slow my breaths and focus on the magic pulsing through my body with each beat of my heart, I feel a small tug to the right.

Turning that direction, the tug grows stronger, and I know, in my heart, this is the direction to go.

I open my eyes and face Lady Alene. "This way."

She nods and says, "Excellent choice."

"Thank you," I say, feeling rather proud of myself as well. It feels good to listen to my own heart. I'm going to do that more often now.

"What do you hope to gain from your studies while you are here?" Lady Alene asks.

The path opens up before us, and the trees give way to an amazing view of the ocean. As it curves slightly more to the right, the path climbs higher.

"I just want to learn what it means to have the power I do. Why I have it. How to prove I'm different from shadow mages."

"Anything else?" she asks.

"Well, learning more about magic in general would be nice."

She chuckles. "Indeed."

Here, there is less vegetation and more rocks. But the rocks glimmer in the sunlight, absorbing the glow and brimming with power of its own. I imagine the light stays within them, well into the night. A stone wall grows on the left, shielding me from the sharp edge of the cliff that drops into the ocean. Birds call out as they fly high above us, and the air starts to smell sweeter. I'm reminded of campfire, and summer.

The sun's rays warm even more and the cooler air surrounds me in a blend that reminds me of the way my magic reacts to Soren, Jesse, Milo, and even Gideon. All around me are signs that seem to signal that I am right where I am supposed to be. That in the end, all will be well.

We edge toward the side of a mountain, where the path leads. The shade beckons to me, and once I'm there, deep green grass covers the land to the right, filled with wildflowers and butterflies. Small huts dot the land every so often and I'm curious what they are for. Bushes with berries sprout against the side of the mountain, and as we round the corner, the path stops again.

There are a couple of benches, carved from the side of the mountain. Lady Alene gestures for me to sit. I do, and she takes a stand next to the bench. The path seems to aim straight with a fork curving off to the right. Both are blocked. I can't see beyond where they end.

"This is the final decision on your path to the house you will belong to. It's often the decision that takes the longest. This is why we have a bench. Perhaps, you would like a snack?"

"Sure." I'm a little hungry. That walk really worked up an appetite.

Lady Alene lifts her left hand and snaps the fingers on her right. An apple fills the palm of her left hand. I smile.

I'm never going to grow tired of this place.

Lady Alene holds the apple toward me, and I take it, biting into the flesh as the sweet juices run out the side of my mouth and down my chin. The taste is amazing. This apple is the sweetest, most flavorful fruit I have ever tasted.

I moan.

"Like it?" Lady Alene asks with a hint of humor in her voice.

I nod as I take another bite. I just can't get enough of it.

"I'm glad."

As soon as I'm finished with the apple, Lady Alene gestures for me to toss it to the side.

"Birds will take it, or one of the critters from the meadow will come and get it. Either way," she shrugs, "it will benefit."

I nod and throw the core toward the meadow to make it easier for them.

After a few moments, the lady faces me and asks, "What moment or event in your past do you think most defines you?"

My eyebrows knit together as I ask, "What do you mean?"

She smiles. "What do you think it means?"

Honestly, I feel like I know, but it comes too easily, and everything that has come to me easily has come with strings attached. Not that this is the same, but it does force me to really think about the question and make sure I am solid with the answer before voicing it.

There are events in my past that have helped make me who I am today. The thing when I was five, my mother dying, my father disappearing, my kidnapping from my aunt's home, living with the trolls… But which one is my most defining?

I sigh. "I don't know."

"It does take some time to consider. Which makes this the most difficult choice. But neither choice is wrong. It all is up to you."

"Will I know beforehand what my choices are?" I ask.

"In terms of which house?"

I nod.

She smiles, clasping her hands in front of her as she shakes her head. "I'm afraid that isn't an option as it's not so much as which house belongs to you, but which one is best suited for you, to not only help you grow, but to support you in all you do."

That didn't help. But I smile and try to make the most connections between her explanation and the question.

"Would it help if I, perhaps, rephrased the question?" she offers.

I shrug and say, "It's possible."

"Very well," she says. "What have you learned in life that you will always carry with you? Wherever you go, this is the thing that has propelled you forward."

"Oh, well that's easy." But as soon as I say it in my mind, I start to second guess myself.

"And that is?" Lady Alene asks.

"It's learning to rely on myself and pick myself up from the ground because life isn't fair, and people will hurt and use me for their personal gain. My choices are to either let it keep me down or rise above it. And I always chose to rise above it."

The path reveals itself.

"You have selected well," Lady Alene says. "Go, see what your new house is."

I smile and skip to the path.

The stone gives way to dirt and is nestled between rock faces. As the opening between the rock widens, thick evergreens stand guard. The smell of fire hits my nose and it reminds me of home. Dead pine needles litter the ground and curious faeries poke heads out from beyond the trees to see who is approaching.

At the end of the path, surrounded by evergreens and mountain, is a chest. Two lit torches stand on either side of the chest, and I'm curious as to what house I'm going to belong to, if Jesse, Milo, or Savannah will be there too, and if not, will we still be friends?

Nah. Nothing can separate us now.

Eagerness fills me along with a sense of nervous excitement as well.

As I come to stand before the chest, I kneel and flick open the latch. Lifting the lid, I find fresh black and burgundy uniforms with the iconic golden, embroidered "B" for Blackbriar. And on top of it all, is a sash with the symbol of the phoenix.

"House of Phoenix," I say. And the sound is like music. It *feels* right.

I grab my things and find an empty black duffle bag at the bottom that has the phoenix embroidered in gold on the side. I slip my things into it, and zip it closed before pulling the large strap over my head, resting it on my shoulder. Walking out, the shadows start to lengthen, and the sun falls behind the crest over the ridge above me.

Soon, I greet the lady again and say, "Thank you for your help."

She smiles. "It's my pleasure. Are you ready to go back to the castle?"

I nod and follow her.

Once back at the castle, I head to my old room to gather the rest of my things. Only, I'm shocked they were already moved.

I shake my head, unable to hide the grin pulling on my lips. Magic never ceases to amaze me, and I definitely hope I can learn everything there is to know in the time I'm here. Though I don't know how long I will be able to stay with so many people seemingly after me, trying to make my life hell.

It won't matter. I will overcome them, as I have everything else in my life. I won't be held back. Instead, I will continue to learn and grow.

Because, I'm Wren Blackwood. That's why.

I return to the main foyer of the castle where the other five initiates who had passed the trials stand in wait to be taken to their houses.

Instantly, I find Savannah and she smiles as she rushes to me. "I'm in House of Kraken! Can you believe it?"

"I can. Congrats! I'm happy for you. I'm in Phoenix," I say.

Jesse joins us, throwing an arm over my shoulders. "Good evening, ladies."

"Who did you get?" Savannah asks, beating me to the punch.

"I'm in Winterwolf," he smiles, eyes glistening.

I laugh. "That suits you. Congrats."

He shrugs. "They couldn't deny me if they tried. Just look at me! I'm perfect for them."

Savannah and I both laugh.

I catch Milo, standing off to the side, waiting for a way into our circle. I wave him over and he smiles in that way he does as he runs a hand through his hair. My magic erupts with both Jesse and Milo near, and I never want to get used to the feeling. I'm becoming partial to it.

"What house did you get?" I ask him.

"Drakon," he says and pushes his glasses up on his nose.

I cock my head to the side. "Yeah, I can see that."

Before long, we are separated and taken to our rooms. I finally get a room to myself, but I can't help but feel lonely. I'm going to miss Jesse and his mischief and flirting.

All my stuff is here already. The only thing left

to do is unpack and make the room my own. Later, there is going to be house-wide celebration where another amazing demonstration will happen. I'll get to meet the house leaders.

One of them I already know, of course.

Soren.

## CHAPTER THIRTY-ONE

The celebration is amazing!

All sorts of fire magic is being demonstrated in the courtyard attached to the wing devoted to the House of Phoenix.

The walkway toward the rounded courtyard is lit by torches with the flame-shaped fire spirits, salamanders, and tiny drakes. And in the center of the courtyard is a large firepit with flames in the shape of the phoenix, the mascot of the house I now belong to. The embers blow, shifting between white, yellow, orange, red, and blue. All the colors of fire.

Belong…

That word alone resonates with me, giving me a sense of hope and purpose.

I love it.

I'm greeted by smiling faces and inundated by numerous welcomes and introductions, but I don't remember who's who as I'm so enamored by the sheer design of the show. That's where my focus is kept.

Warmth rushes through my veins, setting my magic on fire. I feel Soren nearby. As I turn, I find him focused on me as he walks toward me, sending my body through sensations and arousal.

I smile, cheeks warming from the fire burning through my veins.

His gaze is softer, but he still carries himself as a hardened warrior, a man accustomed to being in charge. Once he is standing in front of me, he asks, "Enjoying yourself?"

I nod as I say, "Yes. It's so mesmerizing."

"There are more of these nights to come. Keep up the good work, and you'll be able to enjoy many more of these evenings."

"Good to know." We walk to the edge of the courtyard that overlooks a short span of forest before giving way to the midnight blue ocean with rolling grey waves, and its mirror reflection of the sky above.

"I enjoy this view. I come out here sometimes,

when everyone else is asleep and I can't. The sight helps relax me. It's peaceful."

I turn my attention to him and watch as his focus becomes occupied with the view below. "I never pinned you for the kind of guy that loses sleep."

He laughs under his breath a little and nods to himself. "There's a lot you don't know about me, Wren."

"Obviously," I say. "You don't give much opportunity to unwrap the enigma that is you."

"Still consumed with those burning questions, huh?" he asks and sets his gaze on me.

I swallow hard. I don't know what lies behind his eyes, but there is depth and meaning there, and it's almost an invitation to ask him more. But the gravity of the way he looks at me causes my mind to lose all thoughts, except to stand on the tips of my toes and kiss him.

I don't.

But damn it all if I don't want to.

A fire dancer comes closer to us and spits out fire close by, the sizzling rush of heat and flame licks at my skin and draws my attention to him, breaking the moment. I let out a slow, dizzying breath.

Soren truly is an enigma.

And he's going to be the death of me. I know it.

"This is the last event of the night," he says, facing the show, resting his elbows on the edge of the wall behind him.

I nod and say, "So soon?"

He chuckles. "It's been three hours, already."

I'm shocked. Time really does fly by. I had no idea it had gone by so quickly. But even as I stand here, watching the fire dancer, my eyelids grow heavier, and my bed beckons me.

Before I know it, we all filter into our rooms for the night. Soren escorts me to the room. I give him a quick thank you and promise to see him in the morning for training. As soon as I'm inside my room, I collapse onto my bed. A card shaped letter rests on the foot of the bed, but I don't give it much thought. It's probably a welcome card or something.

Sleep carries me away the moment my eyes close.

My eyes peel open with the glare of the morning's light shining through my window on the other side of the room.

Stretching the remnants of a deep sleep, my eyes fall on the letter still resting on the foot of my bed.

I slip my fingers around it and bring it to my face as I flip it open. But as I read the words, my mind and world spins.

*My Dearest Wren,*

*I hope by the time you receive this, it's not too late.*

*As soon as I heard you were at Blackbriar, I wrote this letter in hopes that when you read it, you will find someone you trust and show this to them. I can no longer protect you, but maybe someone there can. You are in danger. Deacon is bound to find out about you sooner than I had hoped. I suspect he may even know now, but I can't confirm his suspicion. I can't allow harm to come to you, my little bird.*

*You see, my daughter, you are the one they are looking for.*

*You fused with a piece of the meteorite when you were a little girl. It gave you powers that I could barely comprehend. I knew then I had to train you and teach you the laws and rules of magic to protect you. But it was not enough.*

*The Order knew of the existence and coming of the meteor, but not what it promised. They had theories, wild ones, but nowhere close as to what they know*

*now. However, they can't follow through with their plans without the meteor being whole.*

*They have all but the last piece, and they won't stop until they have it.*

*I love and miss you dearly. Someday soon, I hope to be reunited with you. Until then, stay safe.*

*Love,*

*Your Father*

I… I don't know what to think. At first.

But then my body rushes with adrenaline and emotion and I end up re-reading the letter several times, trying to grasp more of a hint to my father than just the paper and ink. A smell, a memory, a brief sense of him being here with me as I pore over the words over and over again.

I'm over the moon he was able to send a letter, but it also worries me. Because I don't know if he was caught, if someone knows of the letter, if he's still okay. After what I saw in the mirror in the cellar beneath the professor's office… I can't help but wonder how much more he could survive.

I make a vow to find a way to save him.

But first, I need to find a way to take care of Professor Lawrence. Because if it's one thing I know, it's the information contained in this letter changes *everything*.

This is it. This is what the professor has been after. Like my father, I suspect he knows. He likely assumes I knew all this time and needed me to somehow share and confide in him that little secret. I just didn't know I had fused with the meteorite. That explains so much. This is probably the reason why I can do magic without a conduit and not lose my soul. But I'm not positive.

The men need to know.

I quickly change and grab the letter, tucking it tightly into my hand as I rush out of my room to find Soren.

I have a feeling I know where he is, but I'm not going there immediately. I need to get Milo and Jesse first. For now, I want to wait to let Gideon know until Soren and the others see the letter. I don't want to overreact, but at the same point in time, I also don't want to involve the headmaster and risk him losing his position.

I don't know who the Order is, or how deep their influence runs, but I have a feeling they are not people to be trifled with. If that is the case, I really need to be careful on every single move I make from here on.

First, I find Milo, in the library of course. He looks at me with concern in his eyes as I approach. But I don't give him a chance to speak.

"Follow me," I say.

"What's going on?" he asks.

"Just come," I say and turn around.

He does, and I'm glad I don't have to offer any further explanation. We walk through the halls until I find Jesse with a group of his housemates. He seems to be in the middle of telling some story of his with exuberant details and wild expressions on his face, but as soon as he sees me, and the look of determination on my face, he stands up. All serious and ready to take action.

"Come, now," I say.

He smiles and says, "Damn I love the way you give orders."

I sigh. "Just come, okay?"

"Yes, ma'am," he says and salutes me. I shake my head and walk off toward the training circles.

As we walk, Jesse is relentless with his questions.

"So what mischief are we up to today? Why so serious? C'mon, Wren, curiosity killed the cat?"

Finally, I stop and pull both him and Milo into an empty hall and keep my voice at a whisper.

"This," I say, holding up the letter. They each

take a moment to read it. Both of them don't seem to make the connection.

"I fused with a meteorite when I was five. Now, Professor Lawrence wants what I have, but I don't think he knows. I didn't even know until this letter showed up."

"Are you sure it's from your father and not someone trying to trap you?" Milo asks.

"I'm sure," I say with a nod. "No one else knows what my dad called me."

"What?" Jesse asks. "Little bird? That's a bit obvious."

"True," I say, "but no one but him has ever called me that."

Milo shakes his head. "I'm not convinced."

"Look," I say and take the letter back, "either way, I'm in danger. I don't know how they would take the meteorite from me, but I also have no desire to find out. It has to be bad. I can't do this alone. So, I need to know, are you with me?"

Jesse snorts. "Is it not obvious?" He winks. "You couldn't keep me away if you tried."

"You already know I am," Milo says.

I ignore the jealous look in Jesse's eyes and say, "Good. Let's go find Soren."

"Yeah, about that," Jesse says and points behind me.

I turn, finding him storming towards us, the anger pouring off him is damn near palpable.

"You'd better have a good excuse to miss training." He practically spits fire as he speaks, and the guy is still fifteen feet away. Even still, his anger is nearly tangible.

"I do," I say, holding up the letter.

"What is it?" he asks as he stops in front of me and snatches the letter, almost ripping it with the force of his movement. I don't answer, I just wait for him to read. His expression changes from anger to shock, and maybe even a little worried. His eyes move to mine. "Gideon. Now."

Oh good. He's back to one-word responses.

"Okay," I say.

He hesitates and his eyes widen a little. "That's it? No argument?"

"Nope," I say.

He shrugs then looks to Milo and Jesse. "You two, go back to your houses and wait there."

"No," I say crossing my arms in front of me, standing my ground.

He levels his gaze on me and flatly says, "No?"

"No. They are in this with me. If you don't like it, tough. Like it or not, they are coming too."

"Awe, thanks, kitten," Jesse says, and I roll my eyes at the endearment of his.

"She's right," Milo says. "We're involved now. There's no point in keeping this from us. Besides, she'll probably find a way to keep us in the loop anyway."

"Damn straight," I say and give him a nod. He smiles and pushes his glasses up on his nose.

Soren crumples the letter in his hands. "We don't have *time* for this."

"Fine. Then it's settled. Let's go." I turn around and wink at Jesse who has a smile of pride plastered to his face.

## CHAPTER THIRTY-TWO

We make it to Gideon's door, and I hear his voice and feel my magic blend with the reaction of the others' and it's a bit dizzying, but I feel stronger and more resolved to take care of business.

Soren opens the door. I follow after him. Jesse and Milo file in last.

Gideon is in the middle of a lecture for a summer refresher course—as is written on the board behind him. He acknowledges us with a nod, never wavering in his speech. We take a spot near the wall at the back of the class and wait for his class to be dismissed.

"Coursework for the next year will start in a

couple of weeks, students," he says. "I expect all assignments on my desk before then."

He levels his gaze on the twenty-or so students and waits for each to acknowledge him.

"Yes, Headmaster Storm," they say in unison, some sounding a bit unenthusiastic about having to fill the rest of their break with more assignments.

"Very good. You're dismissed." He turns and wipes the board clean as students file either toward his desk to ask a quick question before leaving or out the door.

Once the last student leaves, he says, "What's going on?"

We approach his desk, and as I get closer, my magic reacts like a flurry of hot and cold, shifting between buzzing and pulsating. It's almost dizzying. In fact, my magic swirls between all of the sensations the men give me. All the passion, the calmness, the ease, the strength. I force myself to breathe as calmly as possible while my body feels like it's about to vibrate through the room. It's an intense sensation that takes most of my attention, which wouldn't be so bad if I didn't have to discuss my letter.

Soren starts off this shindig, holding out the letter to Gideon. "You need to see this."

The headmaster of the academy scrunches his eyebrows as he looks at the now wrinkled letter. "Did you kill it?"

Soren huffs. "No, but you may want to once you read it."

I step forward and say, "It's a letter from my father. He warns that I'm in danger and that I'm who Professor Lawrence and the Order are looking for." I still don't know who the Order is, or what they have to do with the professor. But it's clear that what they want from me puts me in danger, could have serious consequences, or may kill me. I don't want to even begin to think about what methods they would use to take the shard from me.

I won't let them. I will fight them tooth and nail to keep this. To stay in this world.

Gideon moves his gaze toward me and it's a cold gaze with a bit of dread mixed in.

My heart damn near freezes in my chest.

I don't like that he just looked at me like that. My anxieties rise a little more, and I'm made very aware of just how dangerous everything has become.

He sets his gaze over my right shoulder at Milo and Jesse. "And these two are here because?"

"Wren insisted." His voice is full of agitation.

"They have been helping me," I say. "I'm not going to dismiss them now."

"That's right," Jesse adds, throwing an arm over my shoulders. "And we've proven ourselves invaluable beyond our pretty looks and dashing smiles."

I close my eyes and swallow down the need to roll my eyes. The looks that Soren and Gideon are giving him with his arm around me makes me wonder if maybe that was the wrong move. I gently slide out and give him an apologetic smile. Hopefully he realizes that though I'm okay with his amazing touches, the others may not be, and with everything being so new, I have to be careful of each step I make. Not only where it concerns Professor Lawrence, but with the men I've come to care about too.

Milo says, "We can and have helped. We're not stopping now."

I cock my head over my shoulder to cast my gaze over at him. How about that? I've never seen him so resolute and resolved when it came to anything other than his love of books and knowledge. To hear him refuse to leave my side creates a flutter in my tummy that takes my breath away a little. He meets my gaze and I smile. He nods once.

Well done, Milo. Sticking to your guns on this one.

And I'm grateful too. If anything, Jesse and Milo have never given me a reason to doubt them and have been essential to my time here. I couldn't have snuck into the professor's little hideout without Milo's help, and Jesse… he's been a real comfort for me. And the fact that he refused to let me go in alone speaks volumes to me.

"Very well," Gideon says as he steps around his desk and takes the letter. As he unfolds the crumpled piece of paper, he leans against his desk, crossing his legs at his ankles.

At first, I'm shocked the headmaster didn't have an argument. He seems to accept that I have made friends, hot friends, and he doesn't seem a bit jealous or threatened. He just moves on.

But as I watch his eyes read through the lines on the letter, his expression changes from smooth and unaffected to a mix of confusion and anger. And I don't know what to think about that. Once he finishes reading, he places the letter on the top of his desk then faces me.

I start to squirm under his gaze. My nerves are on fire, and my magic can't seem to make up its mind on what it wants to do.

But as he speaks, he turns his gaze to Soren. "Before we address our next steps, I want to first say, I told you so."

Soren groans. "Yeah, yeah. You were right. What do you want? A medal?"

Wow. I'm truly impressed. He must not be accustomed to admitting he was wrong.

Gideon seems to consider it, but says, "Wren, I believe your fusion with the meteorite is why you can do magic without a conduit. But I will need to research this in more detail."

"What?" Soren's voice seems tinged with horror. He stands taller, angling his body toward the headmaster. "She what?"

"Well this is quite a surprising development," Jesse adds.

Milo grips my shoulder and gives it an affirming squeeze. I smile at him. He knew what I could do. So did Gideon. But Jesse and Soren...

Well, I suppose Soren will go back to hating me.

"That explains so much," Jesse finally says.

I give him a questioning look.

"That night you came home from the trial and your conduit was on your pillow."

Ah. Right. I nod.

"I knew there was something off about you, you

shouldn't be able to do magic without a conduit," Soren says. "But I also know that you are not evil or going dark. I've been around you enough to at least know that much. I owe you an apology for my behavior. There was an event in my past that doesn't excuse my behavior, but perhaps explains it."

Wow, that must have hurt. My eyebrows are raised on my forehead as I gape at him. But my attention is soon reclaimed by the ever-intoxicating headmaster.

"Now is not the time to go into detail," Gideon says.

"I agree," Soren says. "Which is why I plan to explain later."

He settles his gaze on me and my nerves *burn*. I'm surrounded by hot men and my body wants to gravitate toward each of them. Especially him. Soren's amber eyes that see into my very soul.

"I look forward to it," I say. "But I need to know what is going on. I understand this meteorite inside me is what gives me my power. What I don't understand is why."

Gideon nods. "I may have an answer for that."

I cross my arms over my chest. "Go on."

He pulls himself from his perch on the desk and

walks toward a glass globe resting on a stand in the corner of the room. The globe itself rests within a brushed bronze ring, with legs that curve underneath it and the stand is a simple pillar of grey marble.

"Follow me," he says.

We do, and as we get closer, the globe takes life with colorful clouds, until the center is of a vast universe, moving and flowing.

I'm in awe.

Gideon waits for all of us to surround the globe, and as soon as we do, he runs his hands through the air above the glass. The image shifts to that of a meteor, with blue and purple veins of light swirling throughout it. The white aura that surrounds the large object gives it an eerie glow. But the whole thing is beautiful to me.

"There is a fable that tells of a powerful star that died eons ago. The power supposedly contained within the pieces was thought to be so great, it would change the world. Some believed that this power would be destructive and apocalyptic, using it as a story to instill fear into people, while others believed it was simply a gift to bring peace and a new prosperous era."

The image shifts, showing the rock heading toward Earth.

"No one knows if this is the fragmented star that soothsayers spoke of long ago, and though many have watched the skies, with meteors passing the world by, none broke the atmosphere until fifteen years ago. The pieces were scattered all over the world."

"But there hasn't been an apocalyptic event or time of peace and prosperity," I say.

"I agree," Gideon says. "Only time will tell which is correct. But this is just one possibility for what fused with you. I will need to research it more and find out exactly what that power is meant to do."

"Meanwhile, I'm a sitting duck." I cross my arms over my chest, placing my full weight on one leg.

"I will do what I can—"

"We all will," Jesse adds.

Gideon nods. "We will do all we can to figure this out. However, it's imperative that the Order never know of you having fused with the meteorite's power. If they find out, they won't stop hunting you until they drain every last drop of power from you. That will, unfortunately, kill you."

Oh fantastic. Dead woman walking.

Jesse and Milo instinctively step closer to me,

while Soren's hands clench into fists so tight, his knuckles turn white.

"No one will bring harm to her," Soren says, and the growling undertone of his words makes me gawk at him.

I'm... I'm at a loss for words. But my heart flutters as warmth rushes through me, my magic pulsates and buzzes in reaction, and I am *loving* it.

"We will do whatever it takes to keep her safe," Gideon says with a sidelong glance at Soren.

"They will also have to go through me," Jesse says. "Believe me, they will have a hard time trying."

"Indeed," Gideon says. "Illusionary magic is a rare ability that not many have the chance of mastering, and you, Mr. Taylor have made quite the progress on your skills. I'm impressed."

Milo steps slightly in front of me. "I'll do whatever it takes to make sure Wren is safe."

Gideon nods. "Excellent." He sets his gaze on me. "It seems you have made quite the impression on each of us here, Wren."

My cheeks flush with heat, burning up from my neck that seems to be set aflame. So, these men must share in the same feelings I have for them.

I smile.

Awesome.

"I'm grateful for each of you. It means a lot that you stand behind me and care about my wellbeing."

"Of course," Gideon says.

"We will always have faith in you, even when you lose faith in yourself." Milo takes my hand in his and the light in his eyes is intense.

I nod.

This new development comes with some pretty sexy perks. Not only that, I now know why I can do magic without a conduit and not turn dark. That was my biggest worry, Soren's biggest concern, and now, we have to make sure no one else finds out.

"First things first," Gideon says. "Stay away from Deacon as much as possible. Avoid being alone with him. Take Soren with you if you get called to his office."

I nod. Though I'm sure that will not go over well. I refuse to let myself fall into his trap, risking my life for his drive for power. My power.

"Wait, what if one of us is with her?" Jessc asks, gesturing between him and Milo. "You said it yourself, Headmaster, that I'm quite skilled."

"Soren has seniority here," Gideon explains. "He is known for doing things for me. Having him speak on my behalf is both believable and plausible." He pauses for a moment, snaps his fingers, and adds,

"In fact, having you around her constantly may get suspicious. We can't lead Deacon to believe we are hiding something. Perhaps, the four of us should randomly take turns. This will ensure she doesn't fall into the wrong hands."

I frown, leveling my gaze on the handsome as hell headmaster. His bluish green eyes meet my gaze, and I almost forget what I'm upset with.

Almost. But not quite.

"I don't need a babysitter."

"Don't think of it like that," Gideon says. "Simply a bodyguard of sorts. You have developed a relationship with all of us, and so it will go unnoticed having us around a majority of the time."

"That may be, but I'm also friends with Savannah. What about her?"

Gideon shakes his head. "I'm afraid she can't be involved. There are too many of us as it is, and any more runs the risk of being caught."

I stand taller, raising my head a little higher. "I can take care of myself."

Soren says, "No one here is going to argue with you on that."

I narrow my eyes on him, wondering just what he means by that little statement of his.

Gideon sighs. "What he means is, no one is

going to disagree with you. However, your training is not formal. And that is a different horse altogether."

"Hey, how long can this last for anyway?" Jesse asks. "Besides, the time with me will fly by, and leave you wanting more." He puts on his devilish smile and winks.

I laugh and shake my head. "You wish."

"We will see…" he says.

Gideon says, "That is a good point. This is only temporary, until we can ensure your safety."

I huff a sigh and cross my arms over my chest as a pinch forms in my forehead. I don't like giving up what freedom I just got, and I hate the fact that I will only feel babysat while with them.

I don't like it. I won't do it.

"Wren," Gideon says with such a soft voice, full of need. It pulls my attention toward him, and as I take in his eyes, there is so much pleading within them. I almost can't breathe. "Do this as a favor for me. Keep one of us with you, please."

And just like that, I change my mind.

Because, who can resist the headmaster—with stellar kissing skills—when he asks for a favor so politely and in that tone?

I can't. And I think he knows it.

I drop my hands to my sides, giving in. "Fine, but you owe me."

That smile says it all.

I smile back and I realize that he really does know what he does to me. And he's enjoying every single moment of it.

Beautiful bastard.

I shake my head and clear my throat so that I can focus and ask, "What about my father? We need to get him out of wherever he is. He probably risked his life to send me that letter. I can't let him die."

Gideon holds up his hands and waves them up and down. "We will find him and figure out a way to get him out of whatever prison Deacon is keeping him. I promise."

"And what of the Order? Are they really that dangerous?"

"I thought everyone knew the stories about the Order?" Milo says.

I shift my gaze to him. "I lived with forest trolls for six years, Milo. I hardly know anything of your world."

"You what?" he asks, but it goes unanswered.

"No one really knows who the Order is," Soren says. "But there are rumors."

"Like what?" I ask, hoping to gain some clarity into the people behind this group.

"One theory is that they are corrupt, seeking ultimate control. Whereas another is that they simply try to keep the balance aligned, aiding in human growth and survival."

"So, they're like, the Illuminati or something?" I ask.

Milo twists his body to face me, a look of confusion on his face. "When were you going to tell me about the trolls?"

Ah, he's still stuck on that. I shrug. "I'll tell you later. Promise."

He seems to accept that as an answer. And I'm glad, because I really don't want to go into it right now.

"Good example," Jesse states, getting the conversation back on track.

"Exactly," Milo adds, back in the game. "The rumors are what protect them, but unless you are inside the group itself, there is no irrefutable proof of their existence."

Gideon continues, "Unless you are standing in front of them and they tell you they are a member of the Order, you'll never know who is and who isn't or what their motives really are. Their agents could be everywhere. Not to mention numerous."

"Shadow mages, too," Jesse says. "If we're going to give her the bedtime story, might as well give her all the nitty gritty details."

"So, Professor Lawrence could be one of them?"

"Yes." All of them speak in unison.

"Wouldn't that mean the Order does exist? And what does it say to know he is acting against them by keeping my father hostage. He said something about the Order not liking him being kept where he is."

"We don't know, unfortunately," Gideon says. "There could be any number of reasons your father would mention them. If they do exist, rather if he has knowledge of them, we will have to carefully watch our next steps until we know more about their motives."

I exchange looks with Jesse and Milo. This is going to be loads of fun, I can tell.

"For now," Gideon says, continuing on. "Business as usual. Soren, continue training Wren. Meanwhile, I will dig into my research and see what evidence I can find that will prove Deacon unfit to maintain a seat at the school. He may be behind why I can't read not only him but a few others in the school."

"And my letter?" I ask. "What if he finds it?"

"I will hold it for safe-keeping. No one will be able to find it."

"Why not just burn it?" Something about the way Jesse asks the question makes me think he is leaning toward the idea of a fire more than just completely obliterating my letter. His eyes have a hungry glint to them as I catch his gaze. He never struck me as a pyro, but I'm still learning about these men. And with Jesse, one can never know what he is really thinking.

I glare at him. I don't like the idea of the one thing I have from my father being destroyed.

He winks at me and adds, "If it's found, it will be used as evidence against her." He nods toward me.

Ah, he just wants to get a rise out of me. But with his explanation, it's a good question, nonetheless.

"I have a special enchanted safe. Only I can get in and out of it. For now, the letter will be placed there. It may be of use as evidence later to exonerate Wren's father should the Order decide to make him a patsy. They are notorious for planting damning evidence against their enemies and making themselves look like the heroes. Besides, I may also be able to use it to track the area he is in."

I suck in a breath as my mouth starts to form a hopeful smile.

"Don't get excited just yet. It's only a possibility."

I nod. Still smiling.

"So, this is settled?" Soren asks, holding his hand palm down in front of him.

"I believe so," Gideon says. "With luck, we can all get out of this with as little unnecessary involvement with the Order as possible."

I bite the corner of my lower lip and wonder if that is even possible. My father said both the Order and Professor Lawrence were looking for me because of the meteorite I fused with. They want what I have. And there's no telling what they will do in order to get it.

CHAPTER THIRTY-THREE

My mind is buzzing with all the information that was just given to me. I barely slept a wink last night. What little sleep I did get was spent with nightmares of being ensnared by the mysterious Order and Professor Lawrence holding some strange instrument above me, hungrily searching for my meteorite.

I hope that I can make it through my stay here at the academy without the professor and the Order finding out about me. But I know that's not possible.

As nice of a thought as it is, that's not my life anymore.

Soren's steps are smooth and even as he steps in front of me, leading me to a new area of the island. I don't know where he is taking me, but we are supposed to be training. So far, all we are doing is taking a hike.

"I thought the training circles were that way." I point a thumb behind me.

"We're not going to the training circles," he says.

"Oh," I say, eyebrows arched high on my forehead. "Where are we going?"

"You'll see." He looks over his shoulder and there is a smirk on his face that lights up his amber eyes and stills my breaths.

Getting accustomed to the way my magic burns through me when I'm near him has been difficult enough. Now I have to learn to control my sexual urges when he looks at me like *that*. Needless to say, I desperately want to jump him. But I don't. Because, up until recently, Soren has been an asshole that sparks a desperate need for sex. Now, that feeling has sweetened without all the hate that he had for me.

I guess learning about me makes a difference in his view of me now.

"Will you be sharing your story with me today?" I ask.

He looks at me again with questioning in his

eyes. After a moment, he says, "Not today. I will someday."

"It must be a painful story," I say.

"It is." He keeps walking forward, a little more silent than before. I respect his need for quiet and take a look at the scenery that surrounds us. We're on the southeastern part of the island that slopes down and levels out within a forest of green that sits just outside of the academy's walls. On the southwest side is the dock I first arrived on. Where that crazy boat guy rambled off riddles and nonsense.

So much has happened in the two short weeks I have been here. So much magic. So many changes. It's almost like the world I used to know, the one where I was just a human slave to a village of trolls, is nothing but a long lost dream.

Well, nightmare.

As we enter the forest and walk deeper, toward the edge of the island, I'm astounded by the glow of the rising sun burning between the tree trunks. It's beautiful.

Before long, there is a small clearing with a fire pit in the middle. It looks long abandoned with an overgrowth of weeds and a collection of twigs and dead leaves that scatter across the area. Soren faces me.

His eyes are like the rising sun. Bright, warm. *Beautiful.* I can't help but smile.

"This is a part of the island that is forbidden without special permission. Here, you can practice your magic without the use of that conduit," he points to my wrist, "and no one will know."

I nod. "Got it."

He steps closer to me. "You can only do this with me. Understand? No one else."

I angle my head to look up at him and it's hard to keep my mind focused on the seriousness of his words.

"Not even Gideon?" I ask.

"No. One. Else." He speaks each word with a low growl and steps even closer. "This is our place. Just mine," he gestures to himself and then to me, "and yours. No one else can share this place."

I'm at a loss for words. There is so much implication in them, but I also don't want to read too far into the meaning. It's sudden, intense, and mind-boggling. Without breaking from his gaze, I whisper, "Okay."

"Good." His eyes search mine, and I wonder what he is looking for. Then his gaze drops to my lips and I suck in a breath as my heart races. But before he leans in to kiss me, he steps away and takes a few deep breaths.

"Let's go through some of our drills," he says.

It's such a quick switch in the air between us, it takes me a moment to catch on. But by the time I do, Soren is already charging.

I try my best to keep up, blocking a jab here, sending a front kick there, but it's no use, he blocks me every time and I end up stumbling through my moves. Always a little slower than his reaction.

"C'mon, Wren, where's that fire at?" He almost sounds amused and that works to anger me a bit.

I throw my punches a little harder, kick a little faster, block nearly every one of his moves.

But regardless of what I do, he is still faster.

"You can do better than this," he says, and I know he is goading me. He wants me to get angry with him.

I roll my eyes, and breathing a little harder, really step up my game. I land a punch to his shoulder.

"Good. But you hit like a girl," he says.

That does it. I'm angry. And I can't help but wonder why he is trying to get me in this mood. "Asshole."

"That's more like it!" he says with a smile and pins me to him, arm pressed to my back and his chest. His breath runs hot down my neck and I squeeze my eyes shut against the sensation that tingles through my core, settling between my thighs with delicious pressure.

"You want me angry with you?" I pant trying to free my arm, but he only tightens his grip.

"Let's just say it adds to the enjoyment."

His words whisper along my ears and I damn near let out a groan at the way I'm turned on. I don't know what goal he has, but if it's turning me on, then he's done a fine job.

I struggle to maintain focus, using my free arm to elbow him in the face. He catches it, slides his fingers through the crook of my arm, and says, "What are you going to do now, Wren?"

I chuckle darkly and try to headbutt him in the nose. Pressure enters my arm as it's forced into my back farther, and he angles himself out of the way.

He clicks his tongue. "Fiery, that temper of yours."

"You haven't seen fiery yet." I stomp on his foot which works to release me, and spin to face him, fists at eye level.

He nods with a smirk of satisfaction then lowers

himself into his stance. "Bet I can knock you down?"

"Haven't we already learned that outcome?" I ask, never wavering in my position.

As he starts to move, I match the same steps, and we move in a circle. The tension between us is electric and charged with sexual desire. He shrugs. "Call it a re-do."

"What's the wager? I answer more of your ridiculous questions?" I ask, still keeping up with his movements.

"I have something far better in mind." He smiles, and that makes me pause. I have no idea what he means by that. But before I have a chance to figure it out, he charges me, quick as lightning, and the world spins in my view.

As my back meets the ground, I land gently cradled in Soren's arms. One arm is wrapped around my lower back and the other wraps around my upper back with his hand cupping the back of my head. I blink the blur away and meet his gaze.

My breath stops as his mouth collides with mine. I clutch the back of his shirt with one hand and run my fingers through his short hair with my other as I kiss him back. I'm taken aback by the sheer passion with which he kisses me, the desire that makes him rush just a little.

He moves to pull his arm out from under me, sliding his fingers under the hem of my shirt. His mouth leaves mine to explore my neck and collarbone, while his hand travels up my shirt, cupping my breast and massaging it.

My thighs quiver from the need growing between them.

A small voice at the back of my mind wonders what the hell I am doing, but my magic erupts with excitement and my body takes over, and I don't want this to end. Not now. I'm too far over the edge.

His mouth meets mine again as he settles between my legs. His erection presses against my entrance. A soft moan escapes me, which further encourages him to do the same, and the sound is delicious.

As he pulls up to sit on his knees, he takes off his shirt and I'm dazzled by the shape of his muscular body, the angle of his shoulders, and the way his abs are tightly formed into a six pack. I want to run my fingers along his skin, but he doesn't give me the chance as he lifts me up and pulls off my shirt then occupies his mouth again with my neck as he unclasps my bra, running his fingers along my back, setting my skin on fire.

I cling to him, digging my fingers into his back, wanting him inside me more than I could ever imagine I would want someone.

He pushes me back to the ground as I toss my bra to the side and work his pants undone. He lowers the waist enough to set his erection free. My gaze takes his size in, and I bite the corner of my lower lip as my gaze meets his.

He growls with need and says, "The things that you do to me when you bite your lip like that."

I giggle and say, "Good to know I have a secret weapon to use against you."

He chuckles. "Damn it, woman. You'll be the death of me."

"We can't have *that*, now, can we?"

This is it. I'm putting my trust into him. Giving over to him completely. And after this, there is no turning back. Never mind that I don't want to.

He kisses me again, running his fingers up my thighs, pushing my skirt up, and sliding down my panties. He breaks from my lips, trailing kisses along my neck and pausing at each breast, sucking and nibbling, driving me freaking mad with desire.

As he works his tongue around a nipple, his

fingers tease the sensitive folds of my clit, dipping his fingers inside me.

My breathing turns erratic as my orgasm builds. I arch my back and grind against his hand until my apex is reached. His mouth collides with mine as I moan through the waves of pleasure his hand pushes me through.

Once it passes, he angles himself to rest the tip of his cock in just the right spot. Panting, trying to catch my breath, I meet his gaze as he watches me patiently. He smirks, and his eyes darken just as he grips my hips and plows into me.

I gasp.

He continues to thrust, sending me deeper into ecstasy, building another powerful orgasm, and keeping a steady rhythm. This man... he burns me through and through. And the feeling is addictive.

As my orgasm comes, I dig my fingers into his back and bury my face into his neck. He somehow drags out the pleasure, keeping it going until he too joins in and releases hot liquid into me.

I figure, this is where we finish, but I was wrong.

And I'm so glad I am.

Because, instead of stopping, he keeps going. "Oh, I'm not done with you yet."

"Good," I say and kiss him.

Soon, we reach our climax again. He collapses on top of me and I run my fingers through his hair as we both work to catch our breath.

I have to admit to myself, that this man has done me in. I'm starting to adore him and his finicky nature. In fact, I feel the same about Milo, Jesse, and Gideon as well. There's no way I can imagine my life without all of them in it.

Soren pulls away from me and stares into my eyes. He brushes the hair from my face and runs the back of his fingers along my cheek.

"Are you doing okay?" he asks.

I smile. "I'm great. You?"

He chuckles. "I'm good."

He kisses me, and it's a gentle, long, passionate kiss that ignites my entire being. When he pulls away, he says, "We better get back."

I nod and we both gather our clothes, pulling them back on. The memory of us having sex replays, and I'm suddenly aware that I could become pregnant. "What about pregnancy?"

"There is a potion I can give you. It will help prevent that."

I nod.

We walk back, taking our time. He grabs my hand and winds his fingers through mine. I smile at the feeling that gesture brings me. So much joy and hope.

But as we get closer to the academy's walls, he pulls his hand from mine. He seems much more rigid and constantly looks over his shoulder. He stays very close to me, and I get the impression that he is fiercely protective.

He still has his asshole moments, and I'm sure it will be to an annoying degree, but I smile as one thing is blatantly obvious.

He doesn't hate me anymore.

"Is everything okay?" I finally ask.

"So far, yes." It's a short response, but that doesn't surprise me. Not with this being Soren.

He leads me to the kitchen for House of Phoenix and pulls out the ingredients for the potion. I take the kettle and fill it with water, then place it on the stove and turn the burner on.

"Some training today, huh," I say as the silence between us becomes unnerving. Something seems to be on his mind, and for a guy that just had his wicked way with me, I almost expected a little more banter.

He cracks a smile and turns his back to me. "Yeah, it was a good session."

"Hmm," I say.

The kettle whistles and he pulls a mug from a cabinet as I turn the burner off and pull the kettle off the stove. He takes it from me and pours the right amount of liquid into the mug. He hands the steaming cup to me and says, "Give it a few minutes to cool, then drink it all at once. It may make you cramp a little later, but this will prevent a baby's conception."

"Thank you," I say and blow into the contents to help speed up the cooling. "For everything."

He faces me, and his expression is hard to read. "Look, I'm not good with feelings and things like that, so please don't take that personally."

I nod, but I can't help but feel a small flutter of doubt flicker in my belly. "Okay…"

"I won't let anything happen to you, all right? Trust in that, please."

Please? He's using manners with me? Huh. Will the wonders ever cease?

I nod again.

A peaceful silence settles between us. He stands right next to me, shoulder to shoulder, and I lean a little into him.

I don't know where this relationship will go or if it will end, but I know one thing. He's taken up a spot in my heart that will forever belong to him.

"That should be cool enough now," he says.

I nod and gulp it down. It burns the back of my throat and is earthy with a hint of spice. I place the cup in the sink and spin around to face him.

"What should we do now?" I ask. "Shower?"

He chuckles. "You're insatiable."

"Not my fault you released a beast."

"I'll take you to your room so you can shower," he says, still chuckling to himself as he heads for the door.

As soon as we enter my room, and the door is shut, Soren pushes me against the wall, kissing me with unhinged passion. I wrap my legs around his waist and my arms around his shoulders, never pausing in our kiss.

I can already feel his erection pressing against me, and I honestly can't say that I mind. Already my body is eager to be filled with him.

He carries me into the bathroom and sets me down, but doesn't immediately let go of me, he holds me close to him. I can feel his heart hammering away in his chest.

"How hot do you like your showers?" he asks.

"I honestly don't have a standard temp. It's what-ever suits my mood."

He smiles. "Fair enough." He pushes the shower

curtain to the side and turns on the water, twisting the lever for the shower to kick on. As he faces me, he pauses and says. "Want me to undress you again?"

I shake my head and bite the corner of my bottom lip as I pull my shirt over my head and slowly, teasingly remove the rest of my clothes. I keep my gaze on Soren's as he watches me. His lips part, and his eyes darken again. I make the assumption that, that look in his eyes, is his tell on just how turned on he is.

As I shake off the last bit of clothing, I stand in front of him, toe to toe. "Want me to undress you?" I ask in what I hope is a sultry voice.

He quickly removes his clothing and crashes into me, kissing me everywhere as he pushes me against the sink. Steam fills the room as he plunges his fingers into me. But he doesn't let me climax, instead, he pulls me into the shower, closes the curtain, and proceeds to send me to heaven all over again.

## CHAPTER THIRTY-FOUR

Soren sits with me in the library, waiting for Milo to show up. He seems fidgety with the way he bounces his knees and occasionally stands up to pace the space between bookshelves.

It's almost as if he doesn't want to leave me. But I don't give that thought too much credit. Things are still very new, and after the endless series of orgasms he had put me through earlier, it's hard not to give that thought some credit.

"Are you sure Milo will be able to protect you?" he finally asks.

"If the need arises, yes," I say. "Gideon wouldn't agree to it if it wasn't necessary, and we have to have faith things will work out just fine."

He shakes his head. "I…"

I arch an eyebrow. "You what?"

He shakes his head, paces a bit more, then sighs and sits down. "You're right. But I swear if harm ever comes to you …"

I smile and try my best to reassure him. "I'm sure the world will probably quake in fear of your rage. But don't forget, I still can handle myself."

Soren looks like he is about to say something, but movement catches our attention. It's Milo. He looks exhausted, but his eyes brighten as they settle on me. I smile. "Hey, you."

"Hey. All set?" he asks.

"Keep her safe." Soren's voice deepens with the commanding tone he's given me a few times. After a final glance toward me, he nods and walks off.

Milo's gaze follows him as he storms toward the door and when he returns his gaze to me, he sighs. "He's rather intense."

"You have no idea," I say. "You doing all right?"

He nods. "Yup. Stayed up most of the night trying to get more research in. So far, I've come across three different versions of the fable Headmaster Storm told us yesterday, but not much else."

"That explains why you look so tired."

"Wanna go for a walk?" he asks. "This room probably won't be very beneficial to me with my lack of sleep. Would hate to fall asleep on you."

"A walk would be nice," I say and jump up from my seat.

We make our way toward the courtyard and we take a seat on the edge of a cliff overlooking the ocean. A part of me wonders if something is bothering Milo. And after a while of dealing with the quiet between us—which is peaceful, don't get me wrong—I know he's hiding something for my sake. I'm drawn to him, and I want to do so much more than just use words. But I don't know what. Not yet.

"What's eating you?" I ask.

Milo chuckles. "I'm not sleeping well. Been having nightmares since that fourth trial."

I nod. "Yeah, that one is a doozy."

I grab his hand and rest my head on his shoulder. It feels right. My head fits perfectly here. He kisses the top of my head and fluttering enters my stomach. I smile.

"Hopefully, it will pass," he says.

"It will, in time. But you will do me no good if you fall off the edge of this cliff because you fell asleep.

"Good point."

I look and find a tree with a wide base, still near the cliff, but poses little risk in him falling over. "There, go sit under that and I'll come sit with you. If you fall asleep, I'll wake you when it's time to go."

He yawns. "You're right. Maybe a quick nap."

We move over to our new spot, and he takes a seat between roots, leaning his head against the tree. He looks peaceful as his skin absorbs the light of the sun. His glasses reflect the glow, but it doesn't bother my eyes.

He pulls a book out and I leave him be, enjoying the peaceful moment outside of the library walls with him.

Before long, I'm occupied by the shadows flittering through the water. Occasionally, a mermaid pokes its head out and stares at me before dashing under the surface again. Before long, another mermaid does the same. It almost seems like they are trying to figure me out.

Maybe they are the ones that were in my fourth trial and are trying to figure out how I got away.

Clouds pass in front of the sun every now and then, taking the warmth from my back. And as they pass by, letting the rays shine on me again, I'm reminded of the way I feel with Soren.

I smile to myself.

My thoughts drift to what lays ahead of me now that I know what I am and why I have so much power.

"Well hey there, stranger."

A familiar voice pulls my attention, and as I turn to see who it is, I find Savannah taking a seat next to me. I wrap my arms around her and pull her close. "Hey!"

"You're glowing." She smiles knowingly and moves her gaze to Milo. "Is he the cause of it?"

I cover my cheeks to hide the blush. "Milo? No."

"Okay," she says, still smiling. "Who's the lucky guy then?"

I peek at Milo, who is either extremely into his book and not paying attention to the conversation or is playing at that very well. Turning my attention back to Savannah, I say, "It's a secret."

"Well, thank him for me." She winks and bumps her shoulder into me.

I laugh.

"So, how are you doing?" she asks.

I shrug. "I'm doing okay. You?" I want to tell her more. About the meteorite, about Soren, everything. But I don't. Partly because I'm not sure I can fully trust her yet, and partly because, the more she knows, the more danger she is in. And I can't have that on my conscience.

I'll wait for now. Because I know one thing for certain. Savannah has been a big part of my time here as well, and I know friendships won't go on for long without mutual benefit. At some point, she is bound to find out more. Just not right now.

"It seems like you are doing more than *okay*, girlie. But I'll take it as a good enough answer for now. As far as me?" She sighs. "I'm totally crushing on my mentor. But he's in a different house, has a girlfriend. It would be wrong to tell him, right?"

I honestly don't know. Relationships are a new thing with me, and I'm the least qualified to give advice. "Probably," I say.

"He's cute too," she says, nodding in the direction of Milo.

I follow her gaze and see what she is referring to. Poor Milo. He's fallen asleep with his book laying open on his chest. He really is cute.

In fact, he's adorkable.

"I'm sort of jealous you have four guys."

"Four?" I ask, sounding incredulous.

She nods. "Trust me. I know."

I shake my head and laugh. "No secrets with you, is there?"

"Eh, you can pretend, and we will call that even."

"Okay," I say as I laugh.

"So, does your family know you are here?"

I nod. "My father does."

"What does he think about you passing your trials?"

I shake my head. "Haven't told him yet."

"Ah. I see."

I give her a sideways glance. "What do you mean?"

She shrugs. "Nothing. You're just waiting for the right moment, am I right?"

"You could say that," I say and look back out on the ocean. "What about your family?"

She smiles from ear to ear, and it reaches her eyes, taking on a hint of violet as she says, "My family is super excited for me! Almost everyone in my family has come here. Mom and Dad met here, and during their final year, fell in love."

"Oh yeah?" I nod in approval. "That's really neat."

"Right? They know I want to help people. Healing and things like that. Especially for my younger sister. She was paralyzed in a horrible accident." She sighs ruefully. "I miss her so much. And my life back in Georgia."

"You don't have much of an accent for being from there," I say.

She shrugs. "Not all of us do."

"Makes sense."

Savannah brings her bag to her lap and pulls out some cookies. She holds the bag out to me. "I saw these and thought of you."

"Oh, really?"

"Mm-hmm." She smiles. "Just wanted to do something nice for you."

"Thank you," I say and take a cookie from the bag. But I have to admit, I'm shocked. I normally don't just receive gifts like this for nothing. However, it's nice.

"Dude, we're totally friends. And that's what friends do."

"We have to share though," I say, holding out the bag.

She takes a cookie herself and we sit, eating them in relative quiet. The waves down below us crash against the side of the island, sea birds echo their song somewhere in the distance, and the gentle breeze rustles through the trees, making soft rattling sounds.

I check on Milo as he snores softly from his tree.

Savannah and I giggle.

"That boy could probably saw a log in half," Savannah says.

"Maybe." I shrug.

"You certainly surround yourself with hot men. I mean look at him!" She gestures toward Milo.

"Yeah, I'm still getting used to that."

"Well, I'll tell you what. Any friend of yours is a friend of mine." She gestures between us, and there is light within her violet eyes that makes them look like they are glowing. She means what she says, and that makes me grateful.

"Thanks. I really appreciate that." I smile.

"Speaking of, we should go see what your other guys are up to." She bobs her eyebrows and I laugh.

"Yeah, probably should wake him up too," I say as I stand up and dust grass off my rear. Savannah follows me as I approach Milo and kneel in front of him. I shake him on the shoulder. "Milo."

He snorts himself awake, which gives Savannah a good chuckle, and he sits up and pushes glasses up his nose and runs his fingers through his hair.

I start to wonder what it would feel like to have my fingers in his hair, but I catch myself and say, "Savannah wanted to meet you."

"Hello, handsome!"

He looks up at her and says, "Oh. Hi."

"We were just going to go see what the other guys were up to," I level my gaze on him and he checks the time on his watch.

"Perfect timing," he says and stands up from the ground.

We sit on the stairs watching the men practice.

Gideon stands off to the side, watching the forms and calling out orders. Soren and Jesse are with the group, and they move on cue. Their motions are almost mesmerizing.

Before long, Gideon and Soren spar, and I can't believe what I'm seeing. No wonder Soren is so on top of his game. They move in unison, each one able to anticipate the other's next move and are able to counteract with an attack of their own. It's like a well-rehearsed dance.

And, lest my eyes deceive me, Soren is smiling.

Holy crap these men around me are hot as hell.

I smile, knowing they are quickly becoming a part of my heart and soul.

Soren catches my gaze and gives a stern nod. Our, ahem, relations are hush, hush. I nod back and try to keep my cheeks from burning red. I absently cover the one closer to Savannah, in case she sees it. If she has, she doesn't say a word, and that makes me happy.

This thing with Soren is complicated, and I'm still not sure what it even is. I don't know how to describe it. And, to be perfectly honest, I'm not sure I want to.

I have no idea what to think about Gideon. He's the headmaster of the academy, and yet, he kissed me. I lick my lips, remembering the taste of his mouth and I squeeze my eyes shut to ward off the ensuing pheromonal rage.

And Jesse?

I find him stretching. He catches me staring and blows me a kiss. I chuckle and shake my head.

My adorable, ever-joking flirt.

Milo is ever focused on the action in front of him, analyzing every move like he's committing them to memory. He is sitting on the bottom step, watching everything like a hawk, jotting small notes in his book every once in a while. His attention turns toward me, and he smiles in that astonishingly bashful way that he does.

He waves at me and turns his attention back to the training and his book.

My men. My friends. My... well, I don't want to get too ahead of myself, but damn it all if I don't love watching them practice stuff.

I'm always finding myself floored with the way my body and magic reacts to them. And I'm ever grateful to have them by my side. They all want to protect me, and I admire that about them, but I don't like not having freedom to be alone.

Not that I don't understand why I can't right now, but that doesn't mean I have to like it.

Hopefully soon, I'll earn a little me time. Until then, these adorable men are my protectors, for better or for worse.

"You seem lost in thought," Savannah says.

I turn to look at her, she is resting an elbow on her knee with her head propped in her hand. She looks at me curiously, breaking a smile as she seems to always know what's going on in my head.

I open my mouth to say something—anything—but as soon as I do, a click from the intercom resonates through the air.

"Wren Blackwood. Report to Deacon Lawrence's office immediately."

The message repeats, emphasizing my name, and a chill freezes me in place.

"Uh oh, trouble maker, what did you do?" Savannah asks.

I half laugh and look to the four men who demand to protect me. They heard it too. "I don't know," I mumble.

Soren barely shakes his head. I nod. Going to the professor would be like walking into a pit of vipers. That is the last thing I want to add to my day.

Gideon announces, "Soren, escort Miss Blackwood to Professor Lawrence's office."

Soren nods, bows slightly at the waist, and takes off toward me.

I stand as he takes the stairs two at a time toward me. The look in his eyes is dark and serious, full of deadly focus. And as they switch to me, they soften a little, and I try not to react outwardly.

I'm not a giddy schoolgirl, after all.

A schoolgirl, yes. Now. But I have better control over myself than that.

I face Savannah and say, "Thanks for hanging out with me and for the cookies. See you later."

"Damn right you will. And I want a full report on my desk by morning." She smiles and winks at me. As soon as Soren's back is to her, she bobs her eyebrows.

I chuckle and shake my head.

As soon as Soren and I are at the top of the stairs, we share a look. One that says we know exactly what this meeting means, and neither of us is going to like it.

And now, the fun begins.

## CHAPTER THIRTY-FIVE

Professor Lawrence is flipping through papers on his desk as we make it to his office door that's propped open. I stand there, waiting a moment before I lightly rap my knuckles at the door.

He looks up over the rim of his reading glasses, slips them off, and smiles. "Wren, perfect timing. Come in, come in."

I smile in return, trying to keep my nerves in control and step in. Soren follows me. The professor's gaze snaps to him, and his eyes are cold and full of daggers. I gulp.

"This is merely a new student check, nothing to concern yourself over. She'll be out in a few. You can wait out in the hall if you would like."

I cast my gaze over my shoulder at Soren. He seems unfazed by the professor, continuing to follow me in.

"Then," Soren retorts, "make it quick. I have training to continue."

The professor chuckles under his breath and says, "This is a private matter between apprentice and professor. It will be boring and uneventful, I assure you. I'm quite sure there are other, better things you would rather do."

Soren doesn't budge. He joins my side and stays just far enough away that I can feel the heat radiate from his body. "Headmaster's orders."

The professor's demeanor begins to crack. His eyes burn with rage and his hands clench into fists on top of his desk. "How many times do I have to go over this with him. She is *my* initiate. Headmaster Storm has no right to interfere with my dealings with my initiates."

Soren shrugs.

I force back the desire to smile because Soren isn't moving and it's pissing off the professor all the more.

He slams his fists onto his desk. I wonder if there is going to be a battle in the office. Before there is, I need to do something to break the tension. The last thing I want is to be caught in a war between two mages contained in a small room.

I raise my hand.

When they turn their attention toward me, I say, "I don't mind if Soren stays. What do you need, Professor?"

He huffs and leans back in his chair and gestures for me to take a seat. I do, and he asks, "Now that the trials are over, I thought I would visit with you and see how you are doing. Are you taking time to enjoy yourself?"

Ugh. Small talk. And fake too. This guy is stalling. He's acting too pleasant, too fake, even for him. He's buttering me up for something and I have a sickening feeling that I'm not going to like it.

I smile my best faux smile and say, "I've had some down time. Not much though. Busy training."

"What do you do on your downtime? Have you been exploring the castle and island?"

I shrug. "Eh, a little."

But my cheeks warm at the thought of me and Soren. I quickly shove that thought down. Now isn't the time for those kinds of thoughts.

"What do I owe the pleasure of this little visit

for? Surely you didn't call me from training just for small talk?"

He tents his fingers on his desk and says, "I simply like to check on my initiates from time to time as I do have a lot riding on their success. Honestly, you have nothing to fear from me." He plants his plastic smile on again.

Ugh.

"If I didn't know better, it seems Soren is acting as your personal bodyguard. I'm curious as to know why?"

I shift my gaze to Soren then back to the professor. "It's as he said. We were in the middle of training when I was called here. Nothing more. Nothing less."

There's something that passes through his cold eyes, but he nods. "I'm relieved to hear that. I hate to bring this up, but I feel the need to remind you I did help you gain your freedom from the trolls. I asked of you nothing in return." He levels his gaze on me.

I sigh, forcing back the urge to roll my eyes. I'm becoming irritated with this charade and I'm ready for it to end. "I'm fine, but I do have a lot on my mind. I would prefer to return to my training so I can get to bed and get some rest."

"Of course, I won't be much longer. Have you

considered what courses you want to take?" He reaches into his desk and hands me a list of courses.

I take it, glance over it quickly, and hand it back. "Headmaster Storm has already selected my courses. But thank you."

There's the cold-hearted stony eyes he was just flashing at Soren. This guy is possessive. He needs to get a grip because I'm no longer property, and I certainly was never *his*.

But I can tell there is more he wants to say. That much is evident by how he keeps looking toward Soren as he is wording his questions. It's almost like he wants to ask a burning question that he can't voice while Soren is around.

And that makes me even more wary.

Eventually, he clears his throat and hunches over his desk. "I want you to know, Wren, that I stand by my promise. If you need anything, come to *me*."

His gaze switches between me and Soren.

The energy in the room feels tense. There's a heavy, electrical weight to the air. Chaotic.

I stand to leave.

Professor Lawrence stands. "Be sure to let Headmaster Storm know to be expecting a visit from me regarding the matter of interfering with my initiate."

Soren nods and places a hand on the base of my back to escort me out of the office.

And as soon as we are out of range, he keeps his voice low as he says, "The whole meeting was off."

"Oh, you felt that too, huh?"

He gives a curt nod.

"Do you think he knows about the letter or about me?"

"I don't know, but Deacon has always been hard to read. We need to let Gideon know of our interaction. That man is up to something. I can sense it. There may be more Gideon can do, but our options are few since we are stuck on an island."

"Fine, then Jesse and Milo should be there too."

"The fewer involved, the better."

"Nope. You either come with me, or I'm going on my own. They have been a big part of keeping me safe and helping me when I need it. To exclude them now would be an asshole move."

I stop in the middle of the hall and level my gaze on him, almost challenging him to make the wrong choice.

"Wren, please, don't do this now."

I shrug. "Fine. See you there."

I don't wait for a response before walking off.

He made his choice. But I refuse to exclude Milo and Jesse because it doesn't suit Soren's principles.

As I walk away, I hear him growl and mutter something under his breath as his steps follow me.

I can't help the smile that stretches my lips. I knew he would see it my way.

## CHAPTER THIRTY-SIX

If I have learned anything about these men, it's how protective they are.

I stare out the window of Gideon Storm's office, leaning against the sill with my arms crossed over my chest, chewing on my lower lip while the men bicker about a plan to keep me safe. For the most part, I'm not listening. But, every once in a while, I catch bits and pieces of the conversation. Because it never takes long before the testosterone overwhelms the room and the energy becomes static and chaotic.

"We need to come up with a plan to keep Wren safe." Soren mutters, anger brewing within his words, and judging by the crackling electricity in the room, I imagine flames covering his body again.

"Not many options, considering we're all stuck on an island," Jesse says.

"True," Gideon says. "It will be challenging but not impossible."

I remove myself from the conversation, watching the sunlight dance upon the tree tops while the wind rustles the leaves, making them sway a little. The side of the castle glows in a sandy color that seems rather perfect for a summery day on a remote island somewhere in the Pacific. Yet, despite the beauty that holds my attention, keeping me from losing my temper while the men all debate options for me, I'm just not feeling it.

My magic continues to pulsate, buzz, and rush through me with a pleasant mix of temperature and flow. A combination of being around all four men at once. And even though they are annoying me today, they are the only men my magic reacts to. The only men I want my magic to react to.

Despite their misguided need to protect me like I'm a freaking helpless damsel.

"Hold on," I say.

But they don't listen. Again. They don't so much as even acknowledge the fact that I have spoken. And it's starting to annoy me. They didn't simply ignore me at first. However, when I offered something that would help...

"No," they say.

"That's too dangerous," they say.

"Don't know enough yet about your powers," they say.

"Too much at stake," they say.

At least they could all agree on those things.

The bickering increases, and I can't take it much longer. Heat blisters through my veins and I'm starting to feel like I'm about to combust where I stand.

Finally, I groan. "I'm not some goddamn damsel! I—no, we—may not fully understand my powers, but I know how to protect myself. Hell, I survived living with trolls!" My voice finally breaks through to them. Perhaps because I practically screamed at the top of my lungs. But at least I got somewhere this time.

Their bickering simmers down as they take turns shifting their attention toward me.

Hiding behind men, albeit well intentioned men, is not my style.

"Besides," I add. "I don't want anyone risking their life for me. Especially, any of you."

They are starting to stare at me like I've grown a second head. Maybe I have.

"Wren," Gideon starts, "we all want what's best for you."

"But what about what I want?" I point to my chest. "Have you stopped to think that maybe I should have a say in this?"

Soren steps forward. "You need to calm down." His eyes drift along the length of my body and I curiously follow his gaze.

I'm covered in a thin layer of flames.

That explains the heat and strange looks. Interesting.

But I can't marvel at it for long. As I do, my focus changes to the way the little layer of fire dances along my skin. Not quite as potent as Soren's but close enough that I'm taken aback. Too soon, the flames simmer and fade away.

"You take smokin' hot to a whole new level," Jesse says, holding his hand flat above his head, smiling like he's impressed.

Milo just stares at me wide-eyed, and I can see the gears of thought moving through his gaze.

And Gideon? He seems the most concerned out of all of them.

As I take in their gazes, I crack a smile. "That was so cool! How did I do that?"

"The answer to that goes back to needing to know more about your magic," Gideon says. "However, perhaps we should hear you out. You have proven your point. I'm sure we are all willing to listen."

I nod. "Thank you."

Soren nods as I meet his gaze, and there is a bit of hesitation and worry in his amber eyes that I don't like. What I did just now, probably challenges every single thing he has ever known.

I tuck a strand of hair behind my ear and walk closer to the rest of the group. Checking to make sure I have their attention, I notice Soren joining us with caution.

"I don't want protection."

I'm inundated with an onslaught of rebuttals and all of the men are talking at once. I press my lips together as I take in as calm of a breath as I can take and hold up my hand to silence them.

"I appreciate your need to protect me, but that is not what I want. I just want help."

"That's what we are trying to do," Soren says, and there's a tone in his voice I can't place. It's calm, gentle… hesitant.

I narrow my eyes on him, trying to figure out what the hell is going on with him. But I will just have to worry about that later. Right now, I have a point to make, and I need all of them to hear me out.

"I get that is what you think you are doing, but really, I'm feeling trapped and babysat. I need just a little more credit than that. Yes, this magic is new to you. It's not to me. I may not fully understand it yet, but I know what I'm doing." As I take in the questionable gazes each man gives me, I add, "Mostly."

"We all want to be here for you, every step of the way," Milo says. "But we also don't want to see you get hurt."

"Agreed." Soren nods.

"Then let's start acting like a team." My voice raises an octave. I take a deep breath to release the tension in my neck and shoulders as well as the anger still brewing within me.

Gideon nods and removes himself from his desk as he steps toward me. He rests his hands on my shoulders, and I'm filled with that ache that settles between my thighs and undeniable need to kiss him again. His blue-greens settle on my browns and I let out a shaky breath. This man can undo me like none other. "We all mean well, and we are willing to back down a little, but you aren't accustomed to this world as much as Soren and I are. We have seen things we don't wish our worst enemies to see. We know what could come to you, and no one in this room wants to see that happen."

As much as his words feel nice to my fluttering heart and hormones, I'm angry. Because I feel like this is his gentle way of saying, "Hush, child. I know better than you."

I glare at him. "I got everyone into this mess. Everyone here knows the truth about me. That puts you all at risk. I need to help get you out of it."

Gideon sighs and removes his hands. With a nod, he steps back.

Jesse waves his hand in front of himself. "Uh, it's a bit late for turning back now. Sort of married the idea here."

"Me too," Milo says. He smiles in that bashful way of his and gives a short nod.

"I think you already know my position on this matter." Soren plants his feet shoulder-width apart and crosses his arms over his chest.

I look at him, eyebrows knitted together. Does this man really not know how confusing he can be? Seriously?

He rolls his eyes, dropping his arms to his sides. "C'mon now woman. Think."

Instantly my mind rushes with the images of he and I entangled with one another. My cheeks burn, and I look away.

Oh.

Okay then.

Jesse makes a "mm-hmm" sound. I try my best to ignore him, but my cheeks damn near ignite.

Gideon sighs. "I'm not technically allowed to form any intimate relationships with students at this school. But you are very different from just any student, Wren. I will do whatever it takes to keep you safe, as your headmaster, for now."

"You guys mean a lot to me too," I say. "But, I refuse to let you fight alone. And I refuse to let you win this argument. The only solution I see here is we need a compromise."

Gideon chuckles. "You are something else."

No kidding.

"Very well," he adds. "What would you like out of this arrangement?"

Oh, that is a tall order, indeed. My mind starts to carry me off to places involving sheets, and no clothing, but I can't allow my desires to cloud my judgement. Not when I'm so close to getting what I want. Clearing my throat and shaking my head a little, I say, "Some semblance of privacy."

"And?" Gideon asks.

"I want to help fight, research, hunt, whatever it is you guys do… I want in."

"Next?" Soren asks, arms crossed over his chest as he leans against the side of a chair, a look of amusement softening his features.

I raise an eyebrow. "I want to learn to control my magic, stretch its limits, and use it to help do good in the world."

"That's it?" Gideon asks.

I turn my gaze to him and nod. "It's not an exhaustive list. I'll add to it when I see fit."

"I'm not budging on being your shadow," Soren says. "Day and night. I'll stop Deacon if he comes after you."

"I don't need a babysitter! Have you been paying attention this whole time?" I glare at him and his sexy stubbornness.

"Fine." He looks to the other three. "Anyone else want to vote?"

I wave my arms in front of me. "No vote. I need privacy."

In unison, the other three guys raise their hands.

I gawk at each of them.

Gideon adds, "Bathroom time is the only time you will get alone for the foreseeable future, I'm afraid. Your safety means too much."

"Unbelievable! Where is the compromise?"

"That is the compromise," Soren says.

I look at Jesse and Milo who are chuckling under their breaths and trying their damnedest to hide it.

"What are you two laughing at?" I ask, practically seething.

Jesse says, "Do you know how cute you are when you are angry?"

I shake my head and utter a few unsavory words under my breath.

"We still need to discuss one last thing," Gideon says, looking directly at Soren. "I haven't spoken to Lady Alene."

"What?" I ask.

"There's not much time left," Soren says.

"Time left for what?" I ask and look to Milo and Jesse who both seem just as lost as I am. Milo even shrugs.

"I agree. But my hands are tied." Gideon moves to behind his desk. He flips open a black file and runs his fingers along the page. He taps a spot and huffs.

"Will someone please tell me what is going on?" I ask.

Gideon shrugs. "We must trust that she knows what she is doing. She is well aware of the situation."

Okay. I know this has something to do with me. But why they aren't telling me specifics? I don't know, and I definitely don't like it.

"That's the best we can hope for then," Soren says.

I throw my hands up, exasperated. "So, you're not going to let me in on this little thing you two are discussing?"

"We can't," Soren says, and leaves it at that.

I gawk. "Then why discuss it in front of me?"

"Because time is of the essence, and we are here," he simply says and leaves it at that.

"The only thing left to discuss now is who is sleeping where," Gideon says.

I turn toward him. "What?"

"She's sleeping with me," Soren says.

I about-face and narrow my eyes on him. "No. I'm not."

"I can't have her sleep with me," Gideon says. "There are rules I can't even bend. It wouldn't look good and may draw unwanted attention to her."

"Right," Soren says.

I look at Jesse and Milo who watch the exchange and I can tell they are just rolling with the punches. But a glint in Jesse's eye flickers as he stands straighter and says, "Let's take turns."

"I'm not a freaking item to be passed around!"

"Not only that," Gideon adds, "But you and Milo, though talented and powerful, are just as inexperienced as Wren is when it comes to the way things work not only here at the academy, but in the magical world as well."

"Then it is settled," Soren says. "She stays with me."

"It's my room or not at all." I put my foot down, tired of arguing. "Damn it all. If I have to agree to a constant escort *this* is where I draw the line."

"They do have a point." Milo shrugs as I turn my glare on him. "It's true."

"Traitor," I say, but it lacks the punch I wanted it to have. He makes me soft.

"There's always a bit of fun in sneaking out," Jesse adds. He winks as I look at him. I shake my head, but I can't keep away the smile that stretches my lips.

"Like hell," Soren says.

"Look. As endearing as all of your masculine

protection is, I'm putting my foot down. My room or not at all."

Soren clenches his fists and huffs through his nose. "Dammit woman!" He storms toward me and launches me over his shoulder.

"Put me down, you brute!" I pound his back and I hate to admit I'm not putting my strength into it because as much as this man infuriates me, I have a soft spot for him, and I can't help it. I truly don't want to hurt him.

As he storms into the hallway and down the length of several corridors, heading toward the House of Phoenix, I say, "Put me down or I'll blast you into next week."

He snorts. "Please. You would miss me. You can't even hit the broad side of a barn."

"I'll show you broad side of a barn." I start to wiggle and kick with everything in me. It's no use. He tightens his grip around me.

"If you're not careful, I'll have to teach you a lesson later." He purrs the words, completely unaffected by my insults and attempts to wiggle free.

I huff. "Put me down. I'll walk." It's a lie. I just hope he doesn't pick up on that.

"This is for your own good."

"Who's really benefiting from this arrangement? Me or you?"

"You weren't complaining earlier."

I growl and just give in. There's no use in fighting, and I can't even get free from his lock-tight grip. I give up on fighting to get free, but that doesn't mean I'm not livid.

Because carrying me around like a ragdoll, makes me freaking angry.

## CHAPTER THIRTY-SEVEN

As soon as I am completely calm, we reach the door to my room. Once he sets me down, he grabs my shoulders and forces me to look him in the eyes.

"Be quick. The longer you are here, the more likely Deacon will find you."

I level my gaze on him as I frown. "Thanks for the warning, mighty protector."

He huffs through his nose as he tightens his grip on my shoulders. "Please, Wren."

"Okay, okay. Am I grabbing toiletries and all my clothes or just enough for a few days then we can make a trip back?"

He stands in front of me, staring blankly. "Your

choice. Just make it quick. Whatever you can grab and carry."

"Carry while you are carrying me or walking?" I ask with a smile.

"Woman, if you don't get in there right this second, I'm tossing you over my shoulder again and you'll be forced to wear my clothes."

I giggle. "Can't have that, now can we?"

Although, the thought of his clothing surrounding me makes my heart flutter a little.

I stand on the tips of my toes and kiss him on his cheek. "I'll be right back." I turn and face the door. He stands behind me as I walk in. I half-expect him to follow me in, but the door slams shut no sooner than I'm through.

Spinning around, I try to open the door, but it's frozen in place. I can't get the damn knob to wiggle much less turn. Commotion filters through the door, and I can hear a physical struggle ensue. Soren grunts in pain, and my heart freezes in my chest. I know that was him, and he's in trouble.

I bang on the door and call out for him. He doesn't seem to hear me. Or worse, he can't respond. My heart is in my throat as my eyes sting with the threat of tears. I'm panicking, trying to get the damn door to open with no change in results.

A bright white light flashes around me, and a boom vibrates through the air, deafening my ears and shaking me to the core. Just as quick as it starts, it's over, leaving intense silence settling around me.

It takes a few moments, but once I can focus again, I'm in the garden. Lady Alene stands patiently waiting for me to acknowledge her. And as I do, she smiles.

"Hello again, Wren."

"What is going on?" I ask.

"You have been selected for a fifth trial."

"Soren is in trouble," I say. "We have to get back."

The lady's stony brow furrows. Her eyes gloss over for a moment. As she is silent, I'm desperately looking for a way out of here and back to Soren. Finally, Lady Alene says, "No. He's fine. Though I'm not positive what you saw, it was likely a part of the trial."

I shake my head. That was not part of any trial. I know this. It wasn't all some show to set my nerves on edge. What I heard was *real*. I have to get to him. To save him.

The lady rests a hand on my shoulder, and as I take in her expression, she smiles. "Trust me, sweet one. He is well."

I bite the corner of my lower lip and I give in a

little. I'm still worried, and will be until I see him again, but I have been given no reason to distrust Lady Alene before now. I don't see why that should change.

"A word of caution, my friend," she says, placing both hands on my upper arms.

I'm struck by the fact she considers me a friend. I smile, because it's a nice sentiment.

"Once the trial starts, there will be no exit or escape."

I cock my head to the side, wondering if there was an exit or escape on any of the other trials.

"You must see this one through to the very end, no matter what happens. You cannot give up."

Though I don't know what she means by this, I do know what to do. My plan? Get through this as quick as possible so I can see Soren for myself.

Finally, I nod.

"Follow me." She turns and walks along a path that forms to her right. It curves downward, along the face of the cliff. Within minutes, we're at the end of the path, barricaded by two large mirrors. The images within each are as different as night and day. In fact, they are night and day.

I turn my puzzlement toward the lady. "What am I supposed to do?"

She simply smiles and says, "Follow your heart."

I watch as she walks away, leaving me to stare at the mirrors. As soon as she is out of sight, the path disappears, blocking me in with a fence of dense trees. The ocean crashes against the edge of the island and rushes into the inlet behind the mirrors. On my right is the cliff face.

Above me, the sky is stuck somewhere between day and night, bending together above me in a weird, yet beautiful, array of sunlight and stars.

As I rake my gaze around me, everything I take in is beautiful, magical, wonderous. Like a different world, where everything seems to be brighter, more vivid, and full of life.

To get through this and save Soren, I have to focus. "Follow my heart."

I clear away my concern for him if only long enough to complete this trial. I can't mess up now. Not when I'm so close. Not when Soren needs me. Not when I've just found four men I don't want to ever live without.

Breathing in deep the sea air, I face the mirror and repeat, "Follow your heart."

I assume this means to listen to my intuition, like I did when selecting a house, and pick a mirror.

One mirror is day, either sunrise or sunset. I

can't really be sure. The vivid colors of light blend together and shine over a thick meadow of yellow grass dancing in a slight breeze. The border of evergreens stand guard to this small, private paradise, and small white lights that remind me of sprites dance through the air, chasing butterflies in colors that match the rainbow.

It's a peaceful scene that makes me want to take a walk through the tall grass and see what discoveries there are to explore. I see this place, and I think of warmth, happiness, contentment.

But I also know better than to buy into something at face value. Nothing is ever as it truly seems, and that is truer still with anything here at the academy. Especially with trials.

I step to the second mirror and take in its image. This one is of night. A full moon crests over the horizon, larger than I've ever seen. The stars in the sky are an array of different colors that twinkle like glittering gems. The Milky Way swirls over the edges of the trees, glowing bright as the moon. The meadow is alight with glowing flowers in hues of purple, pink, and blue. Sprites twirl and weave through the air in this image as well.

A shadowy creature flies above the meadow, blocking out the moonlight. It almost reminds me of a dragon, but the shape isn't quite right. It disappears into the left frame, just as quick as it came. Whatever creature that was, it was too fast for me to get a good look, but I swear the thing only had wings and a tail. No legs.

With the moonlight unobstructed again, I return to my study of the scene before me. I'm in awe of the beauty of this serene landscape. It reminds me of warm summer nights, running through the grass behind my childhood home. A time where things were simpler. Peaceful.

But I know better than to think that this choice is a simple one, nor should it be hastily made.

But one thing seems clear to me—the day mirror represents light. The night mirror represents dark and shadows. With that respect, picking the day mirror would be choosing the light. Whereas, picking the night mirror would be choosing the dark.

Yet, I stand here, staring at the two images, wondering what the catch is, if any.

Something ripples through both images, and I can feel the heat and warmth of the day mirror's sun. A cool breeze blows into me, and I'm comforted. The night is a sharp contrast to the day, with cooler temperatures, but the sounds of crickets chirping is like music to my ears. It's cool, comfortable.

I feel at ease within both images.

But as I stand here, I'm reminded of the ever-elusive time limit that every other trial has had.

I have to make a choice soon.

Recalling what I did when walking with Lady Alene, when she told me to listen to my heart as I was deciding which path to walk on, I close my eyes and tune into my magic. I trust in it and let it guide me.

Moving toward the day scene, my magic swirls calmly and effortlessly. It feels relaxed, pleasant. Easy-going.

When I step in front of the night's scene, my magic rushes, churning faster, stronger, more powerful.

With a sigh, I pace the space available to me between the mirrors and the trees that seemed to have gotten closer while I was occupied with making up my mind. That makes things a bit more difficult. As if a time limit wasn't enough, I'm being pushed into making a decision.

Awesome.

Nevertheless, the decision still eludes me.

Facing the mirrors, I know what I want.

To be good. Not go dark and become a shadow mage. To do right by those around me instead of inflict pain and suffering. I know this is where I'm meant to be, but I'm worried there is a trick—a clue or hint—that I'm not seeing.

I look behind me again to see if the trees have come closer to me, and to my dismay they have.

I'm almost certain I haven't missed anything. Obviously, there are pros and cons to each choice standing before me, but I don't have any more time to waste.

I step closer to the day mirror, wanting to be good, light, normal. The mirror shimmers as the glass dissolves away from the frame. I close my eyes, take a deep breath, and step through.

## CHAPTER THIRTY-EIGHT

As I step through, wind rushes around me. I open my eyes as the image of the meadow during the day bleeds away, fading into a dark, dank room that smells of dirt and must. It's moist, and cold. It doesn't take much more to realize that wherever I am, it's deep underground. I've never seen this place before, and as I turn to take in all of my dismal surroundings, I question the idea I'm still on the island. It's large enough to be a cave beneath the island, but I can't tell where the way in or out is. The only lights within the room seem to shine down from a ceiling, and they only provide enough light to see the immediate area. Everything else is thick with shadow.

Finishing my survey of where I am, I turn and

find Deacon Lawrence, standing under a dim light no more than five feet from me, smiling like a cat that has finally caught his prey.

"You." My voice comes out flat, but full of the venomous warning that I fully intend on delivering if he decides to try anything crazy with me.

He smiles. "So glad you could join me. Now that I finally found a way to get you alone."

I quirk an eyebrow and set my hands on my hips. "Explain. Now." My magic pulses through me with the now, and I'm getting a very familiar feeling coursing through me. But I can't focus on that for long before my attention is reclaimed by a man that is proving to be a bigger pain in my ass than I originally gave him credit for.

He chuckles darkly. "Sure. All in good time. But first …" he pauses as he starts to pace the ground in front of me. It's a leisurely pace that signals to me that he is completely at ease and comfortable. Like he believes he's already won. "You have been quite the busy little bee, haven't you? I've been told that you were recently in contact with someone very dear to you recently. Who was it?"

"I don't have to tell you anything."

His pacing stops as he faces me. "Oh, but you do, Wren. You are my initiate."

"I'm not your initiate anymore. Whatever it is you are doing here, make it stop."

"You wouldn't even be here if it weren't for me. I can take my token of good faith away, take every last memory of yours and deliver you back to the trolls you hate so much."

"I appreciate your invitation to the academy. Nothing has changed that. But, no, you won't." I shake my head and cross my arms over my chest. "You don't have the power to take my memories away from me."

I admit, I'm goading him into showing his cards. Because I only have one card to show, and that's not going to happen. He may have the power to revoke my access to the academy, but I'll be damned if I allow him to mess with my memories.

"I suppose you will find out soon enough. That is, unless you tell me who it was you were in contact with."

I shrug. "Crappy sources if they can tell you I was in contact with someone dear to me, but couldn't say who. Which really is a shame, because I'm not telling you a damned thing."

I want to ask about who his source is, but I figure it will come out in time. Just need to be patient for a bit and drag this out as long as I can so I can formulate a plan to get out of here.

"Have you considered your new friends?" He asks, resuming his pacing and calm demeanor. "You seem to have gotten close to a few people in your short time here at the academy."

I narrow my eyes on him. "What are you getting at?"

He shrugs and says, "Well, I would just hate for something to *accidentally* happen to them."

Oh, no he did not just threaten my men.

"I'll kill you if you even try." My words come out flat, resolute, with no room to argue the fact. Because, if it comes down to it, I won't even hesitate.

He clicks his tongue. "Now, now, Wren. I'm the one in control here."

"We'll see," I say, never taking my gaze off of him.

He snaps his fingers. The shadows shift and an army of golems appear. My magic is thrown into the familiar sensation of being around my men all at once. And as that thought registers, the golems drag out my men. Each of them have their hands tied behind their backs with a gag covering their mouths. I want to rush to them, to hug them and apologize, but Deacon holds his hand out to stop me. Instead, I watch helplessly as they are thrown to their knees under the light behind Deacon.

A golem stands behind each of them, except for Gideon who has five. His body is bristling with white bolts of light and power. He is seconds from murdering everything in here, judging by the look in his eyes. I have never seen him so furious.

Soren's body is covered in the same flames that coated his skin in my room before, but it seems to do little to burn away at the rope keeping his arms behind his back or the gag that is tied tightly around his mouth.

I frown and clutch my hands into fists.

Deacon laughs. "I'll give you *one* chance to make things right." He holds up one finger, with the other hand behind his back. "You will either give me what I want, or I'll kill each of your friends," he says friends like it's a bitter taste in his mouth, "one by one, ending with your father."

I narrow my eyes on him and my body erupts in heat. But I don't look to see if I have flames covering my skin. I keep my focus on the one man that just threatened every single person I care about. "You'll never get away with it."

"Oh?" he says, and he snaps his fingers one more

time. The golems behind the men each take the shapes of Soren, Milo, Jesse, and Gideon. "You see? No one would be the wiser. I'll simply have these golems take their place."

I shake my head. "Their eyes are lifeless, people *will* know."

"Not when two initiates fail their test and are," he holds up his fingers for an air quote as he says, "sent home."

"They've already passed their trials, you idiot."

"Ah, but not the fifth one. The secret, random one. The one that allowed me to set all of this up," he gestures to the room around him.

"And of Soren and Gideon?" I ask. "How do you propose to pass off your golems in their place?"

"Oh," he waves his hand in front of him as he chuckles. "You mean the most promising cadet in the Academy Special Forces? He simply dies on assignment. And the headmaster is called off to far away missions regularly. One little oops, and a plane crashes or a spell goes wrong, or… well, you get the picture."

I… I have nothing. Nothing to stall this any longer. Nothing to get him to reveal his true intentions with me.

"Time is ticking, Wren," his voice echoes throughout the room. "I'm not a very patient man."

I shake my head.

"Oh, come now. What will it be?"

I stare at my men, forcing myself to think of something—anything—that will get them out of this mess.

Deacon snaps his fingers and the golems attack the men, kicking them, and pulling them up into a position that is geared to snap their necks.

"Stop!" I raise my hands. There's no way I can save them like this.

Deacon smiles. "That's a good girl. Now, tell me what I want to know."

I shift my eyes between my men and Professor Lawrence. If I attack the professor first, I can protect myself. But I risk losing my men. If I attack the golem men, Professor Lawrence will have an open opportunity to attack me. And if that happens, I'm probably going to get hit and hurt. Bad.

But, I'll do anything to keep those men safe. Damned the consequences to me.

I call upon my magic and it courses through me ready and willing. Fire ignites along my arms and I stare the professor in the eyes as my power grows through my hands. In a matter of seconds, my hands are covered in orbs of light and I release them in beams, hitting the golems holding my men hostage.

They disintegrate into puddles, releasing my men from their near deaths.

The professor, as expected, attacks me. I'm hit in the center of my chest with a blast of fiery light, sending me flying backward. I drop to the ground, hitting my head. Dots line my vision as pain throbs through my entire body. I can barely breathe, but I know my men are no longer at risk of having their necks broken.

Another blast of magic blows over me and Soren's battle cry reaches my ears, pulling me back from a darkness I didn't know was so close to claiming me. I sit up, my torso feeling as if I took a hit to the gut by a wrecking ball, and set my gaze on Professor Lawrence.

"Now, you die." As I stand, magic courses through me. I ignore the sting radiating through my chest and the back of my head as I send another blast of light to the man.

He blocks it as I call upon all the training Soren has drilled into me, taking my horse stance and forming a shield of light. It absorbs the next blast, and I'm quick to toss in another of my own. While the professor recovers from the force of that hit, I sweep my gaze over the fighting men, fiercely stemming the flow of more golems coming through. They take out golem after golem, but there are *hundreds*.

Professor Lawrence makes use of my distraction by attacking. But I regain my focus at the last second and take the hit like a champ. But this fight is going to take more than just magic against magic. I have to close the gap between us and fight with everything I have left, despite my agonizing injury.

Biting against the pain, I charge.

The professor smiles, preparing for a fight he obviously thinks he has already won. But he doesn't know me. I don't give up or give in. I'll fight until my last breath. Where he underestimates me, I will use it to my advantage.

I slice at him with my shield, cutting his arm. He growls and takes a few staggering steps backward, but I don't relent. I'm on him kicking, punching, blasting him with magic. Heat coils over my skin and I'm on fire.

He stares at me with wide eyes filled with horror, but I still don't let up. I'm out for blood, and this man not only threatened every single man that I care for, but he damn near killed me.

He looks to his side and shoots a blast of magic at my men. Luckily, they duck in time, but just barely. The ball of fiery light lands in the back of one of his own golems. Standing in front of the melting creature is Milo.

I turn my attention to the professor. "You must really like the idea of dying. Let me help you with that." I kick him square in the chest, he falls to the ground and stares up at me, his eyes alight with the realization that I'm winning.

He throws dirt in my eyes. But I close them in time. A few particles get in, digging into the flesh of my eyeballs, but it's nothing I wasn't used to when the trolls would cheat their way to the horn each year or when they decided I needed a little reminder of just where my place was among them. I had learned quickly to adapt while living with them. And though Professor Lawrence may have pulled a dirty move, I don't stop.

"Even if you kill me, you won't be safe. You won't know a moment's peace." He stands to his feet.

"Is that supposed to scare me?" I say and throw a ball at magic at him. He rolls to his back and flipping over to land on his feet.

He tosses another ball of magic at me as he says,

"Dangerous people know who you are. What you are. You will be hunted. It will never end."

I land a punch to his jaw and graze him across the chest with my shield. "Still not scared."

He pushes back with a forceful, constant blast of magic. Its radiance nearly blinds me, and the heat hurts like hell as I strain against it. As soon as I'm pushed back five feet, it stops. "The easiest thing you can do is to give in to me now. I'll make everything painless for you."

I pant to catch my breath and focus through the pain as I stare him down. "Yeah, well... the easy way isn't always the right way. And I will never bow down to another person again."

Deep down, I touch the depths of my magic. Feeling levels of strength and tenacity and ability I never knew I had. The fire glowing along my skin burns brighter, hotter, surrounding my body in a thicker layer. With everything inside me, I let go of the magic as I aim it at the professor.

The force of the hit is like a bomb going off, I'm knocked back by the explosion, and a dark rim lines my vision as my skin suddenly cools.

But I don't give in. Not yet.

I dig into the deepest recesses of my power knowing I can't leave my men to defend themselves against the golems on their own. I have to end this fight once and for all.

My palms light up once more. But I can't let my magic hit them.

My vision starts to fade. Pain throbs through every inch of my body and it hurts to even blink. I press my hands to the ground as crackling, electric energy snaps around my arms and pours into the ground. The dirt vibrates and breaks open, splintering in an arc away from me, avoiding my men, and latching onto the golems.

The light shoots into them, shattering the creatures as they become frozen.

My men stop fighting against them and watch as the light within the golems pours through every crevice in their forms until nothing of their bodies remain, and another loud boom ricochets through the space of the cave.

Panting, I fall back to the ground. My vision blacks out, and I feel like I'm sinking into the ground.

Echoes of voices I can't make out surround me, but I don't know where they are coming from. My body hurts and all I seem to want to do is rest. Just sleep it off.

Warmth radiates through me, and my magic

switches between pulsing, rushing, buzzing, cooling, and warm. I feel a sense of strength I get only when Gideon is around, and I feel emotions on a level only Milo gives me. Coolness rushes through me like it does when Jesse is near, and the heat… the fire of passion burns through my nerves, encircling me in the way that only Soren gives.

"Wren!"

My name echoes around me.

At long last, I give in to the peaceful rest I earned.

CHAPTER THIRTY-NINE

I awaken with a start, covered in a hospital gown and all four men busy tending to my wounds. "How did I get here? More importantly, where are my clothes?" I ask.

All at once they turn and set their gazes on me, each one showing their relief that I'm okay. They surround the bed I'm on, and though I get only bits and pieces of the view, I can tell we are in the infirmary.

"How are you feeling?" Gideon asks.

I pause. Actually, I feel amazing. I pull down the front of the hospital gown to check the wound on my chest and I'm shocked to see minimal signs of having been shot in the first place. "H-how is this even possible?"

"It must be a sign of your power," Milo says.

"A nice side-effect, if you ask me," Jesse adds.

I look to Soren who has yet to say anything to me. He sits on my right, propping a leg up on the bed, facing me with his hands folded over his thigh. He gives me a short nod. A thin strip of white covers the corner of his left eyebrow. Bruising surrounds the cut that's been pulled closed by the butterfly bandage. I nod back and take in the rest of the guys who managed to scrape by with a few minor cuts and bruises.

"Wren," Gideon pulls my attention back to him, who seems to have endured the least injuries out of the four men. "Can you walk me through everything that happened?"

I nod. "All I know is, as soon as I stepped into my room, the door shut and wouldn't open again. I heard a fight on the other side of the door, and Soren grunted in pain. There was a bright flash of light and I was sent to choose between two mirrors. One of night, and one of day. I chose the day, stepped through, and ended up in that room." I stop to think about if I missed anything. Nodding to myself I add, "I believe you know the rest."

Gideon nods. "Some students undergo a secret fifth trial where they are faced with a difficult decision. It's supposed to serve as final proof of their loyalty and sense of self. It also shows the academy what alignment they have a natural predisposition toward. The goal is to help foster a young mage's strengths and pushes them to always be more inclined toward the light."

"Rather archaic, if you ask me," I mutter.

"In your case, also unnecessary," Gideon adds with a chuckle. He grabs his ribs and winces. Maybe he endured more injuries than I thought he had.

"How are all of you doing?" I ask.

"Aww, I knew you cared about me." Jesse winks, a devilish smile stretching his lips.

I shake my head and smile.

"We are all fine, now that you are awake." Milo's voice is full of relief. His eyes are softer, with a little deep purple in the corners at his nose. Poor guy. He looks exhausted.

"Did I pass the trial?" I ask.

Gideon says, "Yes. You did, of course. It's not a fail/pass trial, so you shouldn't look at it as such, but it did confirm his original suspicions."

I nod. That's good to know. I try to recall everything that happened as the fight rushes through my mind. It all ends in blackness. I can't remember how it ended.

"Is he …" I don't want to say the name or the dreaded word. But I have to. "Is Professor Lawrence dead?"

"Well, if he's not, he's very clever at hiding," Jesse adds.

"That was completely reckless what you did," Soren finally says to me. "Do you have any idea the devastation you would have caused if you had—" He stands from the bed, shaking his head, not finishing his thought.

I feel a little guilty, but that feeling is quickly squashed as I realize the choice I was faced with. "Would you have made a different decision if it were you in my place?" My voice is even, but there is a hint of gentleness that I know he catches onto because he looks at me, and I see the softness in his eyes.

I raise my eyebrows to let him know that I'm still waiting for an answer. "Well?"

"That's not the point." He looks away from me.

"It is very much the point," I say. "And I would do it a hundred times over if I need to, so get used to it."

"There won't be a next time, so get used to *that*," he says.

"What is that supposed to mean?" I ask as I switch my gaze over the men.

Gideon pats me on the leg reassuringly. "Don't worry, Wren. You made it through the trial. Ultimately, your heart is pure. You have an inclination toward the light, and we can move forward training you and researching your powers."

"That's good to know," I say. "What about my father?"

"I have to call on some of my contacts, but you will be involved every step of the way. I'm proud of you." Gideon smiles.

"Uh, we all are..." Jesse says. "I mean, what's not to be proud of?"

"I would love to take notes on your experience, once you're better. Perhaps I can connect a few dots and fill in some blanks while the headmaster researches and digs deeper into your powers?" Milo pushes his glasses up on his nose.

I smile. "Sure."

"No. She will be too busy," Soren says to Milo. To me, he adds, "You will train harder from now on. I saw what you can do, and you have to learn to control your power."

I roll my eyes and let out a heavy sigh.

At least, we're already getting back to normal.

"Have you done anything like that before?" Milo asks.

I shake my head. "I don't believe so."

"Were you completely in control of it?" Gideon asks, his blue-green eyes take in mine.

I become lost in his eyes, lost in the events that run through my head on constant repeat. Everything was too surreal. Too much for me to process.

Was I in control of the power?

Though I would like to think so, I know that if I were to try and repeat the same thing again, I would fail, and likely hurt someone. It was a response. A last-ditch effort to end the fight and save the men that surround me, the men my magic reacts to.

Eventually, I shake my head.

"That settles it then," Soren says. "Training. Learn to control your power so you don't exhaust yourself next time."

I nod. Because, I know there will be a next time. Plus, I still can't get my mind off of the fight. Something nags at the back of my mind, beckoning me to pluck it from the endless array of images. Something important and dire.

Something life-changing.

I remember what the professor had said.

*Dangerous people know who you are. What you are. You will be hunted. It will never end.*

I gasp.

Oh no.

Not only did Deacon know about me, he shared that little nugget of information with others. Likely the people he works for. Maybe even the Order?

"What is it?" Gideon asks.

"What Deacon said." I tell him. "Someone will know I killed him."

He nods. "Only we know about what happened."

I shake my head. "He told someone about me. He had to. He said dangerous people know who and what I am."

I switch my gaze between the four men surrounding the bed I lay on, men I'm connected to, who saved my life.

Gideon nods and rubs my leg reassuringly. "If he somehow managed to discover anything about you and shared that knowledge with these people, no one can gain admittance to the island without expressed permission by invitation. You are safe. Let us handle things on that end."

"And if people ask about him?" I ask.

He shrugs. "It could be as simple as saying he left the island and was killed in some accident."

"Huh," I say. "That's exactly what he said about you."

"I know. It's a bit of poetic justice," Gideon says. "We'll give it some time before we announce the death to the academy."

I nod.

"How's your pain?" Milo asks.

I shrug. My muscles ache with some movement but nowhere near as much as they did before. "I'm a little sore. That's it."

They gawk.

"She's Super Woman," Jesse says with a smirk.

I laugh and wince with the pain.

Milo says, "We have just the thing to help with the pain." He walks to a counter nearby and picks up a mug, pours some hot liquid from a plugged-in kettle, and stirs it with a spoon. Bringing the cup to me, he holds it out and says, "Drink this. It will help."

"It should help you sleep as well," Gideon says. "Which I think we all need to do. For now, she is safe, but if you would feel better, Soren, you can stay with her."

He nods.

Aww, he's so sweet when he's not so focused on being an asshole. I smile.

CHAPTER FORTY

Four days later, I'm watching the ocean roll by the boat. The crazy captain is busy talking to himself and uttering more riddles, but I ignore him for the most part.

Savannah and I share a smile after the captain cracks himself up. I shake my head and return my attention to the ocean.

That man is something else entirely.

Savannah and Soren were given permission to get me off the island for the day. Gideon saw it as a great opportunity for me to get some time away after the incident with Professor Lawrence. I suspect there was more behind that reasoning, but I don't think about it. At least, I try not to. I didn't even care to ask because I know it involves what happened.

And since Soren hasn't let me out of his sight for longer than fifteen minutes since I woke up in the infirmary, I needed some girl time.

I cast a glance toward Soren. He has that ever-present scowl, all serious and no fun, but when he catches my gaze, as he always does, there's a light within his eyes. Though I've seen hints of it before, it's most definitely there now, without question.

So much has changed between the two of us, and I'm grateful they did. He's still an asshole sometimes, but he's always softer toward me, and it seems only me. I wonder if he can feel the same thing I feel when we are near each other. That radiating heat that courses through my veins, my magic's response to him.

In fact, I wonder if all four of them do.

Soon, we dock somewhere on the coast of Washington, in a town called Samish. Once we're off the boat, Soren grabs me by the elbow and says, "I'm meeting up with a guy for something."

I nod. A silent clue.

He's been following leads into finding my father's location and this is one of Gideon's contacts that may have information on where he could be located.

Savannah seems oblivious to it. At least, she doesn't show that she knows more is going on with this trip than she intended.

"Meet back here in three hours." He nods to me once.

"Don't worry, I've got her." Savannah pulls on my arm. "Go do your thing."

I giggle at the cold glare Soren is staring into the back of Savannah's head. He can't faze her, and he probably doesn't know what to think about that.

We find our way to the local spa and are treated and pampered in ways I never thought possible. Who knew a massage could feel so *good*? I take a sip of iced tea as we sit in super comfy chairs with a robe around our body and faces covered in some sort of mud mask.

"So, when did you and Soren become such an intense item?"

I look to her and shrug. "I don't know that we really are. I don't even know what we are."

She levels her gaze on me and says, "Honey, that man has fallen hard for you. He practically has to pick up his jaw each time you walk past him, and let's not forget the fact he follows you everywhere. It's sweet and all, but damn girl."

"What do you mean?" I ask. Admittedly, the constant supervision has been a bit nuts. But I had let slip the mention of Anderson one time when I saw him spying on us in the hall the other day. It took everything in me to keep him from mowing the guy down. He deserves it. True. But not on Blackbriar grounds.

Ever since then, we've been practically attached at the hip.

He's a senior this year, which means he has a lot going for him. He can't go ripping off the head of everyone that touches me or looks sideways at me. I adore him for that, but it's not necessary.

"I mean, you walk through a room and if he's not actively following you, his eyes are. He gives off a deep sense of protection for you."

I feel my cheeks warm. "Yeah, you could say that."

She sits up and faces me. "You should figure out real quick what you two are, because he's already got it set in his mind. And if that's not what *you* want, your best bet is to break it off now, before you break his heart more than it will if you wait until later."

I… wait. What? Break his heart? Never.

I stare at her. "I don't know what label to put on what is going on between me and Soren, but I assure you, I'm not quitting him."

She smiles. "Good." She leans back and opens up a magazine, flipping through the pages quickly before saying. "I believe there is more to you two than what you are saying."

"There really isn't." I shrug, leaning back and looking at the posters of all the exotic locations that are hung on the wall.

"If you say so," she says. "So, ready to talk about your family?"

"I don't really have one," I say. I do, but until I can have him standing in front of me and I can physically touch him, I won't believe my father is safe.

"What happened to them?" she asks, and there's not only concern in her expression, but her eyes and her voice hold it as well.

"My mother died when I was fourteen. My dad disappeared shortly after that."

"Well where did you live?" she asks, leaning closer, sitting up in her chair and facing me now.

"I lived with forest trolls," I say through a sigh. As much as I tried to keep it from her, she probably already knew with the way she knew everything else. Why pretend any longer? Besides, she's been nothing but a friend to me, and I figure I should reciprocate. After all, she told me about her family.

As I meet her gaze, she doesn't so much as even blink an eye. "I wondered when you were going to say something about that."

"Let me guess, you already knew?" I ask. But I can't keep the smile from my face.

"Sort of," she says. "Aside from my power, I also have an over-developed intuition."

I chuckle. "That explains so much."

She nods and smiles. "Yeah. I want to use it to help and heal people. I still adore you, by the way. Regardless of your past. You can trust me to never let anything bad happen to you again."

I laugh. "In that case, have any zacar repellent in your arsenal of goods?"

"I'll see what I can do." She sits back in her seat and takes a sip of her tea.

"As long as it's before Soren gets a moment alone with him," I mutter.

She just chuckles.

"What else have you seen?" I ask, curious.

She touches my hand. Her eyes turn a dark amethyst color and they focus on a spot near my feet. I can't tell what though. A few moments later, she removes her hand and shakes her head. Her gaze meets mine and she smiles somewhat apologetically. "Sorry, I didn't get anything this time."

"Is that bad?" I ask.

"No." She sighs. "It's like you have a suit of armor protecting you now."

"Huh."

Well isn't that something.

We sit back and enjoy casual conversation as we finish our teas.

Before I know it, our spa day is over and we are heading back to the island. Savannah and I continue to be girlie and talk and poke fun at Soren's broodiness, but we're back to the island in a blink and we have to go our separate ways.

"Bye, lady!" she says and blows me a kiss before waving goodbye.

I chuckle. "See ya."

Soon, I crash into Soren's bed and breathe in his scent. He joins me, a wicked smile on his face. I shake my head. "I've created a monster."

"Maybe." He shrugs as he kisses me on my shoulder and nuzzles his nose along my jaw line, sending sensations of warmth and desire straight to the space between my legs.

"How did your meeting go?" I ask, forcing out breathy words.

"We have a location."

I smile and suck in a breath as I sit straight up and face him. "When?"

He chuckles. "Soon. We have to finalize a few things first."

I throw my head back against the pillow with a groan. "Why did you wait so long to tell me?"

He shrugs. "You were doing girl stuff."

I playfully smack him on his shoulder. "You're such an ass."

"And you're the pain in it." He pulls me to him and kisses me with fierce need. I run my fingers along the base of his head, enjoying the way the tiny hairs feel against my skin. He pulls himself over me and teases the hem of the shirt I'm wearing even higher on my body.

He leaves a trail of kisses as he lowers himself down between my legs. And as soon as he situates himself, he teases my sensitive folds with the tip of his tongue and traces the outline of my entrance. I cling to the sheets and moan for more.

Obliging me, he flicks his tongue expertly until my orgasm peaks. He falls to his back on his pillow with a sigh.

"Oh, no. We're not done," I say and straddle him, inching the length of his cock inside me and riding him through several more climaxes, until he finally releases inside me.

I collapse onto his chest and work to catch my breath. He lovingly wraps an arm around me and kisses the top of my head. I close my eyes as a smile stretches my lips. Just as I told Savannah, I could never harm him or break his heart. As long as I have him, and my other men, I will be content. And once we find my father, we will challenge whoever thinks they can take this all away.

**Wren, Soren, Gideon, Jesse, and Milo will be back in *The Shadows of Blackbriar Academy*, coming July 2019.**

**Join the exclusive, fans-only Facebook group to get release news & updates.**

Read on for a special note from the author.

Hey, Babe!

First, I just want to say thank you for giving my first foray into academy fiction a chance.

I dearly hope you fell just as much in love with the story as I did. And there is so, so much more in store. I can't wait to share the rest of this series with you!

Creating this beautiful, magical world full of whimsy and mystical creatures has been such a wonderful journey. Especially Lady Alene! I see her as such a warm, nurturing mother figure. She's strong, knowledgeable, and a really fun addition to this story.

Wren is a girl I think we all can connect to on

some level. She doesn't let her past define her, but only uses it to help her learn and grow. She never once falters in her belief of building a better life for herself and the people around her. I think that is probably the most admirable thing about her. She never lets her past hold her back.

I especially loved taking her through the trials. Testing her, watching her grow. It was such a delight.

Wren faces some pretty difficult challenges during the trials. She grows her confidence. Realizes how truly clever she is. Pushes her limits. And, of course, begins to discover the true depth of her power.

We just don't get to see *how* powerful yet.

What lies ahead for her? Why does her magic react to her men like it does? What is the deal with her past?

She'll be doing a lot of growing through the series, and I hope you're riding shotgun with me through the series so we can watch her tackle some pretty heavy obstacles.

Especially with her four, incredibly hot men that her magic reacts to.

Soren McCallister—yeah, he's a hard ass, rough

around the edges, but he eventually softens toward only her. He's a soldier through and through and knows she has more power than she should. However, the more he and Wren they spend together, the more he lowers his guard. It's a treat to watch such a bad boy get soft. Well, if only a little.

Jesse Taylor—the carefree jokester. He's an illusionist and knows how to get Wren to loosen up and laugh. We're going to see a lot more of him in the next book!

Milo Moreau— the hot nerd who really gives Wren a safe place to explore her ever growing power without fear or ridicule. He expands her knowledge by his resourcefulness and makes her truly *feel*. And he's just so damn easy to talk to!

Last, but never the least, Gideon Storm, headmaster to the academy. Strong, knowledgeable, and makes Wren feel simply *untouchable*.

Yum.

So, who is your favorite guy? Think anyone can stand up to this group? How is Wren going to fit four gorgeous men and classes in her new school schedule?

You'll have to read the next book to find out!

Until next time, babe!
Keep on being your beautiful, badass self.
-*Olivia*

**PS. Amazon won't tell you when the next Dragon Dojo Brotherhood book will come out, but there are several ways you can stay informed.**

1) **Soar on over to the Facebook group, Olivia's secret club for cool ladies,** so we can hang out! I designed it *especially* for badass babes like you. Consider this as your invite! We talk about kickass heroines, gorgeous men, our favorite fantasy romances, and… did I mention pictures of *gorgeous men*?

2) **Follow me directly on Amazon**. To do this, **head to my profile** and click the Follow button beneath my picture. That will prompt Amazon to notify you when I release a new book. You'll just need to check your emails.

3) **You can join my mailing list by going to** https://wispvine.com/newsletter/olivia-ash-email-signup/. This lets me slide into your inbox and basi-

cally means we become best friends. Yep, I'm pretty sure that's how it works.

Doing one of these or **all three** (for best results) is the best way to make sure you get an update every time a new volume of the *Blackbriar Academy* series is released. Talk to you soon!

## OLIVIA ASH

Olivia Ash spends her time dreaming up the perfect men to challenge, love, and protect her strong heroines (who actually don't need protecting at all). Her stories are meant to take you on a journey into the world of the characters and make you want to stay there.

Reviews are the best way to show Olivia that you care about her stories and want other people discover them. If you enjoyed this novel, please consider leaving a review at Amazon. Every review helps the author and she appreciates the time you take to write them.